An Engagement of Sorts

An Engagement of Sorts

A REGENCY ROMANCE

ALENE WECKER

Covenant Communications, Inc.

Published by Covenant Communications, Inc.
American Fork, Utah

Printed in the United States of America
First Printing: August 2021

26 25 24 23 22 21   10 9 8 7 6 5 4 3 2 1

ISBN:978-1-52441-764-2

PRAISE FOR ALENE WECKER

"The influence of Jane Austen's work is evident in the dialogues and narration of the novel. Alene Wecker has infused the conversations with the same sophistication and wit as *Pride and Prejudice*. The mannerisms of the characters, too, reflect the same source of inspiration throughout the book. Despite these similarities, Alene Wecker has succeeded in keeping the story fresh. The characters have their unique personalities and eccentricities. Mr. Paling, the love interest of Anne, is no Mr. Darcy. He is a flirt whose intentions are very hard to decipher. His banters with Anne are clever and very well-written. Our heroine is equipped with a very sharp tongue and an unmistakable wild spirit. She is not a damsel in distress, yet she knows when to let somebody else take charge. With enough plot twists and a brilliant narrative, *An Engagement of Sorts* keeps its audience hooked to the story until the very end. Alene Wecker presents not just a romantic tale, but a story that sheds light on the double standards of society tastefully and intriguingly. Fans of Jane Austen and historical romance will appreciate the engaging plot and the brilliant dialogues of *An Engagement of Sorts* by Alene Wecker."

—*Readers' Favorite* 5-Star Review

To my mom, for being a decidedly better person than Mrs. Fletcher.

ACKNOWLEDGMENTS

Many thanks to Jane Austen and Georgette Heyer for getting me through months of bedrest and to Julianne Donaldson for showing me that contemporary authors can also entertain with wit and charm.

After growing frustrated that there weren't enough books like theirs on the market, my husband encouraged me to write my own novel. I thought he was crazy. But once I began, I fell in love with my characters and writing in general. Many thanks to him for starting me on this path and supporting me along the way. Thanks, kids, for happily eating cereal for dinner so I could work on my book. And Grandma Chuck, you are amazing. Thanks for watching the kids so I could work on my book (and travel to England with your fabulous son).

Natalie Whipple, thank you for your friendship and for reviewing the earliest versions of my first ten pages. Without your intervention, I would still be putting two spaces at the end of every sentence. (That really dates me, doesn't it? That was a very hard habit to break, BTW.)

But I would certainly not have published this novel if it weren't for Cindy Pearson. Within the casual framework of a conversation, she discovered that I had written a book. She asked for my pitch. I stared blankly at her. She took pity on my ignorance and encouraged me to join a critique group and start attending writers conferences. My husband (huge supporter, remember?) asked if I could just join *her* writers group and—miracle of miracles—she said yes. Many thanks to Cindy, Keri, Angie, and Brenda for your insights. The four of you have probably taught me more about my craft than any other source.

I had the opportunity to visit Rushden Hall and—for any who are familiar with the area, this will come as no surprise—found Clive Wood on the premises, painting a wooden horse for an upcoming festival. He dropped what he was doing to give me a personal tour, which was as informative as it was intriguing. (He literally wrote the book on Rushden Hall.) Thanks, Clive, for your time and for your efforts to preserve this little bit of history.

I'm grateful for my beta readers, and a special thanks goes out to Hillary Sperry, who, during an Indie Author Hub writers retreat, donated her miles so I could fly home to be with my son who was sick in the hospital. Even with a delayed flight, I still arrived on time to be there before he went in for surgery.

Jenny Proctor, thank you for going above and beyond, for your encouragement, story edit, and help polishing the first few chapters. And of course, my gratitude goes to Covenant for taking on a debut author who really had no idea what she was doing. Hopefully the gamble pays off for both of us, and we will enjoy many more adventures together.

CHAPTER ONE
October 23, 1812

THE COACH SWAYED, KNOCKING MY head against the window. I scooted infinitesimally closer to Mother, careful not to infringe upon her space. Were I to accidentally provoke her, she would have no compunction whatsoever about turning the coach around and denying me the privilege of tonight's ball. I was lucky enough that she had still decided to come, my sister's absence notwithstanding.

"Remember, Anne," Mother began her threats as we neared Hinwick House, "this ball shall be a test. You must prove to me that you have finally learned to comport yourself with the decency that befits a lady of your station. If you do, I shall allow you to stay home while I take Charlotte to London for her Season. Otherwise, I shall be forced to take you with me—as unpleasant a prospect as that seems—to ensure you don't get into trouble."

I would like to say Mother was bluffing, but I had seen her play faro before; she did not know how to bluff.

Enduring a Season, with all its accompanying strictures and rigid rules of etiquette, was the last thing I wanted. Thankfully, Mother had never inflicted such a fate upon me; she considered it a waste of resources. "Yes, Mama. I am not the same wild girl I used to be." Or maybe I was, but I had learned how to feign submission. In another two years, when I reached my majority and both Lizzie and Charlotte had married and secured their futures, I planned to escape Mother's leash.

She cleared her throat. "You have certainly made progress, else I would never allow you to stay home with no one but Father and John to moderate your nature."

I swallowed my retort. I could point out that John was more reckless than I had ever been, but such entreaties would only bring the sting of Mother's bony hand across my cheek. He was both male and heir; being wild was his birthright. I was the "willful" middle daughter, with neither Lizzie's perfect propriety nor Charlotte's charm.

We turned onto the crushed gravel drive of Hinwick House, its limestone shining like a beacon in the light of the moon. Unlike Rushden Hall, with its mismatched appendages built in every century since the fourteenth, Hinwick House had been constructed all at once and modeled after the style of Buckingham House. It was, in every way, impressive.

The front doors opened, my cloak was taken, and we were brought into the well-lit hall, already filled with guests. Mother and I waited to greet the hosts while I took in the room. A nervous energy fueled me when I saw so many people present, most of whom were completely unknown to me. I always thrilled at the chance to meet new people, especially because Mother granted me a longer tether on occasions such as these.

Angel Skinner and her mother forged through the throng to meet us. Will Skinner, Angel's brother, served as the vicar in our parish. As a member of the only other genteel family who lived within miles of us, Angel and I had grown as close as sisters.

"I didn't know it would be such a crush," Mother said.

Mrs. Skinner, who accumulated and dispensed gossip like a bee collects and distributes pollen, said in her shrill voice, "Yes, the Orlebars have assembled quite the hunting party. People have flocked here from all over. There is even a Colonel Thoroton from Nottinghamshire whom several young ladies have traveled from London to see."

"I would not travel that far for the prince regent himself," Angel said.

Angel spoke from experience. Though she hated the task, she often accompanied her elderly aunt to Bath, Brighton, and London.

"Not everyone is as reluctant a traveler as you," I said. I had never been allowed to go with her. Mother never let me out of her sight.

"Colonel Thoroton is not just any gentleman," Mrs. Skinner said. "He recently inherited Flintham Hall in Nottinghamshire. I hear it's twice—no, thrice—the size of Hinwick House. And he is only four and twenty." She paused to fan herself, obviously relishing in the attention she earned as the gatekeeper of gossip. "Rumor has it that when his father died, the colonel had to leave his post with the Coldstream Guards and is just now on his way to Town to find a wife. You had better acquire an introduction."

Angel leaned over to me, whispering, "Though little good it will likely do you. The man dismissed me without a word. I suppose he has no interest in the sister of a lowly vicar."

I pressed her hand in a show of understanding.

In the next moment, Mr. and Mrs. Orlebar greeted us and chatted amicably with Mother before Mr. Orlebar escorted us to the colonel for the desired introduction. "Colonel Thoroton, I have two neighbors I am pleased to introduce you to. Here are Mrs. and Miss Fletcher."

Were it not for his eligibility, I doubted any who gazed on Colonel Thoroton would have considered him handsome outright, his scarlet regimentals notwithstanding. His face was not scarred from combat, nor was he a corpulent colonel, but a weak chin, a round face, and a stiffly starched collar combined to produce the appearance of jowls. A man of military distinction should know better than to allow himself to be hemmed in like that, I should think.

I curtsied politely enough to impress a duke, but the colonel didn't even glance in my direction. Determined not to be fobbed off, I inquired, "Have you just come from the continent? My sister's husband was in—"

But he neither looked at me nor acknowledged the question, interrupting me with a gruff, "Charmed."

Though I had never been so thoroughly snubbed in my life, I bit back the spirited set-down which would have made Mother balk. Instead, I turned sharply on my heel and collided into another gentleman from the colonel's party. "I beg your pardon," I said, annoyed that he had stolen my opportunity for a haughty departure.

He reached out to steady me. "Not at all. I can assure you the pleasure was all mine."

I scoffed. "Yes. If there was any pleasure to be had, it was most certainly all yours." I wrested my arm from his gloved clutches.

He laughed loudly, drawing my eyes to his handsome face. But wait—

I knew this gentleman.

What was his name? I stared into his eyes as he searched mine but could not find within their depths the surname I sought. I offered a curt curtsy and hurried on my way to rejoin the Skinners with Mother right behind me.

Once out of earshot, I whispered to her, "Who was that gentleman?"

She replied loudly in slow, concise tones. "Colonel Thoroton of the Coldstream Guards."

I forced a smile. "I meant the gentleman I bumped into after the colonel's dismissal."

She looked over her shoulder to appraise him. "The one immaculately dressed in the poppy-colored waistcoat?"

I looked at him again and nodded. I had been too busy staring into his eyes to have noticed his absurdly vibrant attire.

"I have never met him in my life."

But where had we been introduced if Mother did not know him?

Mother situated Angel and me as close to the twirling couples as possible, then distanced herself so we could attract dance partners like lures for fish. I would have enjoyed dancing with a gentleman of the colonel's social standing but was relegated to scanning the ball for more willing partners.

"Where are Charlotte and John this evening?" Angel asked.

"My sister feigned a headache so she could finish reading her novel, and John and Mr. Smith took the barouche." And a good thing too. No doubt Mr. Smith would have found some way to sit entirely too close to me if we'd had to share a carriage. He was the most odious house guest imaginable. "What about your brother?"

Angel shrugged. "Will is around here somewhere."

I could usually depend on the overzealous vicar to offer me the first dance. "Surely our chaperones could have managed more than one introduction before seeing to their own entertainment. I don't recognize a soul past the Orlebars, and they are busy hosting."

Angel fanned herself, causing the loose ringlets that normally framed her face to billow about her ears. "What of that gentleman you bumped into? The one standing next to Colonel Thoroton?"

I looked back at him, willing myself to conjure a surname from his curly brown hair or chiseled jaw. "I am sure I have met him before, but I cannot recall his name."

Angel sent him a coy glance. "His manner and bearing are much nicer than the colonel's. He's more handsome too."

"Why don't you ask your mother for an introduction? Or should I ask her for you?" I winked at Angel.

She swatted me with her fan. "Don't you dare, Anne. Mother's attempts at matchmaking are bad enough without your interference." She grabbed my arm. "I see Mr. Smith. Shall we hide before he spots you?"

"We had better." We turned away from the dance floor and attempted to become wallflowers.

Mr. Smith had come to Rushden to buy one of Father's horses. When Father had invited him to stay for a bit of hunting, I had been struck by his handsome appearance and looked forward to furthering our acquaintance. At the first opportunity to speak without being overheard, Mr. Smith had whispered, "You are gorgeous, by the way." While flattered at first by his attentions, the excitement soured after his eyes slipped with alarming frequency to my bodice. As if that weren't atrocious enough, he came across me alone in the garden one day and not only tried to steal a kiss, but also had the audacity to offer a carte blanche.

That man had some nerve. I had no idea why he thought I might be amenable to becoming his mistress; he never so much as looked at Charlotte, though she was more beautiful than me by far. But whatever the reason for his lechery, I had spent the majority of the week both avoiding him and abusing him to Angel.

My brother and Mr. Smith approached us, our attempts at hiding notwithstanding.

"I have not attended a ball this crowded since London," John said.

I self-consciously fiddled with my hair and checked that the lace of my bodice had not slipped. While I normally thought well of my womanly figure, standing in Mr. Smith's presence was enough to make me feel insufficiently attired. I longed for a shawl to hide in, in spite of the room's warmth.

"Miss Fletcher," Mr. Smith said, "would you care to dance?"

Not with him ogling me for the entirety. But neither did I want to decline and be forced to sit out the whole evening like an invalid. I scanned the ballroom again but saw no one who was familiar enough to approach. Where was Angel's brother when I needed him?

The only person I could see whom I could even remotely call an acquaintance was the colonel and his handsome friend; both men were surrounded by women like barnacles on a ship. The colonel's friend must have sensed my gaze upon him, for he turned and looked in my direction. I smiled slightly. He nodded briefly in return, and that would be all the reprieve I would receive. It would have to do.

Keeping my sights on him, I responded to Mr. Smith. "I am afraid my first dance has already been claimed. If you will excuse me."

Walking away was easy, but heaven help me, I would need a miracle to pull off the charade I had concocted without looking the fool. Though my palms grew sweaty inside my gloves, I gathered all the confidence I could muster and strode to the dandy, whose eyebrows rose lazily at my approach. The other members of his party turned to me, their looks souring and their conversation abating in pace with my arrival.

I addressed the ladies. "I am sorry to have disturbed your lively conversation, but I really ought to offer my salutations to a family friend." Turning to the gentleman, I said cheerily, "It has been so very long. How do you do?"

He pursed his lips as if he were trying to restrain laughter, causing his dimples to press into creases. "It has been entirely too long. How do *you* do?"

I knew a moment's relief, grateful that he recognized me. "I have been better."

He seemed surprised that I gave him an honest response. Men always were.

"But I am glad I have found you and can claim that dance you promised me years ago. Do you remember?" I sent a prayer heavenward that his friendly manner would entice him to play along with this farce.

His searching eyes compelled me to look away. He stepped to the side a few paces, and I followed him, distancing both of us from his acquaintances. His voice came soft and felt far off. "I promised a great many things years ago, but I no longer dance, so you do not have to bestow that foolishly requested favor upon me."

Of course that was his response. How absurd of me to have had the audacity to—

He took one step closer so that I felt his warm breath on my exposed neck as he whispered, "But perhaps I shall grant the next impertinent request that falls from those deliciously pert lips." He was so close that I could feel his mouth pull into a grin, sending shivers down my spine.

I stepped away immediately. I need not guess what sort of "request" he had in mind. Curse my luck; I had bounced from the company of one cad into another. "Oh . . . I am afraid my heart was set on that dance. Well, um . . ." I was mumbling, and I never mumbled. "If you are opposed to dancing in general . . . that is to say, if you are unable . . ." His flirtation had completely ungrounded me. I stepped farther away from him and glanced back at my group, knowing I would be forced to return like a pup with its tail between its legs and accept Mr. Smith's offer. The thought threatened tears.

Mr. Smith, noticing my glance, broke away from the group and came slinking toward me.

That was it. I had to do something. I leaned back toward the unknown gentleman, speaking as quietly as possible so the females of the company, who stood mere paces away, would not hear. "Then perhaps you would be willing to find another scapegoat for me? Any scapegrace will do, really." Could he see my distress?

Not likely, since all he did was laugh raucously and draw the attention of more than his party. But he kept his response to a conspiratorial whisper, again stepping too close to me. "Though many have called me a scapegrace, I have been around long enough to know better than to be goaded by a bewitching woman."

He took a step away, and my lungs filled with air. I had hardly realized I'd stopped breathing. Sweeping his arm to the side, he displayed his group, all female, save the colonel. "To which of my companions would you like an introduction?" His voice sounded too loud, and the malicious look of several ladies indicated they both heard and understood the gist of our tête-à-tête. "The colonel would refuse, and the ladies would prove terrible partners for you, due to their gender." He paused here and took another step closer to me, whispering again. "They also turn jealous when outshined by one so beneath their touch."

I sucked in a breath. His words flattered and humiliated in turns but did not help. Useless dandy.

My body tensed as Mr. Smith flanked me from behind my left shoulder. Since I refused to turn and acknowledge him, I was able to note the appraising glances of the women in Colonel Thoroton's retinue. They must have appreciated Mr. Smith's handsome physique, for though I would have thought it impossible, they all seemed to stand a little taller and smile even more inanely.

"Ah, Mr. Smith, what luck. My good friend here"—If only I could remember his name—"was introducing me to his entourage who might benefit from a fine dance partner such as yourself."

My bet proved well-placed, for many of the women joined us, and in quick order, Mr. Smith led one exquisitely dressed girl to join the dance.

Without the weight of Mr. Smith's presence pressing into me, I smiled cheekily. "Please consider the scapegoat you just provided as a perfectly sufficient substitute for the favor of your dance. It was noble of you to have offered one of your own disciples, even if only because you were too cowardly to place yourself on the altar." I left before I could see his reaction. This time, I did not bump into anyone.

The sound of his boisterous laughter followed me all the way to where John and Angel should have been. But they had gone to the dance floor together, the little traitors. I sighed at their betrayal, but before I could search for Mother, a pair of gloved hands covered my eyes. The familiar scent of dusty tomes assaulted me.

Will.

I wished he would not do such things in a crowded hall where anyone might misinterpret his familiarity. "And where have you been hiding yourself, Mr. Skinner?" I said. "I could have used your assistance a moment ago."

He gave a throaty chuckle and dropped his hands, though his left hand trailed down my arm to clasp my wrist. He used that leverage to turn me to him before he raised my hand to his lips. "No surprising you, is there?"

"Not when it comes to you." His overtures to me were quite predictable, though misguided. We would never suit, and I could not fathom why he failed to see that.

"Someday, Miss Fletcher, I hope to change that. But for now, dance with me?"

I nodded my consent and soon found myself swept away with the vicar and past the dandy with the outlandish waistcoat. I couldn't help but notice the way he alternately smirked at me or glared at Will every time my dance steps brought me closer to him. I wondered, idly, what it might feel like to dance with a man as tall as he.

Though my dainty sister Charlotte always claimed jealousy over my Hellenic proportions, I wished that didn't place my full bodice—which often struggled to contain its burden during the vigorous steps of a country dance— directly into a shorter man's line of sight. Though Will was not short, per se, he still stood an inch or two shorter than me; at least his eyes remained fastened on mine.

I danced with countless partners after Will, but the flirtatious glances the dandy sent me prevented me from giving any of them my full attention. Instead, I found myself wondering what kind of remarks sent his unholy laughter to desecrate the propriety of the ballroom.

Who was he and where had we met? I couldn't recall and decided I had better cast him out of my mind before I misstepped or said something untoward. I wouldn't have a dandy ruin my chances for a little bit of freedom.

In the end, it was the vicar who rescued me from the dance floor. "Would you like a drink?"

I nodded gratefully, and Will escorted me to the table of refreshments in the adjoining room.

"Have you enjoyed yourself?"

"Very much, in spite of dancing with some eccentric and—well, quite frankly, ill-mannered—gentlemen from London." I sipped the punch he offered, thankful for the refreshment after so much dancing. "I had thought the rules of etiquette were even stricter in Town, but I am starting to wonder if Mother has just been pulling the wool over my eyes."

"No, your mother is correct. Things are stricter . . ." He swirled his punch while gathering his thoughts. With a lowered voice, he added, "But ever since the prince regent gained popularity, eccentricities have become more permissible. Maybe that is what you experienced tonight." He finished his drink and set his glass on the table.

Eccentricities? Hope blossomed in my chest like an eagle unfurling its wings. If London was a place where eccentricities were permitted with greater frequency, then perhaps, after my sisters were safely married, I would find a sense of belonging there. I certainly had not found it within my own home.

"Anne, are you all right?"

"Never better actually." I shook away thoughts of London. "So, is that why a gentleman flirted with me something awful tonight? He is of the regent's ilk?" Though my hackles had risen at the dandy's flirtations, at least he never leered at me like Mr. Smith had.

Will's brows puckered into a scowl. "You should not allow gentlemen to flirt with you, *mon enfant.*"

I bristled at his patronizing tone; Will chastised me almost as often as Mother. "I am neither a child nor yours to so label."

"No, Anne, you have always been in your own keeping, even as much as your mother and governess have tried their best to prevent it." He offered a lopsided grin, as if one side of his mouth knew he should not smile at my antics but the other could not refrain. "I pity the man that should someday try to take possession of your indomitable spirit."

"So do I. It's why I shall never marry." I had no desire to trade a mother who ruled over me until I reached my majority for a husband who would lord over me for life.

"Neither is the man without the woman nor the woman without the man, in the Lord. It is your duty to marry and serve your husband."

Ugh, vicars. Serve or slave?

The dandy strolled into the room with a lady on each arm, offering me a welcome distraction. He nudged past Will and me to attain beverages for his companions.

In order to stop the vicar's forthcoming lecture on marriage, I turned to the dandy and blurted out the first thing that came to mind. "What a practical waistcoat you have chosen, sir."

"Practical?" he spluttered, his face contorted in a show of abject horror.

Dash it all. Why had I chosen that word? If only I had spared a moment to think before speaking. In for a penny, I guess. "Yes, quite practical. You may spill punch on your waistcoat to no effect. It may even enliven the ensemble."

His eyes widened while his face flushed. Apparently, one should not criticize a dandy's choice of attire.

Well, at least I had circumvented Will's lecture. Probably.

I placed my glass of orgeat back on the table and stuck my hand out for Will to offer me an escort. He hastily threaded my arm through his, and together, we fled the room. I looked over my shoulder, hoping my comment had not made the gentleman livid enough to create a scene, but he only shook his head, his shoulders lifting in silent laughter.

"Do you know him?" Will asked, stalling our progress back into the still-packed hall.

"We have met before, though I cannot recall his name. Do you know him?"

"No, and I cannot believe you would say something so impertinent to a stranger, Anne. You grow too bold." He frowned at me.

"Please don't tell my mother."

He brought a knuckle to his mouth, pretending to cough. "Are you afraid I shall tattle on you, Miss Fletcher?"

"Perhaps." I might have been brave, but Mother was terrifying. She would lock me in the larder with the rats if she heard tale of my insult, then force me to accompany her to London.

He took my gloved hand in his and raised it to his lips, whispering, "You should know by now where my allegiance lies." His brows quivered eagerly.

I withdrew my hand, both grateful for his loyalty and frustrated with the passion in his eyes which I knew I could not match. Not that I didn't care for Will; I did. He had been a good friend to me, especially when it came to defending me from both our mothers. But, over the course of the last year, he had begun to see me differently. And I didn't like it. Not one bit.

Afraid that someone might have spied his fervor, I glanced back through the open doors into the room with the refreshments. The dandy had been watching me but looked quickly away, bending over slightly to whisper into the ear of his blonde companion; she laughed haughtily.

My blood boiled with the suspicion that they were mocking me. I turned my back on them, prodding Will to escort me to our mothers, who stood talking to an unknown young lady.

Mrs. Skinner grabbed Will's arm, pulling him away from me. "Will, you must meet Miss Loveland. She's a cousin of ours."

"Indeed?" William bowed gallantly. "It's a pleasure to meet you."

As Miss Loveland bowed, curls the color of freshly tilled earth danced about her shoulders. With the same dark eyes and fair skin that Angel and Will boasted, it was easy to see the resemblance. "I am pleased to learn I have cousins in this area."

Mrs. Skinner's voice cut through all the other ballroom chatter. "A distant relation, to be sure." She turned to Miss Loveland. "Now, if I have this right, your father, who is a solicitor, married Pheobe Skinner." She turned to Will again. "Pheobe is your father's cousin, you know."

Miss Loveland gave Will a coy smile. "Yes, that's right—"

Mrs. Skinner did not give her the chance to finish. "She lives in London, but she and her Father are here by special invitation from the Orlebars—her father is their solicitor, you know. But now the poor poppet has naught to do while her papa hunts grouse. You ought to visit her."

Will glanced at me briefly but responded, "Of course. It would be an honor."

"Yes, you must call on me," she said, smiling demurely.

From the corner of my eye, I noticed the handsome dandy extract himself from his entourage and walk toward me with a mischievous grin on his face. Afraid that he would say something scandalous in front of Mother, I pulled her aside. "I am quite tired. Perhaps we had better return home and allow the Skinners to acquaint themselves with their cousin."

Mother consented to an early departure and we made our goodbyes, but the dandy cut off our escape.

"I am sorry to have disturbed your lively conversation, but I really ought to offer my salutations to a family friend," he said affably. "It has been so very long. How do you do?"

Clever man to turn my own words against me in this fashion. Now it was my turn to trip around this conversation without embarrassing myself. "I cannot be much better or worse than I was a few minutes ago when we conversed over the punch bowl." I fanned myself, feigning innocence. "Or perhaps you were speaking to my mother?"

A crease formed between Mother's brows. "I am sorry, but I do not recall . . ." She looked between him and me in confusion.

"Mr. Thomas Paling, ma'am." He bowed and looked at me expectantly.

Thomas Paling? The name was unfamiliar. Had we been complete strangers after all? My stomach twisted at the thought. "Mr. Paling, pray excuse us, but Mother and I were just leaving." I hoped the comment would preclude me from the necessity of offering an introduction, certain that this flirtatious gentleman would somehow use the knowledge of my name against me.

"Perhaps we shall meet again?"

Not if I could help it.

But Mother eyed him with an appreciative gleam, his immaculate dress and bearing testifying to his good name. Thankfully, she remained unaware of the shocking innuendos he'd been tossing my way. "Perhaps," Mother said.

I whisked her away before Mr. Paling could say anything scandalous. Feeling eyes upon me, I looked over my shoulder. Back in the still-crowded ballroom that sparkled in the candlelight, Mr. Paling watched my exit while Will eyed Mr. Paling.

CHAPTER TWO
An Understanding of Sorts

I TRIED NOT TO FIDDLE with my hair while standing before my father. He looked as nervous as I, staring blankly at the shiny mahogany desk rather than meeting my eyes. As a man solely interested in the three Fs— fishing, foxing, and fowling—the cleanliness and order of the room likely unnerved him even more than it did me. Charlotte was the only one who actually used the library.

In the end, it was Mother who addressed me. "There has been a development."

I flinched. Developments were never good. If John lost any more money at the races, the family would be in difficult straits. But then, why did Mother look almost happy?

Father finally lifted his eyes to mine. "I have granted Mr. Skinner permission to court you."

"Mr. Skinner?" My stomach dropped toward my toes. "But I have no desire to marry." I wished Will had asked me first rather than speaking to Father.

Mother dismissed my protest with a wave of her hand, as though it was nothing more than childish folly. "I never thought anyone would be foolish enough to offer for you either. Congratulations."

Married? No thank you. In another two years, I would reach my majority and Mother's reign would come to an end. But if I married, I would never be free. "He is like a brother to me," I said, trying to give an argument which my parents would understand.

"All the more reason to marry." Mother stood and shook out her skirts.

Father rose and started to walk away, but I couldn't let him. "But . . ." I looked at Father. "Please don't force me to marry him."

Father's eyes softened, but after glancing at Mother, his lips pressed together in a light grimace. "I am sure marrying the vicar will be the best thing for you.

Now, if you will excuse me, John and Mr. Smith are waiting for me to join them on the hunt." He walked out of the room without offering me an intercession.

Humdugeon! I knew Mother would be hard to convince, but I had hoped Father might take my side. He had been very kind to me as a child—teaching me to ride, hunt, and fish—up until Mother insisted that I was scaring off Lizzie's marriage prospects. I'd had to trade in my riding breeches for ballgowns and live under my mother's rule ever since.

But marrying—and marrying the vicar, no less—would be so much worse. "You know I struggle to maintain the decorum requisite for a young lady; developing the characteristics to become a proper clergyman's wife might just kill me. Have you forgotten Widow Moulton?"

Mother rubbed her temples, indicating she remembered too well the way I had accidentally set fire to the lacemaker's wares. At eight pounds per square yard, lace surely comprised the most expensive kindling known to man. I had been locked away for a month after that little mishap.

"How could I forget? Thankfully, Mr. Skinner remains unaware. I suggest you keep it that way until it is too late for him to change his mind."

I turned to Mother, feeling desperate enough to openly contradict her. "We aren't well-suited, Mother."

"No, though through no fault of his. *You* are simply unsuitable. But after he marries you, that will no longer be my problem."

I wondered how much joy she would feel once she rid herself of me.

"He should marry Charlotte instead. She would be perfect for him." Amiable Charlotte had never set fire to an old widow's parlor. Not even once.

Mother pressed her temples again. "Mr. Skinner has no desire to marry Charlotte. Besides, she will likely make an excellent match in her first Season. There is no reason to waste her potential on a vicar. But no one else will ever want you."

I adopted my best fighting stance, arms akimbo. "I would rather become a spinster."

Mother pointed her long, slender finger at me, and I knew I was very close to being locked away. "You will marry Mr. Skinner." She turned to leave.

I grabbed her arm as she walked past. "Wait. I'll do anything, Mother. Please don't force me to marry."

She glared at my hand until I removed it.

What could I possibly say to draw empathy from a mother who disapproved of my every move? The only time she had even remotely seemed impressed was . . . "Remember how much attention Mr. Paling showed me at last night's ball? Perhaps if you took me with you to London, I could make an even better match for myself, just like Lottie." Not very likely. I was just buying time.

"You want to go to London?" Mother's jaw dropped. "But you've never wanted a Season before."

True. I had never been this desperate.

"We don't have enough money to turn both you and Charlotte out."

And yet, she had threatened me with just that only last night. Maybe Mother really did know how to bluff.

"It cannot be so expensive now that Lizzie lives in Town." We had no need to rent a home or hire servants; Lizzie would bear the brunt of the expenses for our keeping.

Mother inspected her gloves distractedly. "Yes, if Lizzie's husband had sold out, as he should have, I am sure they would be happy to host us all. But as he insisted on returning to the peninsula and left poor Lizzie a widow who is now living off the grace of her brother-in-law, who may choose to evict her at any moment, it is time for her to economize, not sponsor her two foolish sisters." Mother's lips drew into a tight line. "Do not forget that if Lizzie has a girl, she will be cast out of her home so that the next heir can inherit. And I shall again find myself with three daughters in need of husbands."

I had no need for the reminder. "That is a possibility, but it is just as likely that Lizzie will have a boy and Lottie and I will both make brilliant matches in London. Then you wouldn't need to worry about any of us anymore."

I could see her eyes sparkle as she considered being well and truly free of me.

I decided to press that point. "And I would live much, much farther away. You would never have to see me again. If I lived here, you would see me every Sunday at least."

Mother's frown caused her chin to pucker like prunes. "Still, one in the hand is better than two in the bush. You will marry Mr. Skinner. It really is the best chance we have for a happy outcome."

"Happy for whom, exactly?" I removed my fists off my hips only to ball them tightly at my sides.

"You. You have a chance at real happiness. You have no idea how lucky you are. Mr. Skinner has known you since you were a wild girl who scampered across the woodlands rather than attend to your lessons, and he has still, somehow, found something in you worth admiring."

Her words assaulted me like fiery arrows. "I do not want someone to love me against their better judgement."

She raised her voice. "How could you possibly expect more? You are lucky you have your looks, else you would be doomed to an ignominious life. I have no idea what you think to find in London, but I can promise you, you will never find there what you already have here."

Mother would not be swayed, though that came as little surprise. I backed cautiously out of the library, lest Mother decide to use corporeal punishment to enforce her will. Not until I was up the stairs and locked safely inside my room did I fling myself onto the bed. I screamed into the goose feathers inside my pillow, hoping they would absorb the sound.

He has still somehow found something in you worth admiring.

I wished Mother could do the same, but she only ever rubbed her temples when speaking with me. I was nothing more than a chore to her. I would never do anything monumental enough to earn her love.

She was right, though. Even Will loved me reluctantly, censuring me as often as not. But could I marry him? He would, eventually, expect children, and I couldn't even think of kissing him without shuddering.

Whether I could or couldn't hardly mattered. I would *have* to marry him. Mother would make me.

I tried to tamp down the multitude of emotions that swirled through me, but they bubbled through unbidden. I would need to wind a tourniquet around my heart to prevent my emotions from bubbling through. Who needed a heart, anyway?

Not me. I had no need for such a useless organ.

A knock sounded at my door.

"Go away," I commanded, not bothering to lift my head from the pillow that served as both kerchief to my tears and muffler to my sobs.

"I am sorry, Miss Fletcher, but your mother has sent me to fetch you to sit in the parlor." My maid, Atkins, sounded duly apologetic.

"Is it that time already?" Mother always insisted Charlotte and I join her for her customary receiving hours, though, more often than not, the time passed in complete silence, without any neighbors calling to rescue me from the monotony.

"Miss Fletcher?"

"Yes, Atkins, I shall be down momentarily." I dried my tears and blew my nose. I would face Mother, and she would never know I had shed a tear over her cruelty.

When I entered the parlor, I ignored both Mother and Charlotte and settled on the padded bench in front of the double bay windows. Fog obscured the view of pines and yews that dappled the parklands, but St. Mary's steeple poked through the fog. A shot rang out, and a brace of pigeons scattered in the east.

Fly, little pigeons. Fly away.

"What an idyllic picture you ladies make." I would have recognized Will's resonant baritone if it had wafted over to me from across a crowded hall anywhere in the world, but to hear it now, when I had thought ourselves alone, startled me out of my wits.

An involuntary, inarticulate, and indecorous noise that might loosely be transcribed as "Aaaargh!" escaped me.

He had been walking into the room, but my response stopped him in his tracks. The vicar stared quizzically at me, as if to ascertain my well-being. He offered his familiar, lopsided smile, where one side of his mouth told him it would be improper to smirk but the other won out anyway. Today, it echoed a truth too recently stated: he somehow found something in me worthy of loving, only against his better judgement.

Mother cleared her throat, and Will hurried to rescue me from her censure. "Miss Fletcher, I am sorry if my appearance gives you cause for fright."

"I am surprised, yes, but you could not frighten me." It was a lie; I was terrified.

Mother's eyes bounced back and forth between Will and me before she stood and grabbed Charlotte's hand. She exited the parlor with Charlotte in tow, shutting the door behind her.

Will gazed at me with unmistakable ardor and took a step closer.

I walked in the opposite direction, to the piano, and carefully removed my gloves before I began to play.

Though turned away from him, I could hear Will's approach. When he placed a hand on my shoulder, my entire body tensed. He trailed his fingers down my arm, and a sense of dread pooled in my stomach.

"Anne." His voice was incredibly gentle. "I have a deep regard for you."

"And I for you." But my voice broke.

He pulled me to my feet and turned me to face him, but I kept my head tucked down. "Darling, look at me, please?" He placed a gloved finger on my chin and lifted my face to him. "Are you crying?"

"No." I was very intentionally not doing that. Again.

He chuckled and extracted a handkerchief from his coat pocket and handed it to me. It smelled like Will: a strange mixture of sweat, horses, and dusty books.

"You are such a watering pot," he said.

I gritted my teeth, trying hard to keep the emotions off my face. But I was an open book to him; he knew me too well.

He sighed and scrubbed his face with his hand. "I know what you need. Let's go for a ride."

I bit my lip, pondering a response. I would usually accept an offer to ride, but if he meant to propose . . . "I'm not sure I can. You know my father and John use all the grooms and stablehands when they are on the hunt."

He ignored my objection and tugged on my arm. "Let's just go see, shall we?" Mother was easy enough to find, whispering with Lottie in the corridor just outside the parlor. "Would it be all right if I borrowed Miss Fletcher?" Will asked. "We should like to go for a ride."

Borrowed? Mother would like nothing more than to give me away and never get me back.

"Yes, of course," Mother responded.

"But Price and Charles are assisting in the hunt today. I shall have no groom," I said.

She offered a chilling smile. "Since when have you ever needed a groom, Anne?"

I blinked several times. She always insisted I be trailed by a groom whenever I rode in mixed company.

Will patted my hand condescendingly. "Don't worry, Mrs. Fletcher. I shall keep a good eye on her. I know she has more heart than head when it comes to riding."

I huffed. "True of most things, actually." I wanted to push Will away, hoping he would see how ill-suited I was, but he gave me that tilted smile again. Maddening.

"Thank you, Mr. Skinner. I am sure she will not give you any trouble." Mother's look warned me that I would see a strict punishment if I did not comply.

William Skinner was going to keep an eye on *me* to make sure I came to no harm while riding? His condescension was absurd, at best. But at least I would have the chance for a ride. I needed that; I needed to clear my head.

Atkins helped me into my riding habit, and all too soon, I was ready.

"Enjoy your ride," Mother said almost gleefully. I had never seen her so happy.

Will was waiting for me in the stables. "Let me offer you a leg up." He interlaced his fingers for me to step into.

"Thank you, Will, but you know I prefer the mounting block." Ever since I'd kicked Will in the face during a dismount—and nearly broken his nose—I'd refused offers for his assistance. My tall, broad frame was a stone or two heavier than most people anticipated, and it embarrassed me to no end to hear them grunt and struggle under my weight. Will, both shorter and thinner than me, was no exception. I walked Buttercup to the block and mounted unassisted. "Where shall we ride today?"

Will shrugged. "I told Miss Loveland I would call upon her sometime. Are you up for a ride to Hinwick?"

"That sounds fine." When we left the stables, an autumnal breeze welcomed me. I breathed in as much fresh air as my lungs could hold before hissing it out slowly. Once I brought Buttercup to a gallop, the wind bit my cheeks, but it only spurred me faster. I relished the scent of last night's rain, which had done its work in reviving the verdure of the fields toward Hinwick. Slowly, my apprehension faded, exhilaration taking its place.

Will kept up but allowed me to lead, and I pushed Buttercup until she tired. The poor mare would have to walk the rest of the way. Will pulled up beside me. "Why haven't I ever seen you on the hunt? You ride as well as most men."

I grunted. Maybe this was my opportunity to push Will away—convince him how ill-suited we were. "I used to dress in breeches and join John and Father on the hunt."

He looked at me askance.

I pressed on. "One time I was fast enough to follow the hounds to their quarry. I still remember the keening whine the vixen made as her life bled out all those years ago."

There. A less ladylike statement may have never been uttered.

But he only chuckled. "The mysterious sensibilities of women. Shall I ever understand?"

Not likely. I huffed.

"Anne, I want to talk to you about something in particular."

I tightened my grip on Buttercup's reins. "Don't say anything we will both regret."

His dark brows trembled as he spoke, pain already written across them. "You mean to refuse me, then." His voice trembled. "May I ask why?"

"You know I have never had any desire to marry."

He scoffed. "So you have said. But would you really rather live with your mother all your life? It would be a hell on earth for both of you."

"Yes, but Mother will send me to Lizzie once she has her baby. I plan on becoming the most doting aunt ever."

He raised one of his arched brows at me. "I'm fairly offended you would rather live with Elizabeth than me. We get along much better than you have ever managed with your sister."

He raised a good point. And yet, I would never have to kiss *her*. "I'm sorry, Will, but you are like a brother to me."

His eyes glossed over, and a vein pulsed in his forehead, testifying to his mounting anger. "You are nothing like a sister to me."

"I know." I bit my lip. "Whatever enticed you to offer for me in the first place?"

He studied his pocket watch. "I did not like the way that dandy looked at you last night."

Oh fustian! A little bit of flirtation and now Will tried to wind a chain around my neck. "But you know I have no desire to marry."

He brushed away some invisible fluff. "I thought you were being coy."

I huffed. "William Andrew Skinner, in the five years you have known me, have I ever once acted coy?"

He shrugged. "You are hardly old enough to know your own mind. How could I be expected to know it?"

Listening to me would make a good start. "I would make a terrible wife. I always say and do the wrong things."

He scowled. "Like right now, for instance, where you should be accepting my offer with gratitude."

"Yes, exactly. You don't want someone who quarrels with you during your proposal."

He stuck out his chin belligerently.

Frustration and anger mounted hot as coals, but I swallowed it back. How could I get him to listen to me? Maybe if I played to his vanity? "Like you said, I am still very young and unsure of my own mind. I am certainly too immature to marry someone as sophisticated and responsible as you are. Perhaps if I have a chance to grow up . . . say, in another year or two . . . after I have at least one Season . . ."

He looked at me like I was daft. "Since when have you wanted a Season?"

Since he decided to propose. Besides, if London was—like he said—a place where eccentricities were looked upon with a greater degree of tolerance, then perhaps I could find a sense of belonging there. But even if Town was every bit as stuffy and horrid as I had imagined, it was my last hope. "I realize now that I am too silly to be a dutiful wife. I need a Season to help teach me propriety."

Perhaps if I went away, Will would realize how delusional he had been and swear a voluntary oath of celibacy.

"I sincerely doubt you would find London to your liking."

Yes, but I knew what awaited me if I stayed here: Mother's censure and a forced marriage. "I want a Season."

"You want to attend balls and routes and the theater before you marry? That is not a lifestyle I could afford to support."

"I know."

He scratched his chin. "London might be good for you. If you had been raised there instead of this remote town, I have no doubt you would have learned proper manners by now. You will need an abundance of those once we marry."

Once we marry? I hated that he considered our union a foregone conclusion. "I have no choice in the matter, do I?" I was trapped. I clenched Buttercup's reins in my fists. She slowed, then stopped as a result.

Will halted his horse as well. "You mean to refuse me, but your parents will force you."

"Yes." Finally, he understood me. If I could convince Will to drop his suit, my parents would not be able to force my hand. Of course, they might lock me away for the rest of my life, but that was a risk I was willing to take. "Don't force me to marry. Please."

He gave me a sad look, then urged Phillip into a trot.

I let him take the lead, grateful for the space. But all too soon, he trotted back to me. We walked our horses together silently before he spoke. "Then I suppose we must find a way to get you to London."

"Really, Will? You would do that for me?" I blinked at him several times, hope beginning to blossom.

"I will talk to your mother, tell her that you require a little bit of Town polish. But know that if I do this, I would like a promise from you in return."

My hope instantly deflated. "What promise?"

"If you find someone else in London whom you want to marry, then I shall wish you well. But if you don't, promise to marry me when you get back. I love you, Anne."

I felt like a horse had thrown me. "I . . ." I could not return those words. I didn't know if I ever could. Not to him or anyone else. I had never seen love before and didn't even know how it worked.

He drew closer to me and placed his hand on my arm. "I know you don't love me. I also know that if your parents force you to marry me, you will only resent me. But if I allow you to go to London . . ."

I waited for him to finish his thought, but he never did. "I see. You are betting against the odds that I will garner success as a debutante. After all, a Newmarket horse has poor odds at Ascot." He would dangle London in front of me like a carrot, while hoping that I would end up back in my stall, where I belonged, soon enough. Either way, a marriage would be in my future.

He shrugged. "I suppose, though I find your phrasing vulgar."

Of course he did. He did not approve of horse racing. Or betting. Or me. Why he thought he loved me, I had no idea.

I tapped Buttercup with my crop, nudging her forward a few paces. What should I do? Should I take the bet? Take a chance for happiness in London? What did I have to lose? If I stayed here, my parents would force me to marry.

I slowed Buttercup, then looked into Will's variegated brown eyes and nodded. "If you can convince my mother to take me to London for a Season, and if I do not become engaged while there, then I promise that when I return, I will marry you." My voice trembled at the end, but I said the words.

We had an understanding . . . of sorts.

CHAPTER THREE
Of Horses and Men

WE EMERGED FROM THE COPSE of trees, and Hinwick House appeared before us. I felt suddenly shy to be here. Alone. With Will. What would people think if they should spy us?

What a bumble-broth I was in now. "I shall go back to the woods while you call on your cousin."

"What? Afraid to be seen with me, Anne?"

"A little," I said weakly.

He looked hurt. "We could go back home."

"Don't be silly. Your cousin is the reason we have come."

He nudged his horse close enough that our legs brushed. "The purported reason, at any rate. We could, of course, start making calls together as soon as you would like."

The sight of John frantically trying to beat out the fire in Widow Moulton's parlor burst across my mind's eye. No. I had no desire to attend social calls with Mr. Skinner. Not ever. "I have made calls with John before—"

William tossed his hands in the air, exasperated. "So have I. And I have made calls with Angel. What has that to do with anything?"

I glared at him. If he had allowed me to finish my statement, he would know what a pariah I was and what a trial that would be for a vicar who needed to stay in the good graces of his parishioners.

But he continued. "Though it may feel so to you, Anne, I am not your brother." He glanced to the heavens, probably praying for patience. "While I call on Miss Loveland, you can tend the horses for once. Stables are that way." He pointed to the left of the house. "May you be so lucky as to avoid the manure." He dismounted and handed me Phillip's reins.

I huffed at him but led the horses to a dark and very empty stable; the gentlemen and all the grooms must be on the hunt. That was fine by me, ideal even, for not even a stablehand was around to gossip about my unconventional visit to the stables. Unfortunately, I couldn't see any mounting blocks; I would have to dismount on my own.

I unhooked my right leg, removed my left foot from the stirrup, and slid off Buttercup. But when I tried to turn to my mare to lead her to a stall, I found myself incapable of moving; my skirt must have caught on the pommel. "Confounded riding habit." This never would have happened if I was allowed to wear breeches.

With my limited range of motion, I was unable to reach behind me or bend to find the stirrup. I twisted behind myself with more vigor but was only rewarded with the distinctive sound of fabric ripping. I was well and truly tethered to my mare.

Phillip, whose reins I still held, was eyeing me curiously, and I could almost imagine him sniggering. "Oh, quit laughing and help me out, will you?" I pulled on his reins, and he nudged his body closer. "That's a boy." I was able to coerce him right alongside Buttercup, whereupon I put my right boot in his right stirrup. Hoisting myself up, I reached backwards and was able to extract my skirt from Buttercup's pommel.

"Success," I cried. "I'm free." Buttercup, long accustomed to my boisterous outbursts, did not so much as twitch, but Phillip startled, pulling me away from Buttercup. In order to keep from falling, I swung my left leg up over his saddle, whereupon he took off.

In a flash, he was back out the stable doors. "Easy, boy, easy." He followed my commands on his reins, slowing to a stop, but I could feel the energy boiling inside him. Unlike my mare, who had virtually exhausted herself from the ride here, the black stallion, just old enough to be a colt no longer, was not in need of rest. Like me, he was bursting with vitality, longing for the breeze through his mane, the chill biting his cheeks, his heart pounding with exhilaration.

Will had asked me to care for the horses. Perhaps the best way to do so was to allow Buttercup to rest while I gave Phillip the extra exercise he demanded?

"What do you think you're doing?" A man emerged from the stables with Buttercup in hand.

Where had he come from? I was sure I had been alone. Had he witnessed my struggle and subsequent exposure? Now I would become gossip fodder for sure. "Phillip here started, and I was just going to—" I stopped spluttering an excuse when I registered that it was no ordinary stablehand who held Buttercup's reins.

Mr. Thomas Paling stood there with the smile of a jackal.

"Where did you come from?"

"I asked you first, Miss—?"

"Don't you remember me?" I asked indignantly. "Or did you flirt with so many ladies last night that you couldn't possibly expect to—"

"Of course I remember you," he cut me off. "But you never gave me your name."

Oh. Right. I should offer it now, but I still hesitated. He could tell everyone he knew that he had seen me riding astride, but without a name to attach to the gossip, the scandal couldn't attach itself to me.

Mr. Paling continued walking toward me. "How could I forget a lady who had the audacity to assume an acquaintance with me, approach me whilst in the company of her social superiors, and demand that I dance with her?"

I swallowed the lump in my throat as he listed my terrible breaches of etiquette. "But I didn't assume an acquaintance. We have met before—before last night's ball, that is—haven't we?" Though I was becoming less and less sure of it; dimples as adorable as his would have made a more lasting impression. But I stuck with my argument; it represented the smoothest exit from last night's follies.

He pursed his lips and narrowed his eyes, as if he were trying to remember any other time we may have met. "Believe me, if we had ever met before, I would have remembered, Miss—?"

I decided to deflect his question. "But you seem so familiar."

His eyes twinkled mischievously. "That must be why you acted overly familiar with me. But I can assure you that I never forget introductions to beautiful women."

My cheeks burned, and I averted my gaze, but that only brought my attention to the scandalous amount of my leg currently on display as I straddled the stallion. Not helpful. I pulled my habit down as far as I could. "Then why didn't you tell me I was mistaken when I claimed an acquaintance at last night's ball?"

He reared back. "I would never refuse to acknowledge a woman who claimed an acquaintance. It would be rather boorish of me, don't you think? Besides, that ball was dreadfully dull, and you provided better entertainment than the scads of ladies who flocked around me to get closer to the colonel."

Remembering all the coy glances Mr. Paling had received, I doubted his statement was entirely truthful.

Phillip shuffled restlessly beneath me.

"So tell me, miss, what are you doing astride that horse?"

"He spooked, and I calmed him. What were *you* doing in that dark stable? Alone?" I peered around him. I didn't see anyone, but he seemed exactly the type of gentleman who might agree upon a clandestine meeting with an unscrupulous female.

But rather than tell me, he grinned unabashedly. "You were going to ride him, weren't you? I stopped you just before you tapped him with your crop."

I made no reply. I needed to get out of here. Now. I nudged Phillip toward the dandy and reached for Buttercup's reins, but he pulled his hand back and kept both hands low and away from me.

"Please, Mr. Paling, would you hand me my horse's reins?"

He grinned wolfishly. "No, I think not. I need the use of your mare for a few minutes."

What on earth could he possibly want with poor old Buttercup?

He turned to my horse then back to me with a frown upon his face. "You wouldn't be interested in offering me a leg up, would you?"

What a ridiculous question. How would I even . . . "You are not going to ride my mare."

He shrugged with the grin of a street urchin upon his face. "If you can ride astride that spirited stallion, then I am sure I should be able to manage mounting this docile creature."

"But—" I really wished I could think of something to follow that conjunction; for once, my tongue left me bereft.

He grabbed the pommel and tried to place his left foot in the stirrup, but the slipper was a tad higher than he was accustomed to. His left leg was not quite flexible enough. He began hoisting himself up using only the strength of his arms, but with all the weight on one side, the saddle slipped to the left.

I sniggered.

He glanced at me in annoyance. "This is not as easy as it looks."

"I am quite aware of the fact. But it is easier in breeches than with yards and yards of extra fabric about your legs."

He raised an eyebrow at that. "And you would know?"

"Of course."

He mimicked my voice with his falsetto. "Of course. I can do anything Mr. Paling can." He huffed.

I laughed. "Probably, though I'm sure my mother's punishment for my unladylike behavior would be severe."

He tried to wrestle into the unfamiliar saddle again, letting go of the pommel so he could use both hands to draw his left leg up into the stirrup. He stood there with both legs perfectly straight but at right angles.

I tried not to pay attention to how snugly his buckskin breeches molded to his muscular legs while in this position. "You do realize that any other mare in the world would have dashed off by now. Perhaps we could find a pony for you."

He waved me away, finally bending both legs enough to jump on one foot and give himself the leverage needed to mount Buttercup—without pulling the saddle down on top of him.

Mr. Paling, with his broad shoulders and muscular build, would look quite striking if he were well mounted. But to see a strong, secure man fold in on himself to daintily arrange his legs into a sidesaddle tickled my soul. I laughed too loud to be considered polite, then snorted when I attempted to stifle my levity.

He looked bemused, but his face flushed to a shade more akin to purple than red, belying the embarrassment he tried to hide behind his humor. "Right then. Are you quite done?"

"I think not," I said, though I tried to rein in my mirth.

His next words helped sober me. "Then I shall have the advantage. I'll race you to the copse of trees." And off he went—not in a straight line, for he had no whip and was unable to direct Buttercup with pressure from his legs as he was used to. He whooped and yipped, trying to spurn Buttercup forward. She wobbled like a souse. At last, my mare understood what was wanted and ambled toward the trees.

I tried to sit up straight, but the laughter had put stitches in my side and made it hard to breathe. He had a good lead on me by the time I controlled myself enough to urge Phillip on. A gentle nudge was all that was needed, though, and Phillip shot forward. His gait was so smooth and even. I had never felt so akin to a bird in flight.

Free. I felt completely free. It had been years since I had been able to ride anyone faster than old Buttercup. It was intoxicating. I could do this forever, but I caught up with Mr. Paling in no time at all, outstripping him before we reached the copse of trees.

Having already lost, Mr. Paling slowed Buttercup to a walk. "How on earth do ladies go anywhere on these saddles?"

"We use a crop for the offside."

I returned to him and handed him the whip. He experimented with it, and after a time, Buttercup understood his commands and turned. He pulled her beside me as we walked our horses back toward the stable. "Still, I have never seen a woman ride like you." He looked me over from head to toe.

I glowered at him. A gentleman should have the decency not to look at a lady's exposed ankles.

"How did you come to be saddled with this old lady?"

I pursed my lips as I considered the tale. "Buttercup is the perfect horse for a lady: docile, obedient, and sweet. Mother couldn't cultivate those particular traits in me, so she mired me with a half-dead mare instead. But Phillip here is a fine creature. My father bred him." I leaned forward to pat his silky mane. "Now, Mr. Paling, would you be so kind as to tell me what you were doing alone in that stable and why you did not make your presence known earlier?"

His sheepish expression only served to compound the ridiculousness of his feminine posture. "Perhaps you will not believe me."

"I would not have believed I would ever see a gentleman of the *ton* ride sidesaddle before today. Let us assume you have managed to stretch the breadth of my imagination."

He wagged a finger at me. "And I never would have thought the same lady who raced across the open fields like a mad-capped warrior—and astride, mind you—would be the same woman to command every man's attention in the ballroom." He tipped his hat to me, but I shrugged off the insults and flattery, both of which he obviously had too much experience delivering.

"Don't change the subject."

He sighed over-dramatically, and I could not help but giggle at the femininity it leant his persona. "All the men are riding to hounds, whereas all the ladies of the house seem to be setting snares for me and the colonel. I was hiding."

"Why don't you join the men on the hunt to avoid the ladies?"

"I can't," he whined like a schoolboy. "Several of the ladies have felt inspired to take up the sport recently. I can't hunt, and I can't stay in. I have taken to sneaking off shortly after the hunt commences and hiding in the empty stables. Hinwick is the most boring place I have ever visited in my entire life." Now he definitely sounded like a child.

"Quit the house or tell the ladies to leave you alone."

"I wish I had your strength of character. I could beat them all back with my glare." He chuckled.

The sound warmed me.

We were almost back to the stables when William rounded the corner of the house.

"You again?" William pointed at Mr. Paling.

Oh fustian. A jealous Will was the last thing I needed.

CHAPTER FOUR
A Battle of Wills

WILL THREW A DISGUSTED LOOK at me. "What on earth are you doing astride my horse?"

"Phillip startled . . ."

Will's hands clenched and unclenched. From the redness of his face, I knew he was fuming.

"I was just—" I said.

Will raised his hands. "That's enough, Anne. I'm sure you have a perfectly reasonable explanation for this, just like you always do whenever you get into a scrape. You have feathers where your brains should be."

"The more fool you are for wanting to marry such a—"

Mr. Paling startled me by placing a hand on my arm. He shook his head ever so slightly. "This misunderstanding is completely my fault. You see, I have recently put a bet in at White's that I would learn to ride sidesaddle before my friend Colonel Thoroton became engaged. Miss Anne was kind enough not only to provide the use of her mount but has also offered me invaluable instruction. Would you be so kind as to verify you witnessed the success of my wager at White's whenever you are next in Town?"

William slowly relaxed. "I am afraid I don't subscribe to White's."

"No worries, lad. I shall give you a recommendation, er, once I have the benefit of knowing your name." He looked at me meaningfully.

I reluctantly introduced the two gentlemen.

Mr. Paling dismounted somewhat gracefully and handed the reins over to William. "Right-o, then. Thank you both for your assistance. Mr. Skinner, I will await your visit one of these days at White's. Just ask for me." He offered his uncannily large grin and strode back to the stables.

I watched his retreating form, contemplating the enigma that was Mr. Thomas Paling. The dandy who had not helped me in my time of need last night had swooped in and protected me from William's wrath today, giving both Will and me a chance to cool our overactive tempers.

In fact, Will now appeared giddy, nearly bouncing on his toes. "Do you know what this could mean for me, Anne?" He turned to me excitedly before freezing, registering my exposed ankle and calf. He cleared his throat once, twice, then looked into my eyes. "Well, come on down now."

I blushed. Why did William ogle me when Mr. Paling, the obvious flirt, had shown the decency not to? But I didn't dismount. "Can I ride Phillip a little longer?"

"What? And have me ride Buttercup sidesaddle like Mr. Paling?" The ugly vein pulsed on Will's forehead again. "That would be most unseemly. Now come down before you break your neck."

Of course he wouldn't let me ride him. This was Will, the upstanding vicar. He had no room in his life for public indiscretions. I dismounted his stallion—without incident this time—and mounted Buttercup with his assistance.

"What a strange person that Mr. Paling must be," Will mused once he started Phillip back to the copse of trees.

"Indeed." Strange. And kind. Mr. Paling could easily have berated me like Will had. Instead, he topped my indiscretion with a level of ridiculousness that seemed to have deflated the degree of my sins. He then created some tale about a bet at White's to deflect my shame, all while making me laugh so hard I had completely forgotten about the dreadful arrangement I had just made with Will.

Seemingly from nowhere, the wind picked up. "I think a storm is coming in. We had better hurry," Will said.

Though I tried to urge my old mare, she would likely need the better part of an hour to return home. I gave Buttercup's neck a reassuring pat. "We'd better pray the weather holds."

Even the clergyman's invocation was insufficient to keep the storm at bay. Will and I were caught in a deluge while still a mile out. Rain soaked through my riding habit, chilling me to the core.

The stables were still empty when we arrived; the men of the house must still be out on the hunt. "Are you headed to the vicarage or do you care to warm yourself by the fire first?"

He shivered. "I think I will nip into your parlor for a spell before I continue home."

We dashed across the slick grass, handed our soaked outer things to the butler, and entered the empty parlor, warming ourselves by the fire. I cleared my throat, grasping for a subject matter. "I forgot to ask: how does the enchanting Miss Loveland fare?"

Will lifted one of his delicately arched brows so that it looked like a bird in flight. It was so unfair that both he and Angel could sport that self-same look while my brows held no autonomy.

"She is tolerably beautiful, isn't she?" He fed me a look that I could only suppose was supposed to make me jealous.

It failed.

"But at the end of the day, there are qualities I prize more than being tolerable."

"That must be why you are still friends with the *in*tolerable Fletchers."

He graced me with his tilted smile. "Indeed, you beautiful pea-goose."

His compliment only reminded me of his earlier insult. A feather-brained pea-goose. "I am going to change into something drier. Feel free to stay as long as you would like."

Though he opened his mouth as if to say something, his look of ardent admiration spurred me onward. I did not want him repeating his overtures.

I reached my room and pulled the bell for Atkins. When she saw me looking like a drowned kitten, she tutted and muttered under her breath. "You will catch a cold, no doubt. You know your sister has one already."

"Really? She seemed fine this morning." She had claimed a headache last night, but I had thought that an excuse to have a quiet evening to herself.

"Sore throat and a fever, I'm afraid."

Poor Charlotte. I would have to check on her as soon as I was dressed for dinner.

She peeled the wet fabric off me and handed me a dry shift. "And now you will catch it too."

"Stuff and nonsense. I am hardly ever sick." But I shivered as I pulled the worn fabric over my head. Atkins wrapped me in a woolen shawl and moved a chair by the fire. "Bring me a cup of chocolate, Atkins?"

She nodded and left.

I combed through my hair then picked out a blue gown to wear for dinner.

Atkins returned a few minutes later and helped me into the dress. She artfully arranged my hair while I sipped my chocolate, watching the water course down the window in sheets. "Are the men still on the hunt, do you think?" They would have had a miserable time in this weather, and Mother would want my help entertaining Mr. Smith until the storm cleared. The thought was as appealing as skipping through a coven of cockroaches. I prayed the weather cleared quickly.

"No, miss. Thomas was in the kitchens fetching the hip bath for your father. And your vicar has left too." She gave me a sly look. Apparently, the entire household was aware of our understanding already.

"He is as much your vicar as he is mine," I said stiffly.

"If you say so, miss." Her eyes danced, but her lips did not betray her.

A deafening boom reverberated through my home. I screamed, my heart racing. What in the name of all that was good and holy?

CHAPTER FIVE
Disaster Strikes

THE OAK FLOORBOARDS TREMBLED UNDER my feet, and my ears rang painfully. I ran out of my bedchamber and down the corridor to investigate. From the top of the stairs, I saw servants rush in from all directions. A maid wailed like a banshee while the cook seemed to be shrieking in tongues. All was unintelligible until Mother descended upon the scene.

She made a kind of hoot that would have sounded more appropriate in a hunt than inside the manor, but the sound silenced everyone. I followed her down the stairs and into the drawing room, where the beautiful double bay windows had blown out. Strewn across the floor lay thousands of pebbles of glass, which twinkled in the firelight like stars across an oaken firmament. Wind blew the curtains in, and rain misted into the gaping holes where windows had been.

My attention was drawn to the butler, who stood over a male figure slumped along the sofa. Not until he shifted could I tell that both John and Father lay there, still as corpses. Father's buckskins were blackened, and blood trickled down his face.

I tried to approach them, but Atkins grabbed my arm, whispering in my ear. "Not in your slippers, miss. You will cut your feet to pieces."

I pushed away from her and approached John, who sat up, moaning while gaping his jaw open and shut like a fish.

"John, what happened?" Mother demanded, pushing me out of the way to kneel in front of Father. She placed her hand on his heart. "Fetch me smelling salts."

Atkins rushed forward and pulled some out of a hidden pocket in her skirt, handing them to Mother with a minuscule curtsy. Mother unstopped the vial and waved them under Father's nose. He came to, rubbing his forehead and grimacing.

John continued to make odd moaning sounds while working his jaw back and forth.

"What happened?" Mother asked Father, but he made no response; it may have been the only time in her adult life that Mother had ever been ignored.

The butler cleared his throat. "I beg your pardon, ma'am, but I think the explosion may have damaged their hearing."

Mother turned her too-calm gaze to him. "What exploded? Did you see what happened?"

"I do not know for certain, but Mr. Fletcher returned from the hunt and desired to stand by the fire for a spell before going to change his attire. He still wore his powder horn, which must have ignited as he warmed himself."

Merciful heavens! Father lay on the sofa, moaning and still rubbing his head.

"Weatherford, send for the doctor. Mrs. White, will dinner need to be pushed back?" Mother asked.

Cook came out of her trance-like state, her eyes snapping into focus. "No, ma'am."

"Wonderful. Dinner shall be at the same time, Mr. Smith. Kindly finish your preparations."

How very like Mother to want to keep a punctual mealtime while Father lay only half-conscious. But no one would contradict her.

Feeling eyes upon me, I looked up, only to see Mr. Smith ogling me yet again.

Odious man. I straightened my skirts, turning away from him until he left.

Mother gave strictures to all the servants not employed in the kitchen or dining room as to how the glass was to be swept and disposed of and canvas procured to cover the windows. Rescued from chaos, the servants nodded to their queen bee and bumbled off with vim and vigor to accomplish the impossible.

I fussed over John and Father for a moment but was shooed out of the room by Mother. "They need to be moved to their bedchambers, and you are only in the way. Go finish pinning your hair."

I glared at Mother, but once Price, Charles, and Weatherford began assisting John's massive bulk up the stairs, I submitted meekly; there was nothing for me to do but look.

I proceeded to my bedchamber, pinned the rest of my loose locks, and exchanged my customary satin slippers for hard-soled half boots, in case there should still be glass fragments strewn about.

I went down the west wing, where John was quartered. After tapping lightly on my brother's door, his valet stepped out so I could enter. John lounged in bed, looking none the worse for wear, considering that he had been blasted like a fox out of its den.

"I'm all right," he yelled. "No need to worry."

"So you ca—"

"No use, Anne. I can't hear whatever you are trying to tell me, so stop flapping your jaws." His voice was so loud that I was afraid all the house would hear what he could not. I put my fingers to my lips with a shushing sound, but he continued. "Don't shush me. And what do you want? Did you think to nurse me? I'm in no humor to be coddled. Send Charles back in." With a wave of his hand, he dismissed me.

What a pity that my sharp tongue would literally fall on deaf ears. I still offered a futile fiery retort for my graceless dismissal. At least John seemed to be fine. His hearing was damaged, but his wits remained. I had been afraid he might have become permanently addled or hiding some wound.

As I walked down the west wing toward Father's bedchamber, a door opened, and Mr. Smith popped his head out. "Anne, what a pleasant surprise."

I tensed. The man had no leave to call me by my Christian name.

He met me in the corridor and bowed handsomely, but I only offered the merest hint of a curtsy. As I walked past him, his hand shot out and grabbed my right wrist, pulling me to him.

I turned to retaliate, but he opened the door to his room and backed into it, pulling me with him. Like a nightmare, time slowed, each second processing as if it were a full minute long. I fought him but found that Mr. Smith was too strong. He pulled me into the bedchamber. "If you scream now, you are ruined forever."

No. Oh no. No! How could he be so strong?

The door clicked closed behind me, and he pushed me against it, pressing his body hard against mine. He might as well have been a monolith. I pushed and squirmed, trying to evade his grasp to no avail; he pinned my wrists against the door above my head.

"I love the ones who fight," he whispered.

My stomach threatened upheaval. I was obviously not the first female he had tried to take advantage of. I stood there, terrified. Helpless in my own home. Weak and insignificant.

With one hand, he lifted up my skirt, pressing my thigh. But the motion loosened his now one-handed grip on my wrists. I wriggled free enough for my knee to find purchase on his groin.

He careened away, and I managed to open the door hastily despite my shaking hand. Before it closed, he squeaked profanities in an unduly high register. The closing door cut off the sound of his voice, and I ran to my room, locking the door behind me.

I breathed heavily, my back against the door, adding my body to the weight of the lock in case Mr. Smith pursued me. Blood pounded in my ears, and my breath came too rapidly, too shallow. I longed to cross to my window, sure that I could breathe properly if only I had fresh air, but my legs would not work. They buckled, and I collapsed into a heap, wincing at the pain in my right wrist as I caught myself. I pulled off my glove and inspected the joint; it looked red and swollen from Mr. Smith's death grip, but I uttered a prayer of gratitude that my wrist was the encounter's only serious casualty.

I began shaking uncontrollably as I remembered the feel of his hands on me. Of his hands lifting up my skirts. These skirts. The pale-blue satin felt vile, and I pulled frantically at the fabric, trying to remove it from touching me. But the buttons in the back would not relent.

I felt the knock before I registered the sound. My body went instantly alert. "Who is it?" My voice sounded rough-hewn and strange in my ears.

"Atkins, ma'am. Your family is waiting on you."

Atkins! The very woman I needed. "Come in, please. I need to change out of this dress." I stood shakily and unlocked the door.

She began walking in but stopped after assessing my distraught state. "Miss, what's wrong?"

"The dress is too tight. It's hard to breathe."

She frowned but fumbled with the buttons. "But why are you trembling?"

"I . . ." I couldn't tell her. Not something so vile. I just wanted it gone—the dress he'd touched, the smell of him on me, and the memory of every sick word he'd uttered. Even if I could find the courage to explain, would she believe me? What if she told my mother? No. It was better to pretend that it never happened. Maybe if I buried the shame deep enough, even I wouldn't have to uncover it. "I am distraught at seeing poor Papa in this state. Please tell Mother I shall take my meal in my room."

After a lengthy pause, Atkins murmured, "Yes, ma'am, but you know she will not be happy about it." She finished undoing the buttons, and I slipped out of the vile thing. "What dress would you like to wear instead?"

"Just hand me my dressing gown, please."

She nodded and handed it to me. I tried not to show the trembling of my hands as I pushed my arms through and tied the sash.

"Are you sure you are all right, miss?"

I nodded, afraid my voice would come as a whimper if I tried to use it again.

Atkins hurried to inform Mother of my requested truancy.

I crossed the room to the window, opening it enough to allow the smell of the downpour to wash over me. My rough-hewn breaths subsided. I leaned my head against the window frame, reviewing what had happened. Praise be to the heavens that I had been able to fend him off, but he was so strong! I had no doubt that a slighter female would never have succeeded.

A few minutes later, another rap sounded at the door, followed by Mother's voice. "Anne, unlock the door."

There was no use fighting her. I opened the door.

"What have you done with your evening dress? Are you unwell?" She placed a hand on my forehead. "Atkins said you seemed rattled."

"Yes, my head hurts something fierce." I had never claimed a headache before, but since it worked for Charlotte, it should work for me as well.

"Charlotte has a fever, and John and your father are obviously unavailable. I need you to pull yourself together to help me entertain Mr. Smith."

That was the last thing I needed. "But Mother—"

"You may get sick tomorrow if you like, but I need you today."

Ah, yes. Here was the empathy I had come to expect.

She quickly thumbed through the dresses in my wardrobe, pulling out a white satin with ties rather than buttons. "Slip this on quickly."

I couldn't even summon the energy to glare at her as she pulled the smooth fabric over my head.

Looking at my tear-streaked face, she said, "I know that noise itself was enough to shake the sins out of Satan, and the windows will cost a fortune to replace, but there is nothing to cry over." Of course Mother was concerned about the disruption of her peace and the cost of windows more than the well-being of her own family. Her heart was as cold as ice.

I gave one last futile attempt to be excused. "But Mother, I cannot go down to dinner and face—"

"Nonsense." She grabbed me by my right wrist and tugged. Hard.

I winced, sucking air through my teeth. Of course she used the same maneuver to bend me to her will as Mr. Smith had. I would have bruises for a week. "Unhand me, and I shall follow you like a dutiful dog."

She eyed me, not appreciative of my tone, but released my wrist. I followed her down the stairs, where Mr. Smith waited, looking innocent as a lamb.

My hands sweated in my gloves. It was just the three of us. Absurd.

Mr. Smith predatorily took my arm, his left forearm brushing my bodice, while Mother walked in front. There was no one to observe him or save me.

Mr. Smith dared to speak. "I worried you might deprive me of your company." He gave an innocuous-looking smile—in some way, it was even more frightening than when he leered.

"And I worried you might still sound like a chipmunk," I whispered.

His suavity did not slip as he escorted me to the table and claimed the seat across from me.

Mother began the pleasantries. "Mr. Smith, how did you fare today? I fear the moisture crowded out all chances for success."

"A truly abysmal day, to be sure, but I managed to find amusement enough. I came upon the most beautiful young cub, an energetic vixen, both wily and agile, but while I thought I had her cornered, I am afraid she got the better of me and slipped away." The merest hint of a smile graced his features while he spoke of his prey.

Chills raced down my spine.

"Perhaps you will have better luck later in the season," Mother said, blessedly ignorant.

"I hope so. But I find such pleasing sport here on the whole. Such beautiful game to be had. Thank you for having me."

Only a scoundrel could flatter a mother and offend a daughter with the same words. I could feel his legs searching for mine under the table, but thankfully I'd had the foresight to wear my heeled half-boots. I brought my heel down hard on his toe. With relish, I heard him squeak like a mouse as he removed his foot.

I ate but little and conversed even less. I hoped Mr. Smith would choke on a chicken bone, but destiny held other plans, it seemed.

As dinner drew to a close, Mother said to Mr. Smith, "You will have to excuse us, as my daughter and I will be attending the invalids upstairs. Please make yourself comfortable in my husband's library this evening."

Mr. Smith bowed handsomely. "Thank you so much for your hospitality, Mrs. Fletcher."

"I am sorry that we cannot continue to host you, but with both John and Mr. Fletcher wounded . . ."

"I quite understand. I shall leave at first light."

Well, at least there was that.

As Mother and I left Smith's sickening presence, a sense of relief washed over me. I waited until we were upstairs, away from servants' ears, in the same ill-fated corridor of assault before addressing Mother.

"Was my presence there really necessary?" I whispered.

Mother rubbed her temples. "I have too many things to deal with right now for me to handle your complaints. If you cannot be helpful, go to your room."

But I would not back down. "You must see that Mr. Smith is never invited back into this home. It wouldn't be safe for Charlotte."

She pinched the bridge of her nose. "Has he insulted you? Called you a silly, impertinent chit, perhaps?" Her glower could curdle dairy. "Even if he has, he paid a small fortune for that thoroughbred. He can afford to call you whatever he likes."

I clenched my hands to keep them from trembling. "He offered me a carte blanche." Though Mother constantly found fault with me, I hoped she would believe me. After all, I never lied; it was my unbridled honesty that got me into the most trouble.

Mother paused to face me, her eyes scanning my countenance. "When was this?"

"Three days ago in the garden."

Mother's eyes grew hard. I flinched, expecting to feel the sting of her hand across my face, but for the first time in my memory, her anger was not aimed at me.

"You are certain? He did not jest?"

"No, his intentions were quite clear." I remembered with a shudder the feel of his body pressed hard against mine.

Mother's eyes flashed, and I took a precautionary step backward. "Only you, Anne, could turn a suitor into a scandal."

Of course she blamed me. And she did not know the half of it. "I'm sorry, Mother." And I was. "I certainly did not try to encourage him."

She sighed, venting her anger. "I know. You never do. You run away from perfectly good vicars instead. I really have no idea what I am going to do with you."

I swallowed. "Should we tell Papa?"

She scoffed. "Don't be daft. Your father is always itching for an excuse to use his dueling pistols, and you can lay ten-to-one odds that he would not miss." She shook her head resolutely. "No. I shall make certain that Mr. Smith is not invited back."

Bless Mother. She may have been frosty, but she was still a force to be reckoned with.

CHAPTER SIX
Nightmares

WE SAT WITH JOHN UNTIL the physician arrived. He gave a thorough examination before pronouncing, "Master John may be plagued with some deafness in one ear, but the other ear should be back to normal within a day or two."

Father's prognosis was grimmer. Though nothing was broken, he had bruised his body terribly. The doctor predicted Father would require a week or more of rest before he recovered enough to walk without pain.

We next visited Charlotte. Though her fever was high, the doctor predicted, "With such a young and generally hale constitution, she should recover quickly."

I volunteered to tend to her, grateful not to be alone in a house where I knew Mr. Smith might be lurking. After placing a cool, wet cloth on Charlotte's brow, and with the aid of some powder the doctor instructed me to place in her drink, Charlotte drifted asleep. I changed the damp cloth every so often, amazed that even with such a fever, Charlotte slept peacefully hour after hour.

But I was not happy to be left alone with my memories of Mr. Smith. I picked up the book from Charlotte's side table: *Pamela; or, Virtue Rewarded,* and settled into the chair. Before I could decide whether the book was utter nonsense or worth my time, a knock sounded at the door. My heart pounded. I was sure everyone else in the household had long since gone to bed. Would Mr. Smith pursue me here, while I sat with my sister? Even he would not be so bold. A key slid into the lock, and Will strode into the room.

"What are you doing here?" I whispered. "It's the middle of the night."

He looked chagrined. "I beg your pardon. I had not known you would be here."

I stood and advanced on him. "And if I weren't? You were trying to visit Charlotte in her bedchamber?" Had he been courting me while entertaining assignations with my sister all the while?

He offered a sickly smile. "You always have been a silly child. Beautiful, but completely feather-brained." He reached forward, grabbing me by the wrist—the same wrist that Mr. Smith and Mother had abused—and pulled me out of Charlotte's room. "But since I have found you, there's something I need to show you." I struggled to no avail as he drew me next door, to my own bedchamber. I was helpless. Again.

Mr. Smith waited for me in my room.

"I have found a husband for you, Anne," Will said jovially as he passed me off to Mr. Smith.

I awoke to Charlotte shaking me. "Anne, dear, you must wake up."

She bent over me, placing her hand on my forehead, but it was no fever that caused my heart to pound and sweat to plaster my hair to my face. It had been a nightmare.

I rubbed my right wrist, which was now peppered with bruises.

"Anne, are you ok?" A crease formed between her graceful eyebrows.

"I'm fine. It was just a bad dream. You should go back to bed."

She meekly obeyed, and I followed her, placing another cool cloth on her brow. "Sorry for waking you."

After I cosseted her a bit, her fevered body quickly succumbed to the sleep it needed.

I, however, stayed awake the rest of the night, contemplating my impending marriage to Will.

By the time morning dawned, Charlotte's fever had lessened.

"Thank you for tending me," she said. "I'm sure you would have rather played cards or the pianoforte."

I snorted; entertaining Mr. Smith was the least of my desires. "I am sorry you were actually sick this time, and I never even thought to check on you until Atkins told me, and then there was the explosion . . ." And then Mr. Smith. I shivered.

She smiled impishly. "That's fair. The boy who cried wolf and all that. Besides, the entire household was in pandemonium yesterday. I am sad I missed all the hullabaloo."

I harrumphed, glad that at least she had been safe in her room. Petite Charlotte would never have been able to fend off a lunk like Mr. Smith. "Are you ready to have some food brought up?" Between only nibbling on last night's dinner and spending almost every minute of the night awake, my stomach begged for sustenance.

"I could handle some toast, I think."

Not long after I pulled the bell, Mother came to check on Charlotte, placing her hand on my sister's forehead. "The fever is down. How do you feel?"

Charlotte shrugged. "I still have a bit of a headache, and my throat is sore, but nothing really to complain of."

Mother sighed. "It's a pity you couldn't even say goodbye to Mr. Smith before he left."

"Gone already?" I asked.

"Yes."

I took a deep breath, surprised at how much lighter my body felt. "Well, if you are feeling better, Charlotte, I need to go lie down." Right after I foraged for breakfast.

"Thank you, Anne," Charlotte said.

"Of course." I practically skipped out of the room and toward the stairs when Mother's voice stalled me.

"Anne, I need to speak with you."

I slowly turned to face her, loathe to do so on an empty stomach. I followed her to my own fireless bedchamber.

She walked to the window and pulled the drapes so light flooded in. "I spoke with Mr. Skinner yesterday after your ride."

Really? He had stayed to talk to Mother, even while soaking wet? "What did he say?"

"He will only marry you if I give you a Season first so you can earn some Town polish." She pressed her temples. "So I have decided to send you to Lizzie after all. She needs a companion as she nears her confinement, and I am needed here to help replace the windows and nurse Father back to health. I shall come with Charlotte once she has recovered from her illness and once the household is put back to order."

She was sending me to London. Without her. This was beyond even my stellar imagination.

"Anne." She looked at me sternly, causing my smile to skitter. "I've already written to Elizabeth. You leave first thing tomorrow morning."

"Alone?" I asked, wondering if I had been relegated to ride atop a stage-coach, like any other baggage.

"Of course not. I am sending Atkins with you, and Price shall drive. But remember, you will not have a horse. We will not be spending money to turn you out. And with Lizzie still in mourning, I doubt she will be able to introduce you to society. Do you understand?"

"Yes, Mama."

I must not have looked duly discouraged, for she continued, her voice growing louder. "This is not a Season but an attempt to satisfy Mr. Skinner. When we return to Rushden, you will marry him." She rubbed her temples and lowered her voice. "Besides, I cannot stand to have you underfoot right now. Do you understand?"

The look of disappointment on Mother's face hurt me more than I thought it would. I was being exiled. Banished. But to London, without her ever-disapproving eye?

My smile threatened to return. "I understand."

Even if I did not manage to secure a marriage proposal, I determined that I would take advantage of every blessed unchaperoned moment.

Of course, I would have Lizzie, and like Will had said, we had never gotten along. We were opposites in nearly every way; she was as cold and calculating as I was passionate and impetuous. But I doubted even my strict sister could harangue me like Mother did.

This was the only chance I would be given. It was time.

Carpe diem, Anne. *Carpe diem.*

CHAPTER SEVEN
Falling for a Well-Tied Cravat

WE LEFT EARLY ENOUGH IN the morning that the fog still hung thick as a tapestry.

"The roads'll be smooth," Price said, "for it's the Leeds to London we're on. We'll stop three times to stretch an' change horses, but if you need ought else, just pull the wire." He smiled warmly at me, his grizzled beard reminding me of how many times he must have made this trip while driving the family coach. In spite of his age, he sprung nimbly to the top of the box.

Mother and the servants lined up in front of Rushden Hall as the traveling coach departed. The rolling fog obscured Mother's expression, but she brushed her hands together before she strode purposefully to the hall. I wondered if she felt unburdened now that she had washed her hands of me.

But two could play at that game. The farther I got from the only home I had ever known, the lighter I felt. I was going to London, with no one but Atkins to moderate me. I giggled, then laughed aloud.

Atkins offered no reproof, silently pulling out her knitting needles and setting to work.

We drove past Hinwick, the location conjuring memories of Mr. Paling riding sidesaddle. I looked about, hoping to catch a glimpse of a handsome gentleman with a too-colorful waistcoat, but saw no one. Would I ever get a chance to thank him for saving me from Will's censure?

I pressed my forehead against the window, determined to notice every living thing, the grass, the sheep, the cows as they lazily munched their cud, but before long, I succumbed to a dreamless sleep.

I awoke when the coach slowed and pulled into a posting inn. "Have we come to the first stage already?"

"Aye, miss." Atkins tucked away her knitting and stretched her plump little legs, preparing to disembark.

"Do you know where we are?"

She shook her head.

"I cannot believe I slept through the entire first leg." Though due to excitement and nightmares, I had hardly slept a wink the night prior.

Price opened the door, and Atkins preceded me out of the carriage. I hurried to follow, anxious for adventure. "Where are we?" I asked Price.

"Milton Keyes, miss. I need to find the ostler. You go stretch your legs and have a bite to eat."

The Rose and Crown looked no different than any other inn, with dingy windows that only allowed a modicum of light to penetrate the bar where the innkeeper stood. "What can I get for you, miss?" he asked, wiping his hands on the half apron he wore.

"May I have a chocolate please?"

The innkeeper scratched his head, and Atkins whispered, "They won't have chocolate here, but they might have tea."

"Or rather, I would like some tea, if you please."

"Yes, miss. Right away." The innkeeper beamed at me and disappeared. At this early hour, the common room was virtually deserted save the three men who broke their fast. After a few minutes, the innkeeper presented me with the weakest thrice-boiled tea I had ever had the misfortune of tasting. But he looked on fondly, as if I were imbibing the gods' own nectar, so I forced the grimace off my face. "It is very nice. Thank you."

He nodded, obviously expecting such a response before engaging in a monologue about the tea's heritage. I fled before he attempted to draw its coat of arms.

After we settled in the carriage and Price drove us forward, I asked Atkins, "Is tea such a commodity?"

She shrugged, and only then did I realize she had ordered nothing for herself. Perhaps she could not afford tea. The thought that even the weakest tea in the world might be above an employed woman's privilege discomfited me. "Let us see what Cook has sent with us, shall we?" She nodded, and I unpacked the basket of goodies: bread, cheese, cakes, Bath buns, apples, and a variety of nuts. We made quick work of the buns.

I began to lick my sticky fingers when I was stalled by Mother's voice. *"You should avail yourself of the use of your napkin rather than licking your fingers like a street urchin."* I could see clearly in my mind's eye the way she rubbed her temples as she spoke, but I licked my fingers deliberately, the minuscule freedom making me giggle. "Cook makes the best Bath buns," I said.

Atkins nodded at me. "But only for her favorite Fletcher."

"If Cook has a favorite, it has to be John. I have never seen a person eat a kidney pie with such relish."

She shrugged, her tight copper curls bobbing in response. "She didn't cry when John was sent away from home for the first time."

"She was crying?" I only had eyes for Mother and her relief at having me gone.

Atkins frowned at that, the look foreign on her cherubic face. "They were all crying, miss. All except your mother."

I scrutinized my maid's face but did not see any traces of deceit. Could the staff possibly miss me when my own family did not, or was Atkins attempting to flatter me? I couldn't tell, so I looked outside while Atkins added the clicking of her needles to the chorus of clopping horse hooves.

The next stage crawled by. Restlessness settled in, and I rejoiced when Atkins announced we would disembark soon. We partook of refreshment at the King's Inn and stretched our legs by walking about the courtyard.

Though we were only halfway to London, I sighed as I allowed Price to shepherd me back into the carriage. At least I was not packed in with my long-legged lummox of a brother; I pitied the woman who would someday end up boxed up with him.

I thought idly about the advantages of marrying a short man like Will or a man who could fold his legs into a parody of femininity like Mr. Paling. If he were in the carriage with me now, his improprieties would not stop with the innocent brushing of knees, I was sure. I pushed thoughts of Mr. Paling and his scandalous behavior out of my mind.

My body found it impossible to succumb to the amount of indolence required to sit in nearly the same position for hours on end and could not cease fidgeting. The necessity to stay inert during church services had felt tantamount to torture, but this inactivity was excruciating. No wonder my brother always preferred to ride his own horse or sit atop the box rather than in the coach. I wished I had been allowed to take Buttercup with me; I would take her at a gallop and feel the cool breeze whip my hair out of its Grecian knot.

Atkins had fallen asleep and was, unbeknownst to her, passing gas. The carriage walls closed in around me, pressing into me just as Mr. Smith had. I struggled to breathe, longing for fresh air. I closed my eyes and pushed against the gathering darkness, willing the walls to recede.

In a stroke of inspiration, I remembered Angel's parting gift: *"I hear those London balls can be quite packed. You might need this if you faint,"* she had said, handing me a small, silver vinaigrette.

"Stuff and nonsense. I never faint."

"Then use it whenever the smell of the city overwhelms you. The vinaigrette is scented with lavender and should remind you of home."

I searched through my reticule, found the box, and brought it to my nose. The pungent vinegar did its job, forcing my body to take a deep breath. The darkness receded, but my heart still pounded too painfully in my chest. I massaged the knot out of my sternum, breathing in the acrid scent, but the smell did not ameliorate my nausea.

I needed fresh air. I needed the coach to stop.

Finally, we entered a town, and the carriage began to slow. I laced my bonnet, put on my spencer, and armed myself with my reticule. The moment the coach stopped, I opened the door and sprung out, not waiting for Price to let down the steps or unhand me.

Freedom.

My freedom was short-lived, however, for though I had been able to stretch my knees and ankles in the carriage, my hips had remained at the same angle for far too long; they were less enthusiastic to be put to sudden use. They buckled, causing me to fall face-first into what had once been a gentleman's carefully tied black cravat.

A rather ungentlemanly voice released an oath. "Sakes alive, hussy, watch what you are about." The uncouth man had reacted to my assault by bringing both hands to my shoulders and pushing me back until my chest rested over my own torso rather than on his. "If I had a pound for every woman who threw herself at me, I could make my own fortune." He unhanded me like I might have lice. I looked upward into the gentleman's—no, *Colonel Thoroton's*—scowl.

His frosty look could have frozen the sun, but it flamed my pride. And unlike last time, the threat of Mother's censure could not protect him from my wrath. "Firstly, I would never throw myself at a gentleman—obviously in name only—who is incapable of coming to my aid and instead treats me like a flea-bitten cur." I ticked one gloved finger out at him. "Secondly, if I *had* thrown myself at you, I would have broken your nose rather than crumpling your oriental, which would have served you right as your nose seems bent out of shape for naught. Thirdly—"

Raucous laughter cut off my diatribe. Mr. Paling stood near, cloaked in his usual persona of gaiety and nonchalance.

In strict contrast, the colonel's tone grew menacing as he spit out each word. "It was a mathematical, not an oriental."

"Yes, well." I tried to re-enact his rude turn of voice; I didn't care if he was the emperor of China. No one spoke to me like this. "I am a lady, not a hussy. Yours was the greater blunder."

Mr. Paling nudged the colonel playfully. "She doesn't even know you, and she called your score."

Colonel Thoroton did not smile.

I turned as I heard Atkins open the door; I needed my travel companion before the colonel could strangle me. Atkins descended, addressing me quietly, "Good gracious, Anne, couldn't you have waited for Price to hand you out?"

"Not the smartest thing I have done today." Under my breath, I added, "Which really says something because I have done nothing but sit in the coach."

Mr. Paling's chuckle indicated that he had heard my excuse, so I spoke a little louder, hoping that at least he would believe my innocence. "I have sprung unassisted from this coach countless times before without incident, but today, the long journey stiffened my joints, and they buckled."

"Are you all right?" Atkins asked, auburn brows puckered in concern.

"Oh yes, I was the very embodiment of dexterity as I bobbled."

Mr. Paling's chuckle spilled into a guffaw, which only encouraged me.

"Certainly nothing embarrassing happened, nor was there anyone of consequence around to witness my faux pas."

Colonel Thoroton responded with a distinct lack of amusement. "We are right here. We can still hear you."

I turned to them, as regal as if making my court bow. "Yes, well, I did say there was no one of *consequence* around, didn't I?"

Mr. Paling clapped his friend on the shoulder. "We shall have to see what your mother says of that when we see her next."

I turned to seek the innkeeper before the colonel could throttle me.

Mr. Paling called out, "On your way to London, Miss—?"

"Obviously," I tossed over my shoulder, still reticent to share my surname with one who had witnessed me riding astride.

The bustling inn was in some sort of commotion. I only caught snippets of conversations:

"No. Where?"

"—don't say."

"—bet it was regular—"

"—why I never take the—"

"—up by Burton Lat—"

In the midst of this tumult, the gentlemen joined me in searching for the innkeeper. "What did you say now to set their tongues wagging? And what have you done with the innkeeper?" Mr. Paling accused good-naturedly.

"I did not say anything and—"

"A modern miracle," the colonel interjected.

Humph. That was a good shot from Mr. Conceited Britches. But the return of the innkeeper prevented me from further aggravating him with a response.

"What's all the hullabaloo for?" the colonel asked in his customary terse tone.

"You've not heard? A mail-coach robbery," the innkeeper said.

I gasped. "Highwaymen here? That's practically medieval." The very thought turned my stomach; Atkins, Price, and I were no match for a band of ruffians.

"Well, not here, exactly. It came by a bit ago and said it was robbed somewhere up by Higham Ferrers—"

"That's not two miles from us," Atkins interrupted him. "Was anyone hurt?" Atkins might have a family member on that coach today for all I knew.

"No, ma'am."

I sighed in relief. I thought mail coaches were supposed to comprise the fastest and most reliable form of travel. "How did someone manage to rob the mail?" I shivered and rubbed my arms, smoothing down the hairs that stood on point.

The innkeeper shrugged. "The guard said he left his post on the box somewhere near Burton Latimer, and by the time he went back to it in Higham Ferrers, the lock had been cut and the bags and mail were all gone. Told us all to keep a lookout."

Mr. Paling assumed a serious expression which looked ludicrous on his jovial face. "Well, these women look suspicious to me."

Atkins gasped, affronted.

I cast my eyes heavenward and prayed for patience.

"They already admitted to living close to where the robbery occurred." He must delight in causing trouble, the bounder.

I could see from the splotches all over Atkins's face that she struggled to hold her composure while I was being maligned. I put a hand on her arm to soothe her; this was not her fight. "You think my companion and I would be skilled and stealthy enough to ride beside a coach, pick a lock, steal the mail, and leave undetected?" I asked, smiling as sweetly as possible. "I am flattered at your overestimation of our skills."

"You forgot the part where the guard is distracted enough to leave his box." Mr. Paling rolled his shoulders, reminding me of a cat settling low in the grass right before pouncing. "I can imagine nothing less distracting than a gorgeous woman riding astride a black stallion without any sense of abandon, her hair streaming free, her exposed legs—"

That was beyond enough. "I suppose your imagination needs work. All that poor guard needed to distract him was the sight of a man effeminately crumpled into a sidesaddle, struggling to rein in the most docile of mares. Both horse and rider weaving a line as if they were barmy on the crumpet—"

Mr. Paling's eyes grew wide as I described him, but Atkins prevented my completion of the cant expression with her defense to the innkeeper. "We had nothing to do with the robbery, of course. But we do hail from Northamptonshire, and so we are familiar with the territory."

Mr. Paling leaned closer. "What township again?"

I had no intention of giving him any further information about me.

The innkeeper crossed his arms over his ample belly. "Anyone can see this lady has naught to do with highwaymen. Now what'll it be, gentlemen? I'm enormously busy."

We each made our demands known, whereupon Mr. Paling turned to me. "Perhaps it will comfort you to know that the colonel and I are headed to London and can keep an eye on your carriage. Or perhaps you would prefer if I traveled in your coach with you?" He waggled his eyebrows ludicrously.

I had no desire to enter London with my reputation in tatters. "I would rather take my chances with highwaymen."

His dimples widened into creases as he smirked.

Atkins and I stretched our legs and avoided the gentlemen until Price was ready. We boarded the coach, and I filled in Atkins on my prior experiences, having met both gentlemen at the ball.

She tsked and tutted while I talked but made no indications of censure or approval. It was . . . refreshing.

The last leg proved uneventful. I considered the mail coach, robbed so close to my home, and shivered. If I had been in slightly straighter circumstances—or had displeased Mother any further—I would have been on that coach today. Any belongings stowed in the safe box with the mail would be gone.

A newfound gratitude for Price, Atkins, and the family carriage filled me.

As we drew closer to London, soot, sewage, and sulfur permeated the air like an un-mucked stable that had been set on fire. We drove deeper into the maze of the city with no end in sight. Eventually, the hovels grew to homes, which grew to mansions lined with mature trees. The smell did not permeate quite as thickly here, and I imagined if a lady kept a fine assortment of lavender, roses, and thyme on her balcony, she could probably convince herself that London smelled lovely.

Price pulled up to what must have been Elizabeth's home, and I waited patiently—this time—for him to descend from the box, let down the steps, and open the door for me. I observed the tidy appearance of the townhouse before I noticed it was not Price who held my hand but Mr. Paling.

I snatched my hand away from his as if it were a hot coal. "What is the meaning of this?" I looked back to Atkins for help, but she was still gathering her sundry knitting accoutrements.

"I thought perhaps you found these stairs to be troublesome and you might find my hand a better-suited aid than Colonel Thoroton or his poor cravat." His smile seemed so genuine, I struggled to refrain from returning it.

"You mean to tell me you followed me all the way to my home and acted the part of the footman on the off chance that I would throw myself at you? My, but you are desperate."

He leaned in and I held my breath, bracing myself for the impertinent response he would whisper in my ear, but he only reached past me to help Atkins descend the steps. "I simply could not live with myself if I let two such lovely ladies travel alone when there are highwaymen known to be about." Mr. Paling's eyes twinkled like stars in the moonlight as he whispered, "And now I know where to find you, Anne."

He waggled his eyebrows at me, and I swung my satchel at him for his impertinence. It hit him squarely in the jaw with a resounding crack. I snatched my hand back, but it was too late.

Hornswoggle! I hadn't meant to actually hit him.

Mr. Paling's eyes widened in shock as he brought a hand to his face, prodding it tenderly.

I reached toward him but stopped myself before actually touching his cheek. "Sorry. My brother always knows to move out of the way . . ." I dropped my hand, unduly flustered. "I never . . . Would you care to come in? Perhaps a poultice can be applied to reduce the swelling?"

He grinned, then winced at the pain that motion evoked. "I have been lured into homes on less pretense, I suppose."

I moved as if to swing my bag at him again but held my hand in check. He ducked regardless.

"At least we are coming to understand one another," I said.

"Did Jackson teach you how to employ such a punishing left?" he asked, dropping his hand and oscillating his jaw back and forth.

"Who?"

"The boxer." He grinned. "Since you obviously take exception to me using your Christian name, and you won't offer me your family name, I believe I shall take to calling you Miss Jackson, since he would be proud to call you his progeny."

I glared. "I would prefer if your jaw swelled shut so you could not call me anything at all."

"It just might. But even so, I must admit myself glad that you arrived safely in Town. I cannot imagine what your reflexes may have done had it been your carriage and not the mail coach that had been robbed. I would hate to see your beautiful neck on the noose for the murder of a highwayman." He tipped his hat to me.

I folded my arms across my chest and scowled.

"And I am absolutely certain your presence in Town shall be most diverting." He winked, then sauntered back to the coach he shared with the colonel.

I sighed. I had only been in London for seconds, and I already found myself assaulting scoundrels with my satchel. Good thing Mother would never hear of it. I skipped into the townhouse, grateful for the blessing of independence and a fresh start.

CHAPTER EIGHT
Mornings in Mourning

THE NEXT MORNING, LIZZIE GREETED me with more warmth than I had ever seen from her. "I had been planning to wait up for you last night, but this baby," she rubbed her belly, "likes to keep his own hours."

"So you have determined that it shall be a boy?"

She tittered. "Of course it shall. The future master of the house is practicing his privileges already. If I were having a girl, she would have had the decency to make sure you arrived safely before retiring."

"Very true," I said, glad that she was maintaining her optimism.

She sighed, rubbing her back before she sat at the breakfast table. The carved mahogany chairs favored fashion over comfort.

I gathered a plate of ham and eggs from the small spread, then sat across from Lizzie.

"You have no idea how happy I am that you have come. Life as a widow is terribly lonely." She nibbled on a piece of dry toast, and I wondered if she was still feeling ill.

"It must feel like living in Rushden again," I said. The Skinners were the only other genteel family in a three-mile radius.

She waved away my empathy. "Worse. There we had the companionship of family, but it's just me here." She stoically refrained from sighing.

"You must miss Mr. Ascough very much."

She shrugged. "I probably would if I had ever had the chance to get to know him. I am sure he was a fine gentleman, but I have spent more time as a widow than I ever did a married woman." She rubbed her belly absently. "You know, we only lived here a month before Napoleon started kicking up a fuss in the peninsula. I couldn't persuade him to sell out."

I had no idea how to respond to that, but hoped my words might cheer her up. "Well, you have me here now. And Mother and Charlotte will be here soon. They both send their love."

"I know. I'm glad you are here to lift my spirits, but I am afraid you will find it dull indeed since I am still in mourning. No routes, balls, or even the theater. But at least a young widow can always promenade at Hyde Park. Have you any suitable walking dresses?"

Once I finished eating, we retired to my bedchamber. She spent over an hour inspecting my wardrobe, sorting everything into "serviceable" and "hopeless," laying each item in their appropriate piles on my bed.

"You have too much color here, Anne. White is the color for a girl in her first Season, you know. We shall have to get you a few new things if you want to make a decent impression."

"A few inexpensive things, perhaps. Mother will not pay to turn me out."

"Is that right?" Lizzie gave me a knowing look.

"Yes?"

She pulled something from her pocket. "Then I wonder why Father enclosed this in his missive and instructed me to prepare you for Town." She waved several notes under my nose.

My jaw dropped. "Father went behind Mother's back? For me?"

She shrugged. "He is the master of the house, you know." She pocketed the notes again. "But just to be safe, we had better not tell Mother anything about it when she comes to Town. Deal?"

"You, my strict and law-abiding sister, propose to do something behind Mother's back? You have grown positively devious."

"Surprising, I know." She winked at me.

I cackled with glee. Lizzie had always been stuffy. Distant. Perhaps her independence had softened her. "Widowhood suits you."

She chortled. "It is rather nice to answer to no one."

The butler interrupted us with an overstuffed vase of vibrant daisies. "I believe the flowers are for Miss Anne."

"Impossible," Lizzie declared. "She knows no one in Town."

I took the card and pondered for but a moment the unfamiliar handwriting which read,

> *Miss Anne _____,*
> *Country wildflowers, freshly cut.*
> *To celebrate lively cuts*
> *delivered in the country*
> *by a lovely, wild flower.*

Thank you for enlivening what has always been the dullest of journeys.
—Paling

"Lizzie, have you ever met a Mr. Thomas Paling before?"

Her response was as unexpected as were the flowers. She plucked the card out of my hand without even asking permission to read it. "This is not to be believed. You have not been here one day, and yet you receive poems and flowers from Mr. Paling. Whatever does he mean? Did you cut him?"

"Well, yes. But you see, his friend Colonel Thoroton cut me first when—"

Her eyes widened as she gasped. "Colonel Thoroton? The same Colonel Thoroton whose entry into Town has been gossiped about by every marriageable miss's mother for a fortnight?"

"Well, I do not claim to know anything of London gossip, but I most definitely met a man of that name traveling in the same company as Mr. Paling. What can you tell me about them?" Finally, I had found someone who could spill light on the enigmatic Mr. Paling.

She gave me her prepare-for-a-lecture look. "Mr. Paling, a notorious flirt, was sent to recover his childhood friend, Colonel Thoroton, from his recently inherited Flintham Hall. From what I hear, the colonel has been holed up there ever since being called home from the war, hiding away from his responsibilities of finding a wife." She pounced on me. "But how is it that you met them? You must tell me everything."

I stifled a snort. She would never hear *everything*. "I was introduced to the colonel at the Hinwick Ball, but he did not remember me when I stumbled across him at the coaching inn. But oh, Lizzie, you will never believe the commotion there." How could I possibly have forgotten to tell her about this? "A mail-coach robbery."

I was right. Even after several retellings, she could not be brought to credit it. The mail had always been infallible.

"Never mind the mail. You never told me why you cut the colonel. Or was it Mr. Paling you cut? I forget now. Tell me again." She looked as excited as a child opening a present.

"As I mentioned, I was introduced to the colonel at the ball but not to Mr. Paling. He had an entire entourage of ladies swarming about him anyway, so I'm sure an introduction would have proved futile."

She nodded in understanding.

"So when the colonel cut me at the inn, but Mr. Paling offered an introduction, I thought it best to decline the offer."

She tsked, then looked thoughtful. "And yet, he sent flowers. If you had fawned over him as you should have, I doubt you would have received flowers today. You are as lucky as you are foolish." It was a slight, but a warm one, and from Lizzie, that was much preferable to her cold stares.

I wanted to capitalize on her openness while it lasted. "I understand the impetus to fawn over the colonel, for he is young and has already inherited a large estate. But what of Mr. Paling? Has he a fortune to his name?"

"Not a fortune, per se, but he is well-connected, in spite of his lack of title. And he has a great deal of charm. That surely cannot hurt his position."

Mr. Paling's visage after I assaulted him with my satchel came to mind, complete with dimples, waggling eyebrows, and the ever-present mischief that sparkled in his indecipherably colored eyes. He was charming, surely. But also scandalous and ridiculous and incorrigible. I tapped his card on my knee. "A notorious flirt has sent me flowers, but I don't know the first thing about interacting with flirts and dandies. What shall I do?"

She gave her customary cool, calculating smile. "You use him to gain entry into the *ton*, of course."

I worried my lip. A gentleman like Mr. Paling would use me long before I could use him, just like he had surely used scads of girls before me. "I could never flirt with him."

"That is the wisest thing I have ever heard you say." She gave me an arched look. "Keep that tongue of yours bridled, and your entry into the best circles is all but secured."

I nodded. I needed all the help I could get. "And the flowers?" I asked, admiring their colors, not the customary white but vivid violet, deep lavender, and bright orange. Country wildflowers, he called them, meant to represent me.

"Those are the ugliest sort of flowers I have ever seen. You cannot display them in the drawing room. Leave them here in your bedchamber or, better yet, toss them."

Toss them? Discard the very symbol he had used to describe me: a lovely, wild flower? For shame. Her rejection stung like a whip. "I could never toss them."

She shrugged, and we resumed our previous chore, creating a master list detailing the deficiencies in my wardrobe, followed by lists of what we needed to purchase at each store. She would soon have me shipshape in Bristol fashion.

We scurried like rabbits—or perhaps waddled like ducks, in Lizzie's case—first to the mantua makers, then to the milliners. Feathers. Gloves. Fabric.

Lace. And then home again, to remake my morning and walking dresses. Lizzie was indefatigable, in spite of being in the family way, and I found myself both surprised and touched that she exerted herself so fully on my behalf. We sat there picking stitches, letting out bosoms, and adding lace throughout the afternoon, and I found a sense of sisterly camaraderie that had eluded me for nineteen years.

CHAPTER NINE
Wildflowers

THE NEXT MORNING, WE CONTINUED to update my wardrobe until a visitor called.

"Anne, this is my dearest friend, Maria Bell. She lives next door, has a charming little girl still in leading strings, and the good fortune to be married to an accoucheur."

I was unfamiliar with the term but too embarrassed to ask.

"Well, I don't know if it's fortunate or not," Mrs. Bell said, "as he keeps the strangest of hours and I often find myself alone."

"But it must be a relief to always have a doctor about now that you are in the family way again." Lizzie turned to me. "She and I shall be nearing our confinement about the same time. Can you imagine, having our babies grow up together?"

"Your children will be very fortunate to have each other," I said. I didn't know what I would have done if Angel hadn't moved into the parsonage only a quarter mile off when I was fourteen. "Forgive me if the question seems impertinent, but how much longer shall it be until the two of you are brought to confinement?"

Lizzie glanced at her friend and shrugged. "A month? Six weeks?"

I felt suddenly squeamish. What if Mother was not here before Lizzie's time came? I didn't know the first thing about childbirth.

Mrs. Bell added, "I shall be a little later, though these things are never very certain, you know."

But I *hadn't* known. "So you could deliver *sooner* than a month, Lizzie?"

Lizzie obviously read the panic in my face and offered an equally anxious smile. "Perhaps. But Mr. Bell shall attend me whenever I am brought to bed, and he only lives next door, so I think you and I both shall have nothing to worry about."

"No midwife?" I asked, worried for my sister. I certainly wouldn't want a male present if *I* ever gave birth.

Mrs. Bell answered for Lizzie. "Only the indigent use midwives anymore. It is much better to have a man of schooling there in case any difficulties arise. As an accoucheur, it is Mr. Bell's focus, though, of course, he also knows how to treat various and sundry other conditions and ailments." Mrs. Bell began helping us with our stitches while she launched into a soliloquy about the advantages of modern medicine. From the wink Lizzie gave, I assumed Mrs. Bell often engaged in such long-winded chatter. "But now, Miss Fletcher, you must tell me something of yourself. How did you find your travels?"

I was obliged to again share the story of the robbed mail coach, though Mrs. Bell believed me more readily than my sister had as she had already read about it in the papers.

"And guess who accompanied her on his way back to London," my sister said excitedly.

"I haven't any idea. Who?"

"Colonel Thoroton and Mr. Paling."

Mrs. Bell gasped and, in an excited, squeaky tone, asked, "Is that true, Miss Fletcher?"

"Well, not exactly true. We ran into one another at a coaching inn, which is where we heard of the mail robbery. And they were kind enough to follow me home—not accompany me like Lizzie said—since they were headed this way anyhow."

She nodded energetically. "And what did you think of them?"

I tried to school my features and offer a bland recitation of their character. "I have never seen two such disparate companions: the one always serious and ill-humored while the other is all flirtations and laughter. Do I miss my mark?"

Mrs. Bell giggled, her mouse-like voice tinkling like champagne glasses during a toast. "No, I believe you described them fairly, not that I know the colonel at all. But I am acquainted with Mr. Paling, and he does know how to make one laugh. He is not like his older brother, the heir presumptive, who is a married, more reclusive sort of fellow. Nor is he like either of his sisters, both of whom you will likely meet as they are often about Town."

I wondered if Mrs. Bell would ever need to pause for a breath, but she continued to prattle unceasingly.

"You will never believe the size of feathers Mrs. Slater puts in her hair. She could likely raise an ostrich for cheaper than the cost of purchasing all the feathers separately. You shall know what I mean when you see her. But instead of making it look ridiculous, she always looks just the thing. If I am ever in want of a special dress to commission, I skip the fashion plates altogether and look to Mrs. Slater. I don't know the younger sister well as she is making her debut in society this Season, but I hear she is quite lovely."

She only paused a second to sigh before continuing her discourse on the pedigree of the Paling family. I wondered how my reserved sister had found such a loquacious friend. "I hear the father is a bit dodgy. He likes his mistresses and doesn't make a secret of them the way he ought to."

I paled. "Does Mr. Thomas Paling take after his father?"

"No, I don't think any of the children take after him. Their father is a bit of a recluse . . . stays on his property up north somewhere . . . He doesn't much care for politics and would rather be alone . . . although I believe the children all share his ambivalence to politics, now that I think of it. But no, I don't think Mr. Thomas Paling takes after his father for all his flirtations. None of the ladies he flirts with ever complain of ill use, and his association is often a boon to their reputation. He's quite harmless, I'm sure. Wouldn't be a regular at Almack's if he were less than a gentleman, so you have no worries there."

I allowed myself a sigh of relief as she prattled on.

"It's a pity he will not settle down, though. The right miss might do the job, for if he does not learn to settle his somewhat wild behaviors, I am afraid he might end up the gambling sort. Not that I have heard ought of him frequenting hells or anything of the like, but he is known for his extravagance at betting at White's. You heard, Elizabeth, about that bet he placed that he would learn to ride sidesaddle? Can you imagine?"

The blood drained from my face. He hadn't been lying about that bet just to protect me. Would he need to mention me to verify his bet? If word escaped that I had ridden astride, my reputation would be tarnished for sure and likely ruined completely. No one would offer for me, and I would have to marry Will. I needed to speak with Mr. Paling as soon as possible.

"He will bring himself to ruin if he doesn't settle soon. Of course, I have a mind to see everyone as happy in marriage as Charles and I. I have no patience with unhappy marriages."

Lizzie cleared her throat. "Speaking of unhappy marriages, poor Anne needs to find a suitor before returning home, else she will have to marry the town vicar." She wrinkled her nose in distaste. "We must help her."

"Who told you?" I asked, my voice hardly more than a whisper. I would have preferred if no one knew of my tenuous understanding.

"Father, in his letter," she said without guile.

"I'm surprised he exerted himself." He rarely interfered in my affairs; he considered the raising of girls strictly Mother's domain. But he had told Lizzie of the situation *and* sent money, behind Mother's back, surely. Hope that he might not force me to marry blossomed for a moment, but it was no more fruitful than an apple tree that buds in winter. I had promised myself to Will. Father could not help me. "How does one go about finding a husband?"

The light in Mrs. Bell's eyes reminded me of a child in a sweetshop. She actually bounced in her seat and clapped her hands together in excitement. "First, tell me what sort of man you like. Are you picky or need he only have breath in his lungs and money in his purse?"

If only I knew. I scrunched up my nose as I thought about why Will did not suit. "He must be taller than me if possible." And he must not feel like a brother. "Handsome." I scowled, remembering my last conversation with Will. "And he must not dismiss everything I say without even listening to me; he must be kind and patient with my foibles."

"Of which there are many." Lizzie smiled ruefully.

And she didn't even know about the time I fell in the lake. Or when I burned Widow Moulton's lace. Or attacked Mr. Paling with my satchel.

Mrs. Bell's lips puckered into a pout. "Patient? Kind? A gentleman who listens?" She blew out a breath. "Would you settle for wealthy?"

I sniggered before realizing she was in earnest.

"Are you sure this vicar fellow of yours will not suit?" She drummed her fingers on her knee but continued before I could respond. "You have already been introduced to Colonel Thoroton and Mr. Paling. How do you enjoy the winner-takes-all, cutthroat competition of the London marriage mart?"

I swallowed. "I imagine I would enjoy it more than an amputation of the foot but less than being drained dry by a score of leeches. Lizzie's the competitive one, not me." She always turned every little thing into a competition.

"Ah, no stomach for rivalry, eh? You had better give Colonel Thoroton and Mr. Paling a wide berth then. Don't worry. I'm sure we shall find someone else to your liking. And you, Elizabeth. As soon as you pass your confinement, you will come out of mourning, won't you?"

She nodded.

That didn't give me much time. I had no desire to compete with Lizzie. But before that, Mother and Charlotte would be here, and who knew how long Mother would suffer me to stay. I wouldn't be surprised if she whisked me home again before the Season was even in full swing. My days were numbered, and I didn't have the foggiest idea how to begin searching for a husband.

The butler brought in a calling card.

Lizzie startled. "Give us a minute before you see him in, and have the tea brought immediately." After he bowed himself out, my sister whispered, "Mr. Paling has come to call on us." We hurriedly stowed away the clothes we had been altering.

"Has Mr. Paling called on you before?" I asked, more flustered by his appearance than I cared to admit.

"Don't be daft," Lizzie said sharply.

The answer served well enough. His visit was unprecedented. Nerves buzzed like I'd swallowed a swarm of bees. He was coming to visit me.

Once we had settled ourselves, Mr. Paling entered, wearing an orange-and-pink patterned waistcoat that clashed so fantastically with his green overcoat that I had to assume he had lost a bet and wore this ensemble as punishment. In spite of this flashy attire, he neither simpered nor put on airs, but entered wrapped in a cloak of nonchalance directly disproportionate to my own jitters.

Lizzie looked every bit as calm and collected as he. "Mr. Paling, how do you do?" She curtsied gracefully, in spite of her prominent belly. "I do believe you have met my sister, Miss Fletcher. And, of course, this is my neighbor and friend, Mrs. Bell."

Mr. Paling's bow, though completely correct in both length and depth, held a level of insouciance which bordered on offense. But then his eyes met mine, his lips curled into a bow, and it was as if the sun poked through a cloud-burst. "Ah, *Miss Fletcher*, is it?" My name sounded dangerous on his tongue. "So pleased to have finally been found worthy of an introduction."

Well, the cat was out of the bag, and Mr. Paling now held my reputation in his hands. But in spite of the threat, my lips slid up at the corners. I was entertaining my first caller after all, in spite of Mother's and Will's doubts.

"Did you receive my flowers?"

The expectant mothers sat on the more comfortable sofa and began conversing with one another while I perched on the hard chair directly across from them. Mr. Paling settled into a chair next to me which suddenly felt too close.

"Yes, thank you for the daisies."

He frowned as he looked around for them.

I winced inwardly at their absence. "I had them sent to my chamber as my sister said they clashed too much with her choice of decor."

Mr. Paling surveyed the parlor: white walls and splashes of crimson in the curtains and armchairs. It reminded me of blood on snow. He spoke reverently, as if in church, "Does she do the same with you when you clash?"

"What, send me to my chamber?" The absurd question caused me to speak louder than I ought, and Lizzie sent me a warning look. Mr. Paling nodded solemnly, and I lowered my voice. "I imagine she would, but she already removed that possibility by declaring that my entire wardrobe shall consist solely of white while I am in Town." I gestured to the white linen I currently donned, then sighed. "I shall miss having color in my life."

He offered a roguish smile. "Not to worry, Miss Fletcher. I shall wear enough color for the both of us."

"I'm sure you will," I responded without hesitation.

"And I promise to embarrass you sufficiently to bring some color back into your cheeks," he whispered.

Though Lizzie and Mrs. Bell seemed heedless of his remarks, I kept my voice lowered. "No need. I embarrass myself enough already. Besides, I doubt even your colorful remarks could inspire me to blush as deeply as you did when you rode aside my mare."

Though he maintained an aura of nonchalance, the color of his own cheeks heightened. "I believe you are the first young woman who has succeeded in bringing me to the blush. But beware of retribution."

"I do not blush easily. And as for retribution . . ." I bit my lip, considering my words. "Have you told anyone of our encounter at Hinwick Stables?"

He smiled mischievously. "Have you?"

"Of course not," I whispered.

"I won't tell if you won't," he said conspiratorially.

I had no choice but to trust him. "Thank you for keeping it a secret. And for the flowers."

He held my gaze for a moment while I tried to decide on his eye color. Hazel?

Mr. Paling cleared his throat and resumed speaking at a normal volume. "Daisies are a happy specimen, don't you think?"

I contemplated the question for probably too long, considering the remark was nothing more than trivial. "I cannot imagine a daisy has the capacity to feel happy. If so, don't you think it would feel quite the opposite to be ripped from its home and loved ones and sentenced to death in a stuffy room, away from fresh air and sunshine?"

"Is that what your bedchamber is like?" he whispered. "I should like to see it for myself someday." He chuckled.

Of all the indecencies! I willed my cheeks not to color; I would not give him that satisfaction.

He resumed speaking at a proper volume. "You must forgive me for having uprooted the daisies, but wildflowers must want to see more than the same patch of sky day after day." He looked thoughtfully at me. "Perhaps you could empathize?"

I often dreamed of unchaperoned adventures on foreign shores, but how could he possibly divine that about me? Though drawn to his warm and penetrating gaze, this connection I felt likely meant nothing to him. I steeled my heart and leaned away. "Yes, but death is a steep price to pay in exchange for a break from monotony. No matter how wild the flower, it must rankle to be thus used and discarded. A wildflower is no plaything." And neither was I. I looked him square in the eye, hoping he would understand my meaning.

Mrs. Bell interceded. "But flowers have no feelings."

"Indeed," Mr. Paling said dryly, and he opened his mouth to say more, but Lizzie interrupted him.

"That's enough of flowers. If Anne's account can be credited, you and she both enjoyed quite an adventure on your way here. Can you tell us anything more of the mail-coach robbery?"

His dimples creased even though his lips did not smile. "Is Miss Fletcher prone to give a false accounting of things?"

"Of course not," Elizabeth bristled, straightening her already stiff posture. "I only meant that her tale was so shocking as to warrant itself incredulous."

Maintaining this mock seriousness, he asked Elizabeth, "Tell me truly, what else did she say of our encounter at the posting inn, besides the mail-coach robbery?"

Elizabeth looked to me, an obvious question in her eyes. I shrugged, not knowing what it was Mr. Paling was baiting her to say. Elizabeth wisely settled for the most innocuous bit of gossip. "She mentioned that you traveled with Colonel Thoroton. I'm sure all of society's misses shall be delighted."

I barely managed to cover my snort with a cough. Colonel Thoroton was about as delightful as my mother.

"Yes, I did travel with the colonel." Mr. Paling tossed me a pointed look. "Though I'm surprised Miss Fletcher mentioned as much to you, since she did not even find him worthy of an introduction."

He rolled his shoulders and licked his lips, preparing to pounce. Surely, he would tell her about the way I had bounded out of the carriage and tackled the colonel and then followed up my indecorum with a verbal attack every bit as scandalous.

I hurried to circumvent his words before he could impugn me. "Please forgive me, Mr. Paling, but there was no one to recommend us, seeing as I had just stumbled upon you at the inn."

He laughed at my verbiage. "Very true."

Lizzie's eyes took on a bit of suspicion as she looked back and forth between Mr. Paling and me. "My sister did not behave or speak discourteously, I hope?"

I held my breath. Though Lizzie had been kind to me thus far, she would not tolerate any hint of scandal.

Mr. Paling's eyes sparkled with mischief. "Mrs. Ascough, I would have you know that in spite of the chaos and danger of her surroundings, your sister showed herself capable of great self-possession. I applaud her for her courage in the heart of a truly terrifying encounter."

From his look, I knew he referred not to the robbery but to the colonel's scathing insults. "It's not as if I was told to stand and deliver," I muttered.

The butler created a diversion by announcing more visitors. Mr. Paling stood. "I believe it's time for me to vacate this seat for Miss Fletcher's other admirers. Are you at home on Fridays?"

I looked to my sister, as of yet unaware of her schedule. She nodded.

"I shall call again then." He sauntered off at a pace that inversely correlated to my racing heart.

CHAPTER TEN
Ascoughs

I AWOKE FRIDAY MORNING TO the sound of laughter. My laughter.

In my dreams, I had visited Astley's Amphitheater, where a man accomplished feats of acrobatics atop an ambling colt. He was joined by a lady who rode around the ring in a frothy pink riding habit, complete with lacy parasol. I had not understood the crowd's laughter until I spotted the wavy hair, sharp jawline, and creased dimples of Mr. Paling, his masculine shoulders and muscular legs hidden in the lady's pink riding habit.

I chuckled again at the image my mind had concocted. Mr. Paling had been a clown in my dreams. Literally. A circus clown.

When I noticed the sunlight peeking through the curtains, I offered a prayer of gratitude for the absurd man who had entertained me in my sleep enough to keep the nightmares at bay. Though how he managed to wear pink waistcoats, ride sidesaddle, and stay in society's good graces all at the same time, I had no idea. The man was an enigma, but if he had the power to chase away my nightmares, he was a welcome enigma indeed.

After getting ready for the day, I added a brief description of Mr. Paling in a letter to Charlotte. And though I spoke only truth, I tempered my words a great deal, in case Mother or Father read it. I started a letter to Angel as well but inoculated my words to her even more, lest she share them with Will.

Waiting for Mr. Paling to call on me caused the morning to drag, which was only exacerbated by Mrs. Bell's incessant chatter. "Now, Miss Fletcher, you should not marry a physician, for I never know if Mr. Bell shall be home in time for supper. Last night, he did not come home at all, you know, and I had to eat all by myself. It's a dull life, Miss Fletcher . . ."

I nodded absently every time she mentioned my name.

". . . but at least he does come home to me eventually. And it's not as if he comes home with booze on his breath and without a feather to fly on like I daresay a great many gentlemen do. He cannot afford to be found in his cups when the clients come to call, so he never comes home smelling of liquor but of vinegar or chloroform or who knows what else—nasty smells—he does bring those home with him. And the laundry bills! Never have you seen such a thing. I bet the prince regent himself doesn't buy as many neckcloths as poor Mr. Bell does. Now, I wouldn't have you think him a dandy, Miss Fletcher . . ."

I nodded again.

". . . because that couldn't be farther from the truth. It's just that Mr. Bell is always getting someone's blood on his clothes, and he is given to throw them in the fire as soon as he comes in at night. I have chided him time and again about that, but he says blood stains won't come out, and he would never be hired by the *Beau Monde* if he showed up with someone else's blood on his shirt. I daresay he might be right." She sighed, the telltale sign that her monologue was nearing its end. "But, like I said, at least he comes home to me eventually, which is more than some ladies get."

"For that matter, do not marry a soldier either," Lizzie added dryly.

Mrs. Bell flustered. "How stupid of me, dear Lizzie, to go on about the trials of being an accoucheur's wife while you sit there still mourning the loss of your poor dearly departed—"

I interrupted her, lest she launched into an epic apology which could only serve to throw Lizzie into the doldrums. "So I should not marry a physician, and I should not marry a soldier. And yet, even if I marry a man whose station in life does not demand that he take a profession, he may still come home to me smelling of whiskey and perfume but without a feather to fly on. I have to admit, none of these prospects recommend themselves to me. Perhaps I should have married the vicar when he proposed."

Directly after pronouncing these auspicious words, the butler ushered in Mr. Paling, whose own stiffly starched cravat must be above reproach. He settled on a chair next to me and cleared his throat. I quickly spoke, hoping he had not overheard my last comment. "I am quite jealous of your waistcoat, Mr. Paling. In fact, I used to have a silk dress made of the same powder blue."

His whispered response tickled my ear. "And I am quite jealous of the vicar who has already had a chance to propose to you."

Oh, but he *had* overheard me. His eyes teased, baiting me to banter with him.

"Nonsense," I whispered. "Any man with courage enough and ten seconds of a lady's attention has a chance to propose. Which one do you lack?"

"I—" He choked on his response, then began coughing in earnest, hitting his chest with his fist to dislodge whatever demon he had swallowed.

My sister came to his aid. "Would you like some tea?" While he doubled over coughing, Elizabeth glared at me.

Mr. Paling waved away the offer. "I shall be fine." Cough. "Once I catch my breath," he wheezed.

While he struggled to regain his suavity, the butler ushered in an austere-looking lady and her two daughters.

Lizzie stood and rushed to clasp the older woman's hands. "Mrs. Ascough, this is my sister Anne. Anne, this is my mother-in-law and her two daughters, Miss Ascough and Miss Grace Ascough."

Elizabeth seemed rather fond of her mother-in-law, whose gray hair and crow's feet leant her a matronly appearance. Miss Ascough stood taller than her sister and had warmer coloring, but Miss Grace fulfilled her name's expectations with her beautiful, sunset curls that framed an angelic face and quiet manners.

"And are you all acquainted with Mr. Thomas Paling?"

Mr. Paling had recovered and made a handsome bow. I wondered if he would shift his attention to these beauties as they sat on the sofa between him and Lizzie. But as soon as my sister began a topic with the Ascoughs, he turned to me, saying quietly, "Have you been to Hyde Park yet? If you find yourself in need of fresh air, I would be happy to accompany you."

I did not want to appear overly eager. "I think you stand more in need of fresh air than I, Mr. Paling. Are you quite all right?"

He cleared his throat, coughing slightly. "Yes, I believe I have recovered fully from your piquant remarks." Color raced across his cheeks.

"Oh dear. I seem to have brought you to the blush again." I found comfort in the fact that, though he flirted atrociously, Mr. Paling still found the decency to grow embarrassed, unlike that rake Mr. Smith who seemed to have no moral compass whatsoever.

His angular jaw framed his dimpled smile as he wagged his finger at me. "One of these days," he warned.

"Yes?" I asked innocently, batting my lashes at him.

He sniggered, then returned to the topic at hand. "Could I call on you later this afternoon for a promenade?"

Drats! None of my walking dresses were currently wearable; Lizzie and I had picked apart the hems just this morning to add new flounces. "I'm afraid I shall have to decline your offer. I have yet to be introduced into London's Society and to do so in your company . . . well, I'm afraid I would be expected to know a thing or two about fashion and would never pass muster under the intense scrutiny an introduction on your hand would engender."

While holding my gaze—his eyes looked as blue as the summer sky today, though I could have sworn that, on Wednesday, they had been hazel—and without looking at Lizzie, he said, "I doubt strangers would scrutinize you as much as your sister."

In spite of the conversation flowing between her and her other guests, Lizzie glanced frequently in my direction. Mr. Paling proved that under his guise of nonchalance and absurdity, he was a keen observer of persons.

"Aye. And I believe she does a fair job at reading lips, so you should be careful of what you say."

He grinned mischievously. "But do you suspect that I should say something improper?"

Of course I did. But I decided to demure rather than bait him. "Pardon me for allowing my tongue too free a rein."

His gaze slid from my eyes to my mouth. "I wouldn't mind helping you rein in that tongue of yours if you would let me." He bit his full lower lip.

I stared at his mouth, wondering what it might feel like to—

Dangerous. Much, much too dangerous for me to think about such things. I was supposed to use Mr. Paling's connections, not imagine . . . *things* . . . between us. I needed a distraction.

I picked up a book from the table at my elbow and began to peruse it.

"Miss Fletcher, what distraction have you found?"

I did not look up. "A book of poetry."

"And do you intend to beguile me with sonnets?"

I kept my eyes on the words, but they would not form into meaning. "I would not have you beguiled."

"I'm not sure you have much choice in the matter."

I looked up at him, but there was no sincerity in his eyes; he was simply trying to make me blush. If I followed Lizzie's advice from yesterday and kept my lips sealed, he would find me tiresome and move on to torment some other lady.

But his intense scrutiny unnerved me into speaking. I snapped the book shut. "Would you care for tea?"

He seemed to take a certain amount of satisfaction at my discomfort and obvious blunder; not only had Lizzie already offered him tea, but he had frazzled me into inviting him to stay longer.

"How do you like your tea, Mr. Paling?" Lizzie asked, flashing me a quick look of annoyance for my faux pas.

"Strong and hot. No sugar, if you please." In a quieter voice, pitched so only I could hear, he muttered, "That is also how I prefer people."

"Ah, so that explains your familiarity with Colonel Thoroton."

He let out a bark of laughter.

"If that is what you seek, Mr. Paling, I think you should become better acquainted with my sister."

Lizzie brought him his cup of tea before pouring for the Ascoughs.

Mr. Paling eyed my sister. "A serious one, is she? That is good to know. Thank you for the tip."

I guiltily perused the room, wondering what these virtual strangers thought as I received Mr. Paling's unabashed attention. But though Elizabeth narrowed her eyes at me, Mrs. Bell and the Ascoughs did not look our way. "Honestly, Mr. Paling, look at my sister now and tell me if those are sugary glances she sends you."

He took his time appraising my sister. "No, to be sure. No honey coating either." But her look did not unnerve him out of his smile, which he turned on me, full force.

He drank his tea, then left; my nervousness exited with him.

I sighed and turned my attention to the Ascoughs. While conversing with Mr. Paling, I had learned little about them except that they enjoyed the piano forte. "I should like to hear you play sometime," I said to Miss Ascough.

"Mama, may we have Miss Fletcher and Elizabeth over for dinner soon? I should like them to hear the new piece I have been working on."

Mrs. Ascough looked at me appraisingly, perhaps wondering if I would be a poor influence on her daughters. Though she had not admitted such with as much as a wrinkling of her brow, she had certainly been privy to Mr. Paling's flirtations, and I doubted she approved. But after a moment, she said, "Of course, dear. Elizabeth, do you already have plans for the morrow?"

As she did not, a date was set. I looked forward to the prospect, for with Lizzie in full mourning, there were but few families with whom she could have open associations, and her husband's family was one of them. Perhaps they would even invite a handsome gentleman or two.

Once the Ascoughs and Mrs. Bell took their leave, Lizzie did not inquire after the details of Mr. Paling's and my conversation, but she did say, "That was not very pretty of you, Anne, to flirt with Mr. Paling whilst the Ascoughs came here with the express purpose of meeting you."

"Me? Flirt?" I spluttered. I hadn't meant to.

"While I don't know what you said to him, that little smile of yours was clear enough. You do realize, do you not, that I am only able to live in this house through the grace of my in-laws?" Lizzie looked angry or possibly scared.

Oh, poor Lizzie. "But if you should have a son, the house becomes yours."

She rubbed her belly, looking weary. "Even if I have a son, I would only become a ward to Master Ascough. Either way, they could choose to toss me to the gutters if they wished. I have no claim on this estate, and I reside solely on their good graces, which, thankfully, have been generous indeed. But I am counting on you, Anne. You must stay on your best behavior around the Ascoughs. They will not tolerate scandal."

I nodded my head, only now registering the anxiety that had been hidden between her frequent glances.

"Also, I feel that I gave you bad advice previously. Though Mr. Paling's acquaintance will undoubtedly increase your associations, you do not want the kind of gossip that his attention would offer. I would keep him at arm's length if I were you."

I swallowed, fearing she was right. Arm's length or farther.

⁕⁕⁕⁕

When Lizzie and I arrived the next evening, only Mrs. Ascough, her son, Henry, and the Misses Ascoughs were in attendance. I had thought perhaps Henry and I might get along well enough—Lizzie had already described his generally jovial disposition—but I soon discovered he was barely more than a half-wit.

Dinner was a dull affair.

But what they lacked in conversation, they made up for in musical appreciation. Their applause at Lizzie's and my mediocre performances on the piano forte was so warm that I had wrongly assumed they were inept themselves.

Such disillusions dissipated once Miss Ascough began playing. After my vigorous applause, Miss Grace said, "I adore Mozart. Don't you, Miss Fletcher?"

I decided to own my ignorance. "I do not believe I am familiar with his works."

They looked at me as if I had spoken crudely in the middle of a sermon.

"But if what Miss Ascough just played was representative," I hurried on, "then, yes, I believe I am completely smitten."

Miss Ascough was incredulous. "Have you never heard this before?" She began playing a different piece. When I shook my head, she tried another and then another.

Lizzie intervened. "I would think you ladies might remember the extent of my ignorance when I first met you. Anne was raised on Handel, Hook, Haydn, and the like, just as I was."

Well, "raised on them" was a bit of a stretch. Rather, the music of such masters was practically crammed down my throat by Mr. Killingsby, my music teacher. But I understood her impetus to exaggerate my musical training to impress her in-laws.

"Do you like the operas of Handel, then?" Mr. Ascough asked.

"I imagine I would love them."

He gave me a blank stare.

"As I have only been in Town these few days . . . and there is no theater in Northamptonshire . . ."

Mr. Ascough blinked three times before responding. "You mean to say that you have *never* been to the theater?"

I nodded.

"Why, that's the most absurd piece of fiddle-cock I have ever heard. You must get yourself there."

It was my turn to stare in exasperation, but I remembered Elizabeth's warnings to stay in the good graces of the Ascoughs. I batted my lashes. "And how should a young female with few acquaintances manage that?"

He looked at me with the same vacant expression a trout might employ when baited.

Mrs. Ascough prodded her son. "As Elizabeth is still mourning your brother, she will not be able to take Miss Fletcher to the theater. She would need an escort, and she knows no one in Town."

Mr. Ascough still seemed oblivious, so Miss Grace said sweetly, "Henry, will you take us all to the theater?"

"Capital idea, Gracie. Wonder why I didn't think of that. Join us at the theater, Miss Fletcher?"

I started to squeal in excitement, then tempered my response somewhat. "I would be delighted."

Miss Ascough put a hand on her brother's arm. "Will you take us to see the new Mozart opera?"

He scrunched up his forehead. "Haven't we seen that one already?"

She nodded. "Twice."

He shrugged. "If that's what you want. It's all the same to me really."

Even though the man was as obtuse as they come, at least he was indulgent with his sisters. My own brother would never be so obliging.

As we took our leave, Miss Grace whispered, "Don't worry. I will make sure he rents a decent box."

I wondered what the man might do without a household of women to guide him. Perhaps . . . Perhaps someone as unobservant as he would allow his wife any number of latitudes. If I married him, I could be the one holding the reins; it would suit me better than being saddled by a taskmaster. I decided not to cross him off my list of potential suitors quite yet.

"Congratulations," Lizzie said once we arrived in the coach. "You have managed to receive your first real invitation into London Society. I wish I could go with you." She sighed dramatically. "But it would be impossible. I trust you will be on your best behavior."

"Of course."

She narrowed her eyes in a way that made her look alarmingly like Mother. "As long as you conduct yourself with decorum, this opportunity will garner others. But do not ruin my relationship with my in-laws, or else I will murder you in your sleep."

Charming.

CHAPTER ELEVEN
Mathematicals and Serpents

LIZZIE, WITH HER BOYISH FIGURE and hooked nose, tended to lash out when we stood side by side in front of the looking glass. She had always been jealous of me. Unlike with Mother, where I was never enough, around Lizzie, I was always too much. Too tan, too tall, and too buxom.

I held my breath, wary of her barbed compliments as she surveyed the cut of my newly commissioned dress. But Mr. Ascough would arrive any moment, whether or not I passed muster. The moment could be delayed no longer.

She nodded crisply. "You look lovely, but that has never been your problem, has it?"

The air I had been holding came out in a puff that sounded too much like Buttercup's nicker. I bit back my words before I called her a jealous harpy.

"I wish I could oversee your debut to make sure you don't endanger our standing with the Ascoughs," she said as she placed her own velvet cloak about my shoulders.

"Of course I shall do no such thing. I am no longer a child."

She eyed me. "Yes, but you are still wild." She fingered the daisies adorning my dressing table. "If you want to garner favor, you need to learn to be a wallflower instead of a wildflower."

"Mr. Paling doesn't mind so much," I mumbled.

She gave me an arch look. "But Mr. Paling will never ask you for your hand, will he? He is just amusing himself." She pressed her lips together. "Trust me, marriageable gentlemen are not interested in wildflowers."

She wanted me to be something else, something less brilliant and vibrant. Something more like her.

I had always thought her jealous, but as I looked into her eyes, I could see no traces of envy or malice. Perhaps she had my best interest at heart. "I shall smile and nod and be demure as much as possible."

She looked taken aback by my meek response. "You really have grown, haven't you? But remember, though you were a catch in Northamptonshire, you are no such thing in London. Our family is respected, but neither titled nor ancient. Your dowry is sufficient, but you are no heiress. You shall do very well with the Ascoughs, but do not presume equal footing with those who go to the theater to be seen."

I endured these strictures well, knowing it was Lizzie's duty to deliver them.

The Ascoughs' carriage arrived in the nick of time, for after I entered, it began to rain thunderously upon the conveyance, adding to the chorus of hooves on the cobblestones. No one attempted to speak over the din, so I looked through the fogged windows at the city while it sped by.

We rolled to a stop in front of a disappointingly nondescript brownstone building. Mr. Ascough readied his umbrella and escorted first me and then his sisters out of the coach to the theater's portico. Though it was only rain, he seemed like Lancelot, charging through his foes, protecting fair maidens from the deluge battering his shield.

Too bad he had dunder where his brains should have been.

Once he brought Miss Grace safely to us, we hurried together through the doors. Many a well-coiffured head turned at our entrance, but they quickly swiveled back to their own companions. No eyes analyzed my every move. There were no elbows jabbing neighbors, querying a report of the newcomer who gracefully paraded up the grand staircase. I reminded myself that I received no more or less than my due, but that knowledge did not help to quell my disappointment.

Mr. Ascough rearranged the chairs in our box with only three in front. "Miss Fletcher, you shall sit there where you can be seen by the *crème de la crème*." He pointed to the middle box seats, where some of the elder generation still proffered powdered wigs and painted faces.

I gestured to the open space beside my seat. "But there is room for you too, if you would like an unobstructed view of the stage."

Mr. Ascough grinned, though I had no idea why that statement humored him. He sat behind me and pointed out the titled persons who had already arrived. I surveyed the *haut ton* to distinguish their *je ne sais quoi*. Aside from their fine jewelry and clothing, the only thing that differentiated them was their stillness. As if made of wax, movements were minimal, and every gesticulation appeared fatigued. They were a tired lot.

A tall man with broad shoulders and hair the color of hay came into the box. He mumbled a hello, nodded in my direction, then took up a seat next to Mr. Ascough.

"That's Mr. Kehr," Miss Ascough explained. "Don't feel offended; the man rarely puts two words together at a time. Now, how is your German?"

"Nonexistent. Why?"

She placed a kind hand on my arm. "Because that is the language of the opera."

Oh. I had assumed it would be in English. Or Italian. Or possibly French. But German?

"And I have already seen it twice, so I shall tell you about the story in order for you to understand."

While she launched into an explanation, I noticed Mr. Paling and the colonel enter and assume a box near the middle of the theater. Unlike my arrival, heads turned, elbows prodded, and whispers flooded the room. Mr. Paling had an elegant brunette on his arm, who glided into a seat next to him. He leaned to her, whispering something scandalous, no doubt, and she laughed in response. I wished Miss Ascough would finish her explanations so I could inquire about Mr. Paling's companion, but I had no chance before the music began.

On the stage, three ladies appeared to fight over an unconscious man while another actor was covered in feathers. Judging from the laughter of the Ascoughs, this was a comedy, but I could hardly understand enough to laugh at the appropriate times. And why did the actors speak? I thought everything was sung in opera.

I struggled to pay attention with the same rapt devotion that Miss Ascough kept, though I fared better than Mr. Kehr, whose soft snoring alerted me to his disinterest. I turned away from the stage for a moment to watch his head as it bobbed down onto his chest in the familiar cadence of sleep, only to snap up to alertness before drooping again.

Mr. Ascough caught my eye and winked. I had no idea how I was supposed to interpret that.

Looking at the people in the boxes across from me, I saw hardly one in ten paid attention to the stage, their eyes instead roving over the persons of consequence. I spied on Mr. Paling and his companion, whose heads tilted toward one another in intermittent communication. He was whispering huskily in her ear, no doubt, and she was responding with furtive glances through her heavy, dark lashes. I tried to squash the unpleasant feelings observing them together evoked. Besides, I had determined to keep him at arm's length. Why should I care with whom he chose to flirt?

The music stopped. "Is it over?" I whispered.

"No, this is an intermission," Miss Grace said. "What do you think?"

"Lovely." I tried to pose an intelligible question. "Who is that one singer who sang so impossibly high?"

"Wait until the second act," Miss Ascough said excitedly. "Her revenge aria is spectacular. She is the villain, you know."

"Is she?"

Miss Ascough launched into an explanation while my eyes wandered away from the stage and to the people who popped their heads in and out of boxes like voles stealing vegetables. Colonel Thoroton, Mr. Paling, and his languorous companion certainly made their rounds. They spent an inordinate amount of time in a box filled with particularly frivolous-looking females before disappearing again.

After Miss Ascough finished her plot summary, Mr. Ascough turned to me. "Is there anyone at the theater tonight whom you would like to visit?"

How thoughtful of him. "I would like to visit a friend, but I have none here aside from you."

His brows puckered in confusion. "Surely you know someone here."

"No indeed. The only persons in London with whom I am remotely acquainted, aside from you, of course, are Colonel Thoroton and Mr. Paling, whom I recently met at a ball near my home in Northamptonshire."

"I have heard all about Colonel Thoroton," Miss Grace said. "How charming he must be."

I smiled ruefully. If the man was charming, he hid it well.

"Though your acquaintances are few, you are lucky in them, Miss Fletcher," Miss Ascough said.

I scoffed. "They are hardly acquaintances. I doubt they should even choose to acknowledge me if they saw me in the street."

"Nonsense," Miss Grace said. "Mr. Paling sat conversing with you when we came to call and seemed quite enchanted."

"Mr. Paling—" I began.

"Is standing right behind you," a jovial voice interrupted. Mr. Paling had condescended to visit our box, a smug look on his face. "So you may want to curb your tongue."

Drats! He had caught me speaking of him. He would never allow me to live it down.

He escorted a scowling Colonel Thoroton and the beautiful lady into our box. She leaned to Mr. Paling and whispered into his ear. Straightening himself, Mr. Paling announced, "Quite right, my love."

My stomach twisted into knots at his easy use of the sobriquet.

"It seems introductions are in order. Mrs. Slater, I am pleased for you to meet Miss Fletcher."

Mrs. Slater? The name was familiar, but I struggled to place it. Mrs. Bell had mentioned her, I thought.

Mr. Paling continued. "Colonel Thoroton, these are her sisters-in-law, Miss Ascough and Miss Grace Ascough. I had the pleasure of meeting them when I visited Miss Fletcher the other day." I was impressed that he remembered their names, for he had not said two words to them during his call.

I wished I had paid better attention to Mrs. Bell's long-winded gossip. Mrs. Slater had a large feather poking out of her coiffure . . . feathers . . . Mrs. Slater . . . his sister! I giggled at the realization. He hadn't been flirting at all.

Mr. Ascough cleared his throat, waiting for me to make an introduction. I quickly stammered, "May I present Mr. Ascough and his friend—" I motioned to Mr. Kehr before I remembered he remained fast asleep.

Mrs. Slater cast her eyes heavenward and whispered audibly, "She has even fewer wits about her than your usual entourage, Thomas."

My cheeks flamed at the insult. I averted my gaze so that Mr. Paling would not spy them.

"*Au contraire*, I find her to be quite witty, Edith. Give her a chance."

But she scrutinized me with a look of disdain that rivaled the colonel's, her eyes sweeping over me and lingering on my full bodice. "Yes, I'm sure you admire her for her great wit."

"If it is her figure you object to," he whispered back, "you must concede she has no control over that, and there is even less reason for me to object."

How dare they speak of such things, especially in front of the Ascoughs! Humiliating. "I believe a conversation of this nature would be better conducted at Tatersall," I said.

"Tatersall? They sell horses there," Mr. Ascough said unhelpfully.

"My mistake, then. I thought Mr. Paling and Mrs. Slater must have been discussing the merits of a filly they meant to purchase."

Mr. Paling's loud laughter spilled into the theater, and I looked around self-consciously as our box took center stage. "See, sister?" He nudged Mrs. Slater playfully. "As witty as she is beautiful."

Mrs. Slater had the decency to look abashed for her exceptionally rude comments.

Mr. Paling turned back to me. "And where is your sister tonight? Does she not care for the theater?"

"She would love to attend, but she is still in mourning. Her husband died in the Peninsular War."

The colonel's perennially stern expression visibly softened at this news. "Where? When?"

Miss Ascough answered. "July. Battle of Salamanca."

He nodded gravely. "There were a great many who fell there." He paused, frowning. "I did not know an Ascough, but any fallen comrade is a brother in arms. I am truly sorry for your loss." He bowed to Mr. Ascough, Miss Ascough, and Miss Grace in turn.

Mr. Paling addressed me again. "So this is why you have been cloistered away."

"We are hardly nuns, though to those of the *ton*, we might appear so."

"No one of the *ton* could mistake you for a nun," Mr. Paling said.

Colonel Thoroton coughed. "Well I, for one, envy your sister the capacity to mourn in peace."

I glanced at his black armband and cravat, wondering if the desire to mourn his father was the sole reason for his perpetually cantankerous mood.

Mr. Paling shrugged. "Can't mourn forever, you know."

The colonel only scowled.

"Miss Fletcher, have you no other family in Town, besides your sister?" Mrs. Slater asked.

"No. My mother had intended to attend me but was detained in Northamptonshire."

Mr. Paling sighed. "And so you are forced to observe your sister's mourning customs, like one buried alive. Edith, can't you do something for this poor, sequestered girl? Send her an invitation or something?" He batted his lashes at her; it was nearly impossible for him to turn off his charm, even with his sister.

Mrs. Slater thawed under his supplications. "I shall see you and your escort"—she nodded at the Ascoughs—"are invited to a few things, but that is the most I can do."

Mr. Paling looked benevolently upon her. "See, that's why she is my favorite sister. She doesn't even like you, and she is still willing to do right by you."

After she nudged him in the ribs, an awkward silence ensued. Mr. Ascough broke it by addressing the colonel. "I say, that is a well-tied cravat. The oriental?"

I laughed. "I believe it is a mathematical, and anyone who says otherwise is sure to encounter his ire."

The colonel's lips twitched. "You speak from experience."

"Yes. I have always had a head for maths."

Mr. Paling chuckled.

The colonel's eyes twinkled as he offered what I had to interpret as a conciliatory half smile. "I hope your head does not ache too much from the last encounter. Had I known you would be here this evening, I would have, perhaps, chosen the oriental."

There, but I do believe that the colonel jested.

Mr. Ascough, blissfully unaware of how literally I had come into contact with the colonel's cravat, exclaimed, "Now, don't say that. You have tied it wonderfully."

Colonel Thoroton laughed, and Mr. Paling cuffed him on the shoulder. "I have missed that sound, old friend." Turning to me, he asked, "And how are you enjoying the opera, Miss Fletcher?"

"I can safely say that I enjoy it better than Mr. Kehr." I nodded at his still-sleeping figure. At the mention of his name, his head again rose to an approximation of alertness before sagging against his chest. "I have been musing on the Sisyphean effort of keeping his head up, only to have it roll back down again. Poor fellow."

The colonel grunted. "The lad needs a drink, not a lullaby."

Mrs. Slater's lip curled in disdain. "No doubt the chap has been deep in his cups already."

I desired to defend the sleeping innocent whom I had dragged into this conversation. "Perhaps it's Tamino's magical flute that lulled him to sleep, though I think Tamino would prefer to call Pamina to bed rather than Mr. Kehr."

Though the men chuckled, Miss Ascough covered her mouth with her hand.

"What? Have I misunderstood the plot?" I whispered to her.

Behind her hand, she hissed, "You should not say such things."

Miss Grace bent her head but could not hide the signs of a blush. Mr. Ascough looked down his nose at me.

Drats! I had offended Lizzie's in-laws after she expressly instructed me not to. I would have to find a way to make it right. I assumed as meek a disposition as I could. "I do not mean to be crass, but how am I to discuss the plot of an opera that deals with love and all its sordid affairs if the merest hint of a dalliance on the lips of a lady becomes taboo?"

The colonel coughed into his hand. Mr. Ascough rubbed the back of his neck. Mrs. Slater's gaze softened slightly, but Mr. Paling was the only one who responded. "Mm. Dalliance on the lips of a lady. Indeed." He chewed on his full lower lip while gazing at mine.

Mrs. Slater rewarded her brother's innuendo with an elbow planted in his ribs.

"Thank you," I said. "I have wanted to do that for an age at least."

Mrs. Slater's eyes narrowed into slits. "Tell me, Miss Fletcher, what other intentions have you toward my brother?"

That was rather bold of her. She must consider me so far beneath her touch that she did not worry about such niceties as polite speech.

"Target practice with your satchel, perhaps?" Mr. Paling asked, expressionless.

I ignored his provoking statement and decided to answer with the same kind of bold declaration Mrs. Slater had employed. "I intend to stay as far away from him as possible. Chasing after Mr. Paling seems tantamount to a death sentence."

"I beg your pardon?" she asked, obviously offended.

"You see, my reception this evening has been pleasantly indifferent until Mr. Paling condescended to admit himself into our box. Now scores of ladies stare daggers at me. Surely one of them will slip something in my tea or run me over with their coach-and-four."

Mrs. Slater looked around, satisfied at the amount of attention her party garnered. "You are a silly girl to mind it. But even so, you must be aware they regard neither you nor my brother and have eyes only for the colonel."

Colonel Thoroton blushed in response.

Musicians began to re-tune their instruments. "Come, Thomas, we should leave Miss Fletcher to her anonymity." She held her arm out, waiting for her brother's escort, but he did not step forward.

"You know, Edith, I would prefer to stay." Mrs. Slater and I glared at him with the same visage of disbelief. "Colonel Thoroton, I recommend you escort my dear sister back to her seat. Between your snarl and her snobbery, you should be able to keep the swarming ladies at bay."

They both huffed but turned and left.

"If you prefer not to have everyone's eyes upon you, Miss Fletcher, I suggest you not hang over the balustrade like a bonbon in the confectioner's window." He pulled two chairs together near the back of the box. "Here. Sit."

I looked to Mr. Ascough for rescue, but he seemed oblivious to my need. He retained his seat next to the slumbering giant.

The orchestra began to play in earnest.

I sat behind Mr. Kehr and felt decidedly better until Mr. Paling relaxed into the other chair, his leg brushing against mine.

I scooted over, though I had effectually pinned myself between him and the wall. "Why are you still here?" I whispered.

He leaned in and removed a curl that dangled in front of my ear so he could whisper back. "I find you entertaining."

Situated as we were in the rear of the darkened box, my heart pounded; I convinced myself I was angry. Yes. Definitely angry and not at all interested in feeling his smiling lips pressed against my neck. "Is the theater not entertainment enough?"

He backed away from me, but in doing so, his leg brushed mine again. "You made the colonel laugh, you know. No one has done that for some time. Not even me. I own that I am in your debt."

"Is he a good friend of yours, then?"

He nodded. "He never used to be this surly, you know. War and death have changed him."

I looked at my gloves, pondering what I could say. His hands were placed on his knees, inches from mine. "I'm glad he is recovering, but I would rather not be the object of his laughter, if you know what I mean."

He looked at me askance. "You would rather be the object of his heart?"

I snorted, then covered my mouth with my glove, but no one turned to glare at me. "If he indeed has a heart lurking beneath that scowl of his, I would rather not be the lady tasked with unburying it."

Mr. Paling pursed his lips, but I couldn't even distinguish the coloring of his eyes, let alone the schemes that swirled behind them. "That is probably for the best. He is most likely going to marry an heiress like his father and grandfather before him. You would not happen to be an heiress, would you?"

"No," I whispered. "I am afraid my dowry is of the more modest sort."

He nodded. "I didn't think you were, but you have an uncanny way of surprising me." He elbowed me playfully.

The feeling was mutual. "Are you his matchmaker, then?"

He huffed. "Something like that." He gave me another sideways glance. "And now that I am in your debt, would you like for me to secure a match for you as well?" He waggled his brows at me.

I suppressed the urge to slap him across his chiseled jaw. "You and the heavens above know that I can use all the help I can get."

He chuckled and leaned closer, again removing the curl in front of my ear. His gloved hand brushed my neck. Shivers coursed down me. "I wonder what sort of payment we could arrange for services rendered."

He would likely exact payments in kisses—or worse, the scoundrel. I planted my left elbow firmly into his ribs.

He winced and backed away. "Well, I suppose if you don't want to be introduced to a few eligible gentlemen, you could just say so."

"Not if all the gentlemen you know are scapegraces like you."

He grinned wickedly at the insult but maintained his distance.

"If you do happen to know any ladies—not in mourning, mind you—or well-mannered gentlemen, an introduction would be priceless," I said.

"Priceless but not free. Nothing in this world is free." He gave my hand a condescending pat, seemingly unaware of how much his touch unnerved me. "But you should treat the fairer sex as if they were serpents."

I pulled my hand out from under his. "Come now. We cannot all be so venomous."

"Venomous, no. But I have yet to meet a snake that did not bite eventually. Even you, Miss Fletcher, I shall have to be wary of. My sister dubbed you silly, but I see you as dangerous. After all, it is the youngest of the serpents, the ones who cannot control their venom, that prove to be the deadliest." He took my hand again and raised it to his lips. "And so, I shall bid you adieu."

He stood and left with an urgency I had yet to see him employ. I shivered at the loss of warmth, even as I told myself it would be better not to be cozied up with him in the relative privacy that had been afforded us.

The orchestra stopped playing, and the dialogue continued, but I had no idea what was being said. I soon succumbed to the same fate that plagued Mr. Kehr.

I was roused by the sound of clapping.

Oh dear. I hoped I hadn't snored! My cheeks flushed, but it would seem that none of the Ascoughs had witnessed my inattentiveness.

Mr. Kehr silently exited the box, and I made to follow, but Miss Ascough placed a hand on my arm. "Not yet. We wait just a few minutes for the lower level to exit first. Plus," she lowered her voice, "it gives gentlemen a chance to call on us if they wish."

"How did you like the opera?" Miss Grace asked pleasantly.

"Very, much. I thank you."

The girls both nodded, but Mr. Ascough said, "Not to worry, Miss Fletcher. I fell asleep my first time too."

My cheeks heated. Miss Ascough glared at her brother, but he seemed as oblivious as always. "When did Mr. Paling leave?" he asked too loudly.

I glanced over my shoulder to make sure he did not materialize while I spoke of him. Again. "Before the orchestra finished their first piece."

His brows knitted together. "That's good. I don't think he is the sort . . . er . . . that you should . . . uh, encourage."

Well. If even Mr. Ascough felt compelled to warn me off, then I really ought to listen.

Miss Grace defended me. "She didn't encourage him; he sought her out. And a good thing too." She swatted her brother with her fan. "Without her connections, we never would have met the colonel. And Mrs. Slater has promised us an invitation to boot."

Miss Ascough continued where her sister left off. "You should have introduced her to all your friends rather than chastising her for speaking to her only acquaintance. I don't believe Mr. Kehr uttered more than two words all evening."

Mr. Ascough shrugged. "To his credit, he never says much of anything, which is more than I can say about the two of you."

Miss Grace scowled. "Of all the people in the theater, Mr. Kehr should have paid the most rapt attention since he speaks German. Instead, he fell promptly asleep."

They continued chatting with the friendly banter of siblings. I wished Lizzie could have been there so I could have someone to talk to in moments like these.

In the end, we left the box without receiving any visitors.

I did not see Mr. Paling or the colonel again that night, but several ladies offered me cruel looks as they whispered behind their fans. A few gentlemen appeared faintly curious about me, but no one deigned to introduce themselves.

As I left the crowded theater, I had never felt so alone in my life.

CHAPTER TWELVE
Brothers and Fiancés

I RECEIVED A HIDEOUS PLANT the next day with a note from Mr. Paling. As I opened the letter, an invitation to Mary Paling's ball fell out. It had been written in an unfamiliar and decidedly feminine script. I set it aside and read Mr. Paling's note.

> *Dear Miss Fletcher,*
> *I hope you have not found your tea poisoned. Just in case, here is some chamomile to ease your pain before you die. I sent the entire plant, pot and all, so that it may live a long and prosperous life. I hope you do as well.*
> *With sad regard to the dangerous situation I have placed you in,*
> *—Paling.*
> *P.S. Chamomile is impossible to find at the florists. This particular specimen was dug out of Mother's garden. It may not look like much now, but I am told it will blossom in the spring as long as you care for it.*

I considered the spindly green plant that looked more akin to a weed than a flower. And yet, Mr. Paling had obviously gone to some trouble to bestow it. In spite of its barren leaves, my heart danced when I looked at the plant.

I set it next to the wilting daisies in my bedchamber but quickly decided they would suit the balcony better. It was a perfect place for the inconspicuous plant to watch the street sweepers muck the mews, unbothered by the more ostentatious blossoms flowering below.

As I bent to place the potted plant, a voice hollered, "Ahoy, who goes there?"

I looked down and saw none other than Mr. Paling. I instinctively put a hand to my chest, then backed toward the door.

"Come, don't be frightened. Have a stroll with me. Bring that serious sister of yours."

But Lizzie was not at home. And I did not need him hollering at me as if I were a Juliet in need of a Romeo. He would have every tongue on the block wagging in no time at all. I turned and went in, not giving a response.

The butler soon found me, handing me Mr. Paling's card. "I told him you were not at home to visitors today, but he insisted I check again."

Of course he did. The man showed no respect for propriety. I took his card and tapped it against my leg as I considered a response. Keeping Mr. Paling at arm's length was soon becoming as difficult as it was imperative. "Please tell him the nuns prefer to be cloistered today."

Simmons raised a brow but did not comment on my cryptic remark. He turned to fulfill my request.

I hastily added, "But thank him for the invitation and flowers." Though being near him had grown dangerous, I couldn't afford to offend him either.

After Simmons had sent Mr. Paling away, I paid a quick call to the Misses Ascough, and they delivered the *on dit*. Not only had they received a similar invitation, but they would put off their other engagements so they might escort me to Mary Paling's—Mr. Paling's younger sister—coming-out ball.

Though only three days off, time crawled as slowly as if I'd been locked in the larder. Between the incessant rain and my sister's mourning, we found ourselves completely at the mercy of those who bestirred to venture into Lizzie's drawing room. Few did, other than Mrs. Bell. I had only my sister and my correspondence to entertain me.

Charlotte's letter was woefully nondescript. She had overcome her illness, John had recuperated, and Father was still on the mend. She and Mother would come to London as soon as Father recovered.

I tapped my hand upon my knee in a nervous gesture. I had been in London for ten days already but was no closer to securing a proposal now than I had been when I left. And doing such would only be harder under Mother's scrutiny and with the illustrious Charlotte outshining me at every step. Maybe I should start flirting with Mr. Ascough.

Angel's letter brought happier tidings. After several visits to the vicarage, Miss Loveland accepted an invitation to stay for a week. Knowing Mrs. Skinner, she indubitably planned to throw her son and his cousin together. Perhaps they would fall in love and Will would let me off the hook, but Angel was suspiciously silent on that point. In fact, she failed to mention her brother at all.

I wrote to her, demanding more details and giving my experience at the opera.

And then I waited. Waited for visitors to call. Waited for more correspondence. Waited and waited and waited.

The rain stopped just before Mr. Ascough came to collect me for the ball. As I walked toward the coach, the clouds parted, revealing countless stars in the heavens. The sky, purged momentarily of all traces of smoke, soot, and sulfur, smiled upon me.

"Beautiful, is it not?" Mr. Ascough asked, spreading his arms to encompass the heavenly expanse.

"Absolutely breathtaking." I craned my neck to take it all in, including the moon, which peeked over Lizzie's townhouse.

"I could not agree more."

But when I finally tore my gaze from the sky and looked at Mr. Ascough, he was staring at me rather than the sky. Of course, if he had been Mr. Paling, the serial flirt, I would have dismissed the attention right away. But with Mr. Ascough, the lack-wit? Perhaps he was musing on the height of the feather perched upon my head. One might never know with him.

I took his proffered arm, and we ascended into the coach, where the Misses Ascoughs chattered excitedly. "I wonder who shall be there? You know, Miss Fletcher, the Palings run in different circles, so I shouldn't wonder if we have only a few acquaintances."

"Nonsense," Mr. Ascough said, puffing up his chest. "There is hardly anyone in Town the Ascoughs do not know."

The Misses Ascoughs shared a look, obviously used to their brother's bloated sense of consequence.

"I shan't hardly care who is there as long as I spend the evening dancing," I said. I needed to meet as many gentlemen as I could if I was going to make a match this Season.

"Henry, you must secure partners for us all. It's a good thing you know everyone."

Mr. Ascough, impervious to his sister's teasings, promised he would see to it.

We soon arrived at Barkley Square, were divested of our cloaks, and made our way upstairs to the hall. The moonlight streamed through the east-facing windows, throwing ethereal light onto the ladies who floated around like specters in their spotless white.

Even though I wore the same color, I felt immediately out of place. I was an imposter, and judging by the cold glances people proffered me, they knew it as well as I.

I clung to Mr. Ascough's arm for protection as we spoke with Mrs. Slater. "I am glad you were able to come," she said. "I was afraid the invitations might reach you too late."

Before I could respond, she introduced me to her mother. Though of advanced years, a twinkle in her eye belied a sharp wit that had not diminished with age. "Good grief, but you are tan. Where are you from, Miss Fletcher?"

I had the decency to feel abashed for my lengthy escapades outdoors this past summer. "Rushden in Northamptonshire."

"And how does London compare with your part of the country?"

"It's certainly vaster." At my vague response, I expected her to dismiss me, but instead, her eyes narrowed. I reluctantly decided to offer a less perfunctory answer. "And here, everywhere I turn is a beautiful lady." I nodded to Mrs. Slater. "It is rather alarming. I now understand my brother's difficulty in selecting a wife."

Mrs. Paling's lips twitched, reminding me of her son. "But are the lovely ladies not equally tempered by lovely gentlemen? Perhaps it would be less unnerving to focus on them instead."

"Yes, Mr. Paling gave me the same advice, though I believe he told me that women were nothing more than venomous serpents."

She tsked. "I shall have to talk with my son," she grumbled. "I would introduce you to my daughter Mary, but she's dancing just now." She pointed out a girl, younger than I, with mounds of golden hair piled atop her head. She sported the self-same dimples as her brother, and her smile seemed genuine enough.

"If ever she has a break from dancing, I should be delighted to receive an introduction," I said.

She nodded at the statement and then spoke briefly with the Ascoughs while I scanned the room for outlandish waistcoats and scarlet regimentals.

My heart nearly stopped.

Mr. Smith stood among a group of gentlemen near the fireplace. I wanted to feign sudden illness and ensconce myself in some cranny, but the Ascoughs took their leave of Mrs. Slater and began to cross the room, bringing me toward Mr. Smith. I would have to face him. Again.

With the memory of being pinned between his body and the door, the sense of being trapped returned to me. I struggled to breathe, and my peripheral vision grew dark.

I needed an escape.

I made for the nearest balcony. As soon as the cool night air brushed my skin, my breathing slowed, and the spots of blackness dissipated. The scent of wet earth still hung heavily in the air, and I gazed at the stars.

Mr. Ascough found me moments later. "There you are, Miss Fletcher. Why have you come out here?"

"I couldn't breathe." I took a slow breath and held it for a few moments before letting it out.

He placed his hand solicitously on my elbow. "Are you unwell?"

Yes. Most certainly unwell. I considered my options. I could ask to be escorted home, I could hide on the balcony all night, or I could go back in there and face the scoundrel without allowing him to ruin my night.

But before I could decide which course to take, a giggle and a set of whispers reached my ears. A throat cleared, then an all-too-familiar voice announced, "Now that we are alone, I have something to ask you, darling."

Darling? I turned to verify the voice. Though his back was to me, I would have recognized him by his profile. William—my Will—bent over a lady's hand. She was a dainty beauty with a strong, Roman nose.

What on earth was Will doing in this intimate position with another lady while ostensibly engaged to me? It had only been two weeks since he had claimed to love me, and yet, here he was with someone whom I had never seen before.

The woman who had been looking into Will's eyes raised her gaze to consider me. "We are not quite alone, Will," she giggled again, pointing to me with a toss of her head.

He dropped her hand and spun around, his brows twitching in their fight to display multiple emotions at once. "Miss Fletcher." He bowed. "May I present Miss Smith?"

I huffed. He had done that well enough already. And what a presentation it was. I guffawed at the absurdity.

Miss Smith's eyes widened at my cackle.

Will cleared his throat and nodded to Mr. Ascough.

I very belatedly took his hint. "Right. Mr. Ascough, this is Mr. Skinner, the vicar of my very own quaint town of Rushden. Miss Smith, Mr. Skinner, this is Mr. Ascough, my brother-in-law."

I wasn't sure why, exactly, but even though I did not want to be engaged to Will myself, the fact that he had replaced me so easily wounded some part of me. Had I ever meant anything to him at all? My eyes began to sting, but I would not cry in front of Will. Not over this. Not when he had done exactly what I had wanted him to do: find someone else.

Miss Smith gazed at him with a fervor more akin to worship than love, and I had to wonder what she saw when she looked at him. Certainly not a brother, like he was to me. I wanted to be happy for him. Truly I did. But there was no room in my soul for such a charitable emotion, not when I felt like such a fool. I had thought that he cared for me, maybe even loved me. But obviously I had been wrong.

Will grinned at his newly acquired darling; I had the most absurd urge to wipe the smile off his face. I placed a territorial hand on Henry's arm. "Mr. Ascough has been such an attentive escort tonight."

Will's lips puckered into a frown. "That is very kind of him."

"Not at all," Henry said. "I had to accompany my sisters anyhow."

Ugh. Couldn't the man tell when a woman was trying to flirt with him? I ran my hand down Henry's arm. "And we had a delightful time at the opera. A good escort is invaluable when you know no one in Town."

The vein across Will's forehead pulsed ominously. He was clearly jealous, but why? He had been about to propose to another woman.

Miss Smith placed her own hand on Will's arm, marking her territory. "Very true. I would not be here at all tonight if it weren't for Will." The sugary glances she sent him made me want to vomit.

I addressed Miss Smith. "Did you know that only a fortnight ago, Mr. Skinner proposed—"

I summoned what I thought was a convincing cough, relishing in the look of panic which blanketed Will's expression. He pulled on his cravat as if it had grown too tight, but then clasped Miss Smith's hand in his own, as if for strength.

I narrowed my eyes at their hands and cleared my throat. "Excuse me. Only a fortnight ago Mr. Skinner proposed to visit me in London. My, how the time has flown."

Miss Smith giggled. "I concur. It seems as if Will and I only met yesterday." She giggled again.

They probably had.

Will sent her an annoyed glance then licked his lips.

Wait. I had played too many rubbers of whist with Will to miss that particular tell. Will was bluffing.

I stopped bemoaning my own tragic life long enough to really look at Will. His jealous glare, his twitching fingers, and the way he kept looking at me with those same puppy brown eyes, practically begging for scraps of my love. And I knew. I knew he was lying.

But to what end? Did he want to make me jealous? And would he really come all the way to London—and bring this poor woman too—with the idea of a romantic ruse? The very idea was absurd. And yet, it made more sense than Will coincidentally ending up on the same balcony as me, out of all the places in the world where he could have been tonight.

I decided there was only one way to know for sure. I had to call his bluff and see where the cards fell. "May I be the first to offer my felicitations on your upcoming nuptials?"

Both their faces blanched and Will began stammering, "No! But we are not—" Will waved between Miss Smith and himself. "You have misunderstood."

"Oh?" I said, with a smug smile. "I think I understand well enough."

"That is—" Will stammered, sweat plastering his pasty white brow.

Ha! Served him right for trying to manipulate me into loving him. I should let him sweat it out a little longer before I—

Miss Smith spoke tremulously, "Though I would certainly accept, should he choose to offer for me."

Wait. What? I thought I had ended their charade. Why was she still blushing and batting her lashes? This made no sense at all.

"You would?" Will asked, dumfounded.

I couldn't tell who was more stunned, me or Will.

She nodded eagerly and leaned forward to whisper something in his ear.

A smile spread across Will's face as slowly as the coming dawn. He took Miss Smith's hand in his, removed her glove, and placed a kiss on the back of her hand. "Julia Smith, will you marry me?"

"Yes!" She rose up on her tiptoes so she could kiss him on the cheek.

Will preened, sticking out his chest and swaggering a smidge in the wash of her affection. "Well, Miss Fletcher," he gloated, "*now* you can be the first to congratulate me."

But I was too shocked to respond. My mind replayed the last few moments. I'd called his bluff, but Miss Smith held the trump card. And I had forced her to play it. What had I just done?

"Congratulations," Mr. Ascough said cheerily, oblivious to all of the emotional currents that had just passed under his nose.

They looked at me expectantly, so I tried to gather my own thoughts into a cohesive response. "Yes. Thrilled. Ecstatic. Charmed, I'm sure." What was I even saying? I curtsied then turned to make a hasty departure.

Will reached out and grabbed my arm. "Miss Fletcher, would you save a dance for me?"

Honestly, I would rather dance with an orangutan at the moment, but I needed the opportunity to speak privately in order to begin processing all the thoughts and feelings flying chaotically through me.

I nodded to Will and stuck my hand out for Mr. Ascough to escort me away. Thankfully, he took the hint and we moved back into the hall. As we skirted the edge of the dance floor looking for the Misses Ascough, Henry asked, "Have you known Mr. Skinner a long time?"

"Yes, ever since he became the vicar some five years ago."

He nodded sagely, as if my comments had somehow enlightened the whole of our relationship.

But my mind still reeled. Was Will truly engaged to another? I'd seen it with my own eyes, but hardly believed it. And if he was, did that mean that I was free? What would Mother say when she heard of the engagement? Would she allow me to stay in London? Did I even want to stay in London once Mother was here? My mind felt like the contents of a reticule which had just been upended.

Henry located his sisters, who chatted animatedly with the more taciturn Mr. Kehr. The group had been pushed to the room's periphery and stood next to a group of sour-looking chaperones who posed along the wall like austere busts in a gothic church's alcoves.

Moments after rejoining them, Mr. Smith approached me. His sudden appearance startled me as thoroughly as if I'd been thrown from a horse. What with the recent revelations, I had somehow forgotten about the degenerate.

"Miss Fletcher, what a pleasure to see you again," Mr. Smith said melodically. "And who are your lovely companions?"

At the sound of his voice, my skin crawled like a snake had slithered up my skirts. I introduced him to the Misses Ascoughs as discourteously as possible, but they still curtailed their conversation to bat their lashes at the handsome rake.

He smiled beatifically at Miss Ascough through the introduction. "Would you do me the honor of accepting the next dance?"

It was like a nightmare I'd had many times: a child stood in the road when a coach and four whipped around a corner, and there was no way for me to save her. Time moved slowly, and I reached out my hand, as if to prevent Miss Ascough from certain destruction. But I was powerless. She agreed.

He turned to Miss Grace. "And perhaps I could tempt you with the dance that follows?"

She nodded her acceptance.

Mr. Smith turned to me and offered an innocent-looking smile. "Has your family all recovered from the explosion?"

"An explosion?" Miss Ascough gasped.

"Everyone is fine. Thank you."

"What explosion?" Mr. Ascough asked.

I had no desire to share the tale that would surely cast a less-than-impressive light on my family. "There was a minor hunting accident. That's all."

But Mr. Smith launched into the tale with gusto. I blushed to hear Papa's folly discussed with such a want of delicacy.

"Have they recovered their hearing yet?" Miss Grace asked solicitously.

"They have. According to Charlotte's letters, John has recovered completely, but my father still keeps to his bed."

While I offered this brief response, Mr. Smith leaned towards Mr. Ascough and dropped a word in his ear. Henry snapped his gaze to mine, shock clearly written on his face.

Fear pricked down my spine, leaving gooseflesh in its wake. What sort of aspersions was Mr. Smith casting? I would have to find out, but for now, the group was abuzz, exchanging inane niceties.

The music stopped and Mr. Smith took Miss Ascough to the dance floor.

"Miss Grace, may I have this dance?" Mr. Kehr asked.

She nodded shyly at the quiet Mr. Kehr, and they also went, leaving me alone with Mr. Ascough. I felt his gaze upon me but would not peel my eyes off of Mr. Smith long enough to return his glances.

In a low voice, I warned him, "Keep a close eye on your sisters as Mr. Smith dances with them."

"What do you mean?" he asked too bluntly.

I groaned inwardly, annoyed that the man required things to be spelled out for him. "He does not always act the gentleman."

"I see," he said, though I had to wonder if he really did.

But Mr. Smith neither ogled Miss Ascough nor caused her to blush. To all the world, he seemed a paragon of virtue.

While keeping my vigil, I hadn't noticed Will and Miss Smith until they settled in front of me, blocking my view of Mr. Smith. The poignancy of my feelings toward Will had lessened; with Mr. Smith around, I had more important things to consider than my own wounded pride. I stepped closer to Will and whispered, "Did you know that Mr. Smith is here tonight?" I nodded to where he danced with Miss Ascough.

"Yes, and if you had allowed me to continue speaking with you on the balcony," he censured, "then you would know that Mr. Smith is my newly minted fiancée's brother."

An uncontrollable shudder swept through my body. Mr. Smith—that monster, that vile, reprehensible man—was going to become Angel's brother-in-law. What had I done?

CHAPTER THIRTEEN
Vision

I FELT SUDDENLY DIZZY, AND reached a hand out to steady myself.

"Are you all right?" Will whispered.

I realized I had clutched his arm and that he had wrapped his other arm around my waist to steady me. I hurriedly stepped out of the almost embrace and glanced guiltily at his fiancée.

"Miss Fletcher, are you well?" Miss Smith asked.

I waved her off. "Yes. Yes, I'm fine. I just . . ." What in the blazes could I say to her? That her brother was a predator? Did she already know? Had he ever . . . assaulted her? I shivered at the thought of being related to such an unconscionable man. "I'm just a bit warm." I nodded toward Mr. Smith again. "He is your brother?" I managed.

Miss Smith's mouth moved excitedly, but my brain, still processing the implications of this relationship, could not register the words she spoke. Then she laughed, a reaction so incongruous with mine that, to my ears, it sounded like waves of broken glass tumbling into shore. "I understand your confusion. With a name like Smith, one can almost assume anonymity. And we are only half-siblings, after all." She smiled again, and now I could see the resemblance. They had inherited the same Roman nose, from whichever side of the family they shared. And while his features were dark as ebony, her coloring was a touch lighter, and her beauty as delicate as china.

"And you are only half-siblings, you say?"

She nodded. "Different mothers."

I looked at her askance. She did not look as if she had ever been . . . mistreated, though I wasn't certain what that would look like. I wracked my brain for any details Mr. Smith might have shared about his family situation but came up empty. After his offer of carte blanche, I had avoided him at all costs. "Mr. Smith is a great deal older than you, is he not?"

She nodded vigorously. "Really, he's more of a father to me since both our parents have passed on. I'm actually his ward." She beamed.

I sighed in relief. No one could be that cheerful in the face of their abuser. He must have only acted in such a way with me, though the heavens only knew why.

Will surveyed me with concern, and I forced a broad smile upon my face.

"Miss Fletcher, may I claim that dance now?"

"Of course," I said, though the music for the current set was only half done.

Will led me toward the dancing couples but stopped when we were a few feet shy. "Please let me explain. I know of your predilection for mishaps, so when I heard of the mail-coach robbery, I worried. I came to London to make sure you were all right—"

I scoffed. "And yet, you have not even called upon me once, choosing to visit with Miss Smith instead?"

He sighed and rubbed his hand across the back of his neck. "I *did* check on you. I spoke with Mr. Paling . . . and managed an invitation to this ball . . ."

I tapped my foot impatiently. "And? Is this all the explanation you intend to give?"

He stiffened. "I don't see why you should care. You've made it abundantly clear that you would rather flirt with Mr. Paling and Mr. Ascough than marry me." He straightened his cravat. "Although, really, I ought to thank you for helping me propose to Miss Smith. She is a very nice sort of girl, and I'm sure she will make a better clergyman's wife than you."

I scoffed. *Anyone* would make a better vicar's wife than me. Honestly, it was a good thing he had finally come to recognize that. But to Miss Smith? "You need to know what kind of family you are marrying into."

His raised brows displayed his confusion clearly enough.

"While he was a guest in my home, he cornered me in the garden and tried to kiss me."

Will gave a lopsided smile. "That is nothing so extraordinary, Anne."

"And offered me a carte blanche."

"Odd." He cocked his head to the side, pursing his lips. "He is a bit of an eccentric, I'll admit, but there is nothing in that which would—"

I pressed on. "While he was a guest in Rushden Hall, I had the misfortune of running into him in the corridor. He tried to drag me into his bedchamber."

Will's gaze flicked rapidly from one of my eyes to the other and back again before he blinked several times. "If he did something like that, you should have told me."

I blushed profusely. "Why would I? There was nothing you could have done."

His hands clenched into fists. "I could have called him out."

"And that, right there, is one of many very good reasons to keep you in the dark."

He scowled. "I could have . . ."

But there was nothing he could do, and we both knew it. "Just . . . be careful. She may be a saint, but he is not, and I am sure that, as a vicar, you will not want to be associated with him."

He nodded, though anger still flashed in his eyes.

"Do you still mean to marry her?" I asked. "I certainly won't make you."

He paused a long moment, emotions warring on his face. "This puts me in a delicate situation. I'm not certain that . . . What do you think I should do?" He looked at me eagerly, with that same visage of adoration that Miss Smith had employed on him.

And I knew that in spite of his engagement with Miss Smith, he still wanted *me*. Was he expecting me to claim my right to marry him? After all, he had promised to marry me if I returned from London unengaged, and I was most certainly still single.

But whether or not that was what he wanted, I knew I could never look at him with that same level of devotion. And it would be cruel of me to encourage him. "I sincerely wish that you and Miss Smith will find all the love and joy which you deserve. Just keep an eye on Mr. Smith, especially around your sister."

"I promise." The amber streaks in his brown eyes danced in the candlelight as he took my hand in his and raised it to his lips. "Come, Miss Fletcher. The music has stopped. Let's take our place in the next set."

My surname felt wrong on his lips, as wrong as the way he looked at me as he was engaged to another. I glanced at Miss Smith several times, ashamed and embarrassed every time Will stood a little too close or held my hand a touch too long. But Miss Smith beamed at him, regardless.

When the dance finished, Will returned me to my escort.

I turned to Miss Smith, wanting to befriend her—to see this paragon of virtue so well-suited to be a clergyman's wife in spite of her vile brother—but Mr. Kehr turned to me and stuttered, "W-w-would you like to dance?"

"Of course." In my introduction to him at the opera, I had not heard a speech impediment, but he had only said a word or two.

"Y-you don't mind if I st-st-steal her from you, do you, Ascough?"

"You cannot steal what I do not own," he said without rancor, though I wondered why Mr. Ascough's eye twitched as he spoke.

But I had little time to reflect upon that as I accepted Mr. Kehr's hand and allowed him to escort me to the dance floor. With his tall frame and muscular build, I knew we would partner well. His hand engulfed mine as we began to dance, and I had to look up to smile at him. Perhaps we were kindred spirits, joined together by our similar proportions and the tendency to be lulled asleep at the opera.

He said nothing as we danced but continuously glanced at his feet.

"Are you from London, Mr. Kehr?"

He only grunted, too occupied with the steps to be capable of more.

"Have you any family in Town?"

Sweat glistened across his brow. "P-p-please," he said, still concentrating. "Not now."

This dance, of necessity, must be a mute one. But at least the poor fellow understood his limitations and did not allow himself to become so distracted as to fall out of time. There were a few close calls, but I managed to keep my toes out of his path. He frequently looked down, and on the occasions that he did look into my eyes, a flush crept up his neck. The man must be dreadfully shy.

"Thank you for the dance," he said when it ended.

"Of course. I am always happy to dance."

"I am s-sorry I could not c-c-converse earlier. It is hard en-n-nough for me to speak well w-w-when I am not trying to pay attention to my feet." He shrugged.

"I understand completely."

Mr. Kehr's brows furrowed, and he opened his mouth to speak, but then he shook his head and began to escort me back to Mr. Ascough. Before we were halfway there, he stopped suddenly and opened his mouth again.

Our unexpected stop caused someone to collide into my backside.

"I beg your pardon," Mr. Paling said, clutching my shoulder as he steadied himself.

I trembled at his touch. "Not at all. I can assure you the pleasure was all mine."

He cocked his head to the side, his smile gouging deep creases into both of his cheeks. "Yes, if there was any pleasure to be had, it was most certainly all yours."

I laughed—not only at the memory of our first meeting—but in the evidence that Mr. Paling had remembered it too. We held one another's gaze, but this time, I did not search the depths of his eyes to conjure a name. No. This time, I searched his eyes to discern his intentions in seeking me out. I came away as empty-handed now as I had then.

Mr. Kehr coughed.

How embarrassing to be caught mooning over Mr. Paling like that!

"Miss Fletcher, would you care to dance?" Mr. Paling asked.

"I thought you no longer danced?" I asked.

"What kind of person comes to a ball if they have no intention of dancing?" Mr. Paling said dryly.

What kind of person indeed?

Mr. Kehr bowed and left us.

I frowned at his retreating form, wondering why such a strong, handsome man felt as insecure as he obviously did. "Now look what you have done, making Mr. Kehr feel like an interloper."

Mr. Paling sighed. "I thought that dance would never end."

"Oh? How long have you been watching me?"

Mr. Paling gave a mischievous look but did not answer. "Have you enjoyed yourself this evening?"

"You should know."

He honored me with one of his smiles and, if I wasn't quite mistaken, the hint of a blush. "Have you not danced with enough men? Shall I matchmake?"

Ooh, that was exactly what I . . . wait . . . I *didn't* need his help with introductions any longer. Will was engaged to another woman.

I was free.

I cackled, then covered my hand with my mouth. "I am afraid I know one too many gentlemen here, actually."

He bit his lip, and I could see he was trying to calculate whether he was the offending straw on the proverbial camel's back, especially after I had refused to see him the day he had brought me chamomile. I was too distracted by the sight of him nibbling on his lip to reassure him.

"If you are too tired to dance . . ."

"Don't be ridiculous. I was referring to the same blackguard whom I had been evading when we met at the Hinwick Ball." I nodded toward where Mr. Smith, Mr. Ascough, and Mr. Kehr conversed.

He scowled, his normally jocular face assuming a hint of menace. "Do you want me to call him out?"

I scoffed. "What good could that do?"

He chortled. "I have no idea. It's just an idle threat to scandalize the ladies."

"I have very little experience with idle threats."

A look of concern puckered his graceful brows, but he changed the topic. "And what of the ladies? Have you made any acquaintances while here?"

"None. They avoid me like the plague."

"How I envy you," he sighed over-dramatically. "Shall we take our places, then?" he asked, offering me his arm.

As he led me to the dance, I became acutely aware of the increased level of scrutiny I engendered at Mr. Paling's side. The discomfort only increased after we made our bows and began the familiar steps. Everyone—well, the women, at least—focused their attention on us by either pouting at him or glaring at me. Feeling as stiff as a dandy's cravat, I focused on the putrid green of Mr. Paling's waistcoat, but it did little to settle my nerves. "That is a very . . . green waistcoat."

His eyes laughed at me, but his lips did not so much as twitch. "Yes."

Though not quite as tall as Mr. Kehr, Mr. Paling was much lighter on his feet. His hand, when touching my glove, was not so meaty, and his scent was decidedly less sweaty. While I did not enjoy the feeling of being on display, I did thoroughly enjoy dancing: the music, the movement, the swish of my skirt, the light touch of my partner's hand.

When we finished dancing down and had a moment to ourselves as the outside couple, Mr. Paling said, "I had no idea you were such an excellent dancer. I was a bit dubious given the display you and Mr. Kehr offered me just now."

It was hard to be mad at him for his insult, especially coupled with the compliment. "You would have known if you'd danced with me the first time I was in need of a scapegoat."

He chuckled. "What was that all about, anyway?"

"I already told you. A loathsome man invited me to dance, and you were the only person I *thought* I knew capable of extricating me."

He nodded but said, "That seems all too reasonable for you, Miss Fletcher."

"Come now. I am quite often reasonable."

He eyed me dubiously, so I changed the topic. "Do you own any waistcoats of more subtle hues? Grays or creams or whatnot?"

"Yes, of course. But life is too short for wearing drab colors like that, don't you think?"

"I agree with you in general, but I do have to wonder what inspired this particular choice tonight." I had never seen a garment made to match the hue of fetid waters in the late summer sun before.

"Ah, that's easy. You inspired it."

I looked quickly into his eyes but could not decipher anything beyond the layer of mischief that always blanketed his face. "How is this?"

"I know my sister shall serve split-pea soup tonight, and I did not want to chance ruining a cream-colored waistcoat. This option seemed the most practical." His eyes twinkled.

It had been exactly a fortnight since I called his poppy-colored garment practical, yet he had remembered. Was there any comment, no matter how flippantly delivered, that Mr. Paling did not heed?

Though he could hardly contain his humor, his words sobered me. I had come to expect flippancy and outrageous flattery from him, which was as painless for him to deliver as it was for me to cast aside. But I could not laugh away the flattery of being heard. Of being seen. Of being thought of.

I looked anywhere but into his enigmatic eyes, and I knew from the jealous stares that assailed me that he made everyone feel this way. This was the secret to his popularity.

We rejoined the other couples, though his attention had sobered me sufficiently to remove the spring from my step.

"Anne, are you all right?" he whispered as his steps brought him near.

No, I was not. I did not want him to see me. I did not want his powers of perception to unravel me. Even his mother stared at me now. "You have no leave to use my Christian name. And why is your mother watching you like a hawk?"

He scanned the ballroom until he found her, then shrugged, a gesture that fit his posture of nonchalance so well. "She probably assumes I said something outrageous." Then he added, almost reluctantly, "And I told her about you."

"You what? Why?" This was getting worse and worse. Outrageous flattery I could handle, but his sincere regard threatened to undo my resolve to keep him at arm's length.

"I told her you knew no one, and she should help you if she could."

"Why do you care about me?" I had not intended to speak the words aloud. But I could not recall them, and he did not answer. We spent the rest of the dance in an uncomfortable silence.

When the music ended, he whispered, "If you allow me a moment of your time, I shall give you an explanation." At my raised eyebrows, he ushered me to the same balcony where I had seen Will. It was empty now.

I gazed at the white roses in the garden below that glistened like silver in the light of the full moon. I leaned over the balustrade to soak it all in. "It is so beautiful tonight."

"Truly." The awe of his voice matched mine, but when I leaned back enough to glance at him, he gave me a tired look. Maybe it was the moonlight reflecting off his putrid waistcoat, but his face looked more haggard than I could have expected on his perpetually youthful countenance. He seemed older . . . realer . . . and the authenticity of this persona made me wonder how often he hid this personality behind his carefree flirtations.

"I care about you because you are different," he said in sober tones.

I snorted at his unflattering remark. "Tell me something I do not already know."

"You do not like being different?" he asked, taken aback by my bitter response.

"I despise it. I want to belong somewhere."

He nodded solemnly. "What you do not understand, Miss Fletcher, is that being different is infinitely preferable to belonging."

"That is easy for you to say, as you are welcome wherever you go, no matter how horrid your waistcoat."

He looked at his putrid garment and smoothed it self-consciously "Horrid?"

I felt guilty at my thoughtless remark. "Case in point: A lady should flatter rather than insult, and yet, my tongue has a mind of its own and constantly lashes out. Try as I might, I never can rein it in or school my emotions." I pouted a bit, further accenting my point.

But he chuckled and dragged the knuckle of his index finger across my cheek and onto my protruding lower lip. "I would not worry about that vice if I were you. It is one of your better qualities." He must have known the effect this touch would hold over me, for he withdrew immediately as he gave me a sideways glance. "Have you learned to waltz?"

"Yes, of course."

"Excellent. Would you do me the honor of saving the first waltz for me?"

Should I? Mother would never allow such a thing. That sealed my decision. "I will, but I have yet to hear them call a waltz all evening."

He placed his hand on his chest in a gesture of having been offended. "Miss Fletcher, I am disappointed at your lack of faith. Did I not contrive for a whole pot of flowers to be delivered to your door so that they would not suffer the loss of their companions? And have I not garnered you an invitation to this very ball? Arranging a waltz should be no large contrivance."

With that charming smile, I would not be surprised if he could get whatever he wanted.

"Adieu until the waltz, then." He bowed and left.

In spite of the November air, I felt feverish where his finger had trailed across my lips. Though it had been imprudent, I longed for him to touch me like that again. But he was a flirt with no other intentions. Nothing good could come of dwelling on that feeling.

Heaven help me school my heart.

CHAPTER FOURTEEN
A Feather's Kiss

Mr. Ascough found me alone on the balcony. "Must I remind you that Mr. Paling is not the type of man whom you should allow to lead you off into private places?"

"Thank you for your kind attention, but I can assure you, it is not my intention to allow any man to drag me away." A sudden pain in my chest threatened to discompose me as I remembered Smith dragging me into his room. I massaged my sternum with the heel of my hand in an attempt to alleviate the pressure.

"Are you feeling unwell?"

I nodded and dropped my hand. "A little. It is why Mr. Paling took compassion on me and led me here for a breath of air." I felt a fierce need to protect him. "Of course, as soon as we discovered we were alone, he removed himself." Too soon or too late, I still wasn't sure which.

"Should you like to leave early?"

"I can wait until your sisters have finished their amusements." And until after the waltz. A chill wind blew, giving me the shivers.

"Let's go inside before you catch cold." Mr. Ascough escorted me back to his sisters and brought me some refreshment before excusing himself to play cards with Mr. Smith and Mr. Skinner.

Miss Ascough coughed discreetly into her hand, drawing my attention so she could keep her voice low. "Mr. Paling seems very attentive."

"Yes, to everyone," I responded, noticing that he again held court like some Adonis with a gaggle of worshipers at his side.

"But he offered you marked attention."

"I should hardly think it possible for anyone to mark such a thing, since he flirts equally with everyone of his acquaintance."

The giggles of the girls in his company punctuated my point. But he did not seem to enjoy the fruits of his labors. He reclined against a wall with a broody expression, his brow furrowed and his lips pursed in thought.

Miss Grace remained unconvinced. "He has not asked anyone else to dance."

"And I daresay he shall not," Miss Ascough added authoritatively. "He is not known for dancing. He does not even accept vouchers at Almack's anymore, so they say." She snapped her fan shut and pointed it at me. "What did he say to you? Why is he brooding?"

I shrugged. "Perhaps it is because I called his waistcoat horrid."

They gasped at my insolence, but I did not offer a response as the waltz was called. Mr. Paling walked into our circle and claimed my hand, leading me next to his younger sister, Mary, to whom I still had not been introduced. She had been dancing all evening.

"Watch this. It's my favorite part," he whispered.

"What is?"

"Let's see how many people Lady Willow turns away."

He indicated a lady whom I thought I had seen dancing near the top of every dance. A man came to ask for her hand, but she declined. By the time enough couples had joined us in a circle and we began to promenade, she had rejected no less than four gentlemen.

"Lady Willow positively refuses to waltz. She claims the postures are too crass for her, but I think she has never learned the steps. She's a hesitant dancer to begin with."

"Those poor gen—" I gasped as he drew me close, his arm about my waist.

"Are you sure you have done this before?" he whispered in my ear.

I didn't want him to know how his touch sent thrills across my body. "Would you like it better if I told you this was my first time?"

He chuckled darkly but gave no response as we continued our intimate steps. Together. Away. Arms up, framing his face. March. "I have never danced with a lady of your height," he admitted as my hair brushed his sleeve in a move where I stepped underneath his upheld arms.

"Be grateful you are taller than Mr. Skinner. He needs the arms of a monkey to enact that particular move with me."

"Or perhaps you should be grateful that I am not Mr. Kehr; he might decapitate you out of negligence."

"Don't be unkind. I would much rather dance a waltz with Mr. Kehr."

His face fell, and he opened his mouth to speak, but I stalled him. "Whenever I dance with you, everyone stares at me."

He drew me closer and whispered, "You are supposed to be so entranced with me that you don't notice what else is happening in the room."

I tried to ignore the way his whisper tickled my ear. "But then I would never see how closely your mother watches you."

He cursed under his breath, then gave me an apologetic look. "I beg your pardon, Miss Fletcher."

He was a model of propriety from thenceforth. He may well have been the dancing instructor for his lack of flirtations.

When the dance ended, however, he plucked the feather from my hair, its shaft sadly bent and drooping. "It appears I accosted this feather during the waltz. Please forgive me." He raised the feather to his lips, bestowing on it a light kiss, then extended it to me. It brushed my ear, across my cheek, and tickled my lips.

I could hear my heart pounding as I looked at how the candlelight flickered off his multi-faceted eyes. "Your mother is watching you."

"Blast," he muttered, looking around for her.

I let him search for a moment while I regained my composure. "I don't actually know where your mother is. I just like making you swear."

"You . . . you little minx." He smiled so winningly that it was hard to breathe. "You are not the first woman to make me swear, but you are the first to ever admit to liking it."

And apparently, I was the first woman in a long time who had convinced him to dance. The knowledge made me float back to my escort. But Mr. Ascough stood there with his arms crossed, practically glaring daggers at Mr. Paling.

Drat. Both men positioned themselves as if they were cocks preparing for a match. I quickly placed my hand on Mr. Ascough's arm. "I haven't seen you dance all evening." I batted my lashes at him, hoping he would take the hint and ask me to join the set.

But he shook my hand off. "I'm afraid I have already ordered the carriage." He turned away from me and to his sisters. "Come. Let's leave this blasted party."

I looked to them for answers, but their countenances displayed the same questions as mine surely did. We made a speedy departure.

Mr. Ascough sat uncomfortably close to me in the coach.

"Did Mr. Smith say anything amiss?" I whispered.

His response was as violent as it was quiet. "What reason have you to think that he should say anything amiss?"

"I thought, perhaps, he had danced with one of your sisters and—"

"Mr. Smith has been nothing but a model of propriety all evening. But I was quite shocked when he told me you tried to tempt him into an assignation while he was visiting Rushden."

"What?" I spluttered. "I would never . . . *He* tried to kiss *me*."

"I have no doubt he did, after the brazen wantonness I saw from you today."

But what had I—the feather? Was this all about a kiss on a feather?

"In the card room, everyone was talking about the new trollop Mr. Paling had acquired, whereupon Mr. Skinner and Mr. Smith both shared stories, none of which were flattering to you. I left the card room only to find you dancing a waltz with him."

"But I was told the waltz was only taboo at Almack's."

His look could freeze the Thames. "I saw him whispering in your ear. Did you plan an assignation?"

I stared blankly at him, though the coach was so dark it was hard to make out his features. "Never. How could you think that of me?"

"I won't risk you sullying my sisters with your reputation," he said before he turned his back to me and apologized to the Misses Ascoughs about leaving early. He claimed I had been feeling ill, but they were astute enough that I had no doubt they were capable of gleaning the truth from our words.

I huddled in on myself as I looked out the blackened window, trying to ignore the thickness in my throat as I held back tears.

Perhaps it would not have been possible for Mr. Ascough to have withstood Mr. Smith's lugubrious slander, but the fact that Will had contributed to the trouble rather than defending me felt like the greatest betrayal of all.

CHAPTER FIFTEEN
Villainy

I LONGED TO RIDE A horse down Rotten Row but kept the sluggish walking pace that Lizzie and Mrs. Bell set. Even if they hadn't been in the family way, our progress would have been impeded by the need to exchange a word or two with their acquaintances. It seemed the whole fashionable world had decided to capitalize on the finally dry weather by promenading Hyde Park today. I had been introduced to a dozen ladies at least before I ran into Miss Smith, accompanied by her loathsome brother on one arm and her fiancé on the other.

I desired to give Mr. Smith the cut direct, but the chance of refusing the acquaintance was taken from me as my sister gushed uncharacteristically. "Mr. Skinner! I had not realized you were in Town. Anne, did you know?"

Mr. Smith and Mr. Skinner both bowed.

"Yes, I had the fortune of seeing Mr. Skinner at the ball last night. And may I introduce you to his fiancée, Miss Smith?"

Lizzie's eyes bulged like a toad's for a second, but then the rest of the introductions were made.

Mr. Skinner turned and whispered something into Miss Smith's ear, and she nodded in response. He turned to me, extending his arm. "Miss Fletcher, would you care to walk with me?"

Once I accepted, Mr. Smith and his sister began strolling a few paces ahead of us, with Mrs. Bell and Lizzie following behind. I could hear the ladies whispering together, and though I could not distinguish any words, my ears burned.

"And what do you think of Hyde Park? Is it as you imagined?" He looked at me fondly while I tried to reconcile his adoring glances with the knowledge that he was affianced.

"No. In fact it is far larger than I anticipated. I have yet to explore it as thoroughly as I might wish to." I planned on remedying that once Charlotte was here.

"And you have not brought Buttercup. However do you manage?" He offered a lopsided smile.

"It's quite simple. In lieu of riding and walking, I dance." It was a bald-faced lie, but for some reason, I wanted Will to believe I had spent all my time in other men's arms instead of stuck in my sister's sitting room.

Mr. Skinner scowled. "About that," he gave my hand a condescending pat, "I want you to stop associating with Mr. Paling. He is dangerous."

"Not as dangerous as your future brother-in-law," I muttered.

"Anne." He sighed. "I spoke with Mr. Smith for quite some time last night and can assure you that you are mistaken about him."

I withdrew my arm from his escort. "*I* am mistaken?"

"Yes," he said simply.

I huffed. "There is no mistaking his actions when he tries to drag me into his bedchamber."

But Will only chuckled. "I have often wanted to drag you into a room myself to scold you for your impertinence. I know how provoking you can be. What did you say to anger him?"

Tears welled in my eyes, threatening to blind me. Will didn't believe me. Or worse yet, he *blamed* me. "I did nothing wrong. It was the day of the explosion, and I happened to walk past his room after checking on John."

Will gave my hand another condescending pat. "Oh, I know. Just like you did nothing wrong when you fell into the lake and I had to rescue you, pushing us together in your nearly transparent dress. Or the time you almost broke my nose, then tried to clean the blood off my waistcoat by undressing me. You never mean to get yourself into these situations, Anne, but you do. It's almost as if . . . as if you wanted to be compromised."

His words felt like icy water dousing my soul. "You accuse *me* of—" My throat hurt from the effort of holding back a sob. "I thought I was your friend. You even said you loved me. So how can you choose to trust the word of a man you hardly know over me? Especially when you expressly promised to stay vigilant around him?"

But Will patted my hand. "Don't worry, Anne. I understand why you did it. He is quite a catch. But you really ought to be more careful from now on. Not everyone will be as forgiving as I am."

Will actually thought I had tried to ensnare Mr. Smith! I could hardly blame Mr. Ascough for believing such slander—after all, he hardly knew me. But Will? We were friends. At least, I thought we were. "I am mistaken?" I asked again, my voice raw.

He nodded.

I stopped walking and turned to face him. "You are right. I am mistaken. I have never been so wrong about anyone in my life, Will. Heaven, as my witness, knows that I never believed you could be so cruel."

His eyes widened in shock as he registered that I was referring to him.

His look tore a hole in my heart, but there was no amount of bandaging I could use to salvage it or our friendship. A gentleman who thought me capable of something like this was no friend of mine. "Please do not ask to speak to me again. If you do, I shall have to cut you."

I began walking back to my sister, who, by this time, had trailed quite far behind, but was interrupted by an arm at my elbow. "Unhand me, Will."

But it was Mr. Smith's oily voice that responded. "Ah, yes. There is the fiery vixen I have come to covet." He used my elbow as leverage to turn me around before threading my arm through his.

"There is nowhere to drag me to this time," I said, heartened by the throng of people surrounding us.

He smiled, a cold look that could not reach his eyes. "Yes, I believe such pleasures shall have to wait for another time."

I tried to pull my arm away, but he held it as if in a vice.

"Now, don't be like that," he pouted. "I am only trying to help."

"I do not want your help."

He smiled softly. "Maybe not yet, but I imagine you will grow tired of polite Society eventually. They will never accept you, you know. You are not one of them, and you never will be."

I tried to allow his words to roll off my back like water off a duck, but they resonated too fully.

I would never belong.

"Once you have finished accumulating their scorn, what do you plan to do? Return home to become a spinster?" His eyes roved over me. "With your genteel background and other assets, it seems a waste. You could become rich."

My face grew hot as I realized what he meant. "Do you . . . do you run a business of ill-repute?"

He shook his head. "Nothing like that. Brothels are for the masses. I help provide certain—*ahem*—services, for those of a more distinguished palette."

"I am not a piece of mutton."

He smiled. "But you would make a nice piece of muslin. And with the way your brother gambles away your inheritance, you will never get a better offer. Do you have any idea how indebted he is?"

Dread pooled in the pit of my stomach, mixing with nausea. I knew John had run into a bit of misfortune, but was it so bad that even Mr. Smith knew? Or was he bluffing? "I'll not be sold off to pay for my brother's sins."

He shook his head. "You already were. You were denied a Season, and then John convinced Mr. Skinner to offer for you. You've been sold off. Cast aside."

"No," I said through clenched teeth. "You'll not have me. And I'll tell everyone what you are."

He offered me such a debonair smile that I wanted to box his perfectly straight teeth in.

"I've seen the way your family treats you. They won't believe you. They will turn on you just like Mr. Skinner and Mr. Ascough. You are completely friendless."

No . . . I . . . I . . . My heart constricted. Why did his words hurt so much? Because they were true. I was friendless. Alone. Powerless. "You are despicable."

He placed a self-righteous hand on his chest. "I'm not the one who cast you off. I'm the one offering you wealth. Opportunity. Power."

I scoffed. "The piece of mutton is not the one holding the carving knife."

He dropped his facade and began speaking in earnest. "You think Parliament wields power? The Prime Minister's mistress holds more power in her pinky than all of the House of Lords. What you are describing, little lamb, is marriage. If you want to be good and innocent and holy all your life, by all means, find some man to rule over you, take your dowry, and waste it as he sees fit. I'm offering you a way out. I'm offering you freedom."

I could see the vision he painted of the women who pulled the strings from behind silk screens, the Madames de Pointiers and de Pompadour who ruled over the court and the kingdom. Was this the freedom and sense of belonging I had been searching for?

"No!" my heart and I exclaimed at the same time.

He shrugged. "Stick to your moral high ground then if that pleases you. There are plenty of other women out there. In fact,"—he rubbed his chin—"I was just thinking of how lonely your sister must be. Perhaps I shall have to find another reason to buy a horse from your father. He could use the money, especially if you become a drain on his resources."

No. Not sweet little Lottie. She was no match for him physically. My stomach threatened upheaval; I doubted I could speak without casting up my accounts. I tried to wrench my arm free again, but he held it firm.

"Or there was a lovely vixen at the vicarage. She's what? Twenty-two? Twenty-three? Almost on the shelf. As the sister of a vicar, she is on the precipice of poverty. Surely working an honest wage would be better than dying destitute."

"How many women have you ruined?" I asked, anger replacing the shame I experienced when he threatened me alone.

"Ah, but a gentleman never discloses his conquests."

"You are no gentleman."

He shrugged. "I am gentle sometimes, but I prefer violence. One day, I think you will come to enjoy the sensation of being ravished, just like your sister and Miss Skinner will."

He must have seen how green I looked, for he released me before I could unload the contents of my stomach onto his shiny Hessians.

I rushed back to Lizzie and Mrs. Bell before disassembling into a sobbing mess.

"Oh, you poor dear," Mrs. Bell said.

They ushered me to a bench facing the serpentine, which allowed a modicum of privacy. I sat and looked at my boot points while they stood guard on either side of me.

"Why didn't you tell us Mr. Skinner was engaged?" Lizzie said.

Mrs. Bell rubbed my back consolingly. "It must have been quite a shock to her. No doubt she would rather not talk about it."

I sniffed and dashed away my tears; I could not be seen crying with half of polite Society as witness to my weakness.

"Honestly, Anne, you didn't even want to marry him," Lizzie scoffed and folded her arms. "Now you are blubbering because he has chosen to marry someone else."

I didn't try to correct her false assumptions. Mrs. Bell placed her arm about my shoulders, offering a slight embrace.

Lizzie tapped her foot impatiently. "For heaven's sake, school your emotions."

"I would if I only knew how," I mumbled.

"It's easy."

I scoffed.

"I'll show you." She hooked a finger under my chin and turned my head until I was looking into her eyes. "Repeat after me: 'You are obtuse. I am so much better than you.'"

Mrs. Bell tittered.

"Hush," Lizzie said to her friend. "It really works. Say it in your head, Anne."

You are obtuse. I am so much better than you. A distance, cold and disapproving, enveloped me. "I feel like Mother."

"You look like her."

I shuddered, but I needed that distance right now.

"Say it again," Lizzie counseled. "Repeat it over and over if you have to."

You are obtuse. I am so much better than you. You are obtuse. I am better than you. You are obtuse. I am better. It was more comfortable this time. I sat up straighter, more confident, more distant.

"I use that little parlance whenever I am tempted to laugh at you but I know it would not be proper." Lizzie nudged my leg playfully.

"Oh," I said in a small voice. "I thought you despised me."

She sighed and put her arm around my shoulder. "Of course not. But that distance is the price you pay to school your emotions. With a little distance, you see that others are not worth your tears, nor do they merit your laughter. Try it again until the tears dry themselves."

You are obtuse, Mr. Smith. I am better than you. You are obtuse, Will. I am so much better than you. You are obtuse. It was working. It didn't soothe the turmoil of Smith's threats or fill the aching hole of Will's absence, but it removed me from them somehow.

I stood and took a deep breath, disconnecting myself from everyone around me. We resumed our walk, and I even managed to receive a few introductions without disassembling. The maxim repeated seamlessly in my head while I thought of what I had to do to keep Mr. Smith away from Angel and Charlotte.

What could I do? Could I stop him somehow? Go to the Bow Street runners and tell them that a gentleman . . . what? Set up mistresses? Was that illegal? I didn't think it was. Disreputable, certainly, but not against the law.

I could tell my family, but *if* they believed me, what could they do? What could anyone do?

I might not be able to do *anything* to prevent Mr. Smith from his devilish work, but could I at least prevent him from gaining access to Angel and Charlotte?

Yes. I had to. I had to convince Will to break off his engagement with Miss Smith. If only I had known earlier about Mr. Smith's nefarious occupation and the depth of his depravity, I would never have encouraged that relationship!

But would he listen to me if I tried to talk to him? He hadn't believed me before and was even less likely to speak with me now that I'd cut ties. Cut ties, then set them on fire.

There was only one way now. I would have to force him to honor his previous understanding with me. Then Mr. Smith would not have a connection, marital or otherwise, to the Skinners. And with Will on my side, we could convince my father not to do business with Mr. Smith again. Charlotte, Angel, and I would all be free of the scoundrel.

Marrying Will was the right thing to do; the only way to fix the mistakes I had created.

Lizzie nudged me, and I became aware of my surroundings. I looked past the fine pair of bays to the gentleman in the curricle.

Mr. Paling.

CHAPTER SIXTEEN
Heroism

He cleared his throat. "Woolgathering, Miss Fletcher?"

"As per the norm," I said without chagrin. *You are obtuse. I am so much better than you.* I was determined to not be provoked.

"Have you been taken around the park in a curricle, yet, Miss Fletcher?"

"No."

"Then I daresay you have missed the best of Hyde Park. Come. I shall take you for a turn."

I complied woodenly, the verbiage looping through my mind.

He hopped down lithely and assisted me into the carriage. Once he brought his bays to a walk, he offered me a sideways glance. "Why do you look so much like your sister today?"

My facade cracked as I smirked. "Because I have decided to start schooling my feelings. I was doing pretty well, wasn't I?"

"Entirely too well." He actually shivered. "And did I not just tell you that honesty was one of your most endearing qualities?" He nudged my knee playfully with his, but I was in no mood to have it.

You are obtuse. I am so much better than you. "No. You made some kind of innuendo, I believe, but I do not think you ever mentioned my honesty."

"What's the matter?" he asked brusquely.

Somehow, I doubted that telling him, "*My dearest friend, my sister, and I were threatened in the most vile and reprehensible nature by someone who would soon become a near relative and neighbor,*" would make an appropriate topic of conversation during a leisurely drive in the park.

"What have I said?"

You are obtuse. I am so much better than you. "It's nothing *you* have said." And then I started crying. Drats! Where had that blasted facade run off to? I willed myself to look into Mr. Paling's brown-green-hazel eyes while repeating silently the words *You are obtuse. I am so much better—*

"Who then? Is this about Mr. Skinner? Or his friend Mr. Smith? Isn't that the man you were evading when you asked me to dance at the Hinwick Ball?"

I had no desire to unleash my burdens on him. What would he do with such heavy things but cast them off and me with them? But he surprised me again with his attentiveness.

"Well, isn't he?"

I sighed. "The very same. You helped provide a scapegoat for me that time, but I am afraid you cannot help me now." I would be the sacrificial lamb. I would marry Will to keep Mr. Smith away.

"Did he harm you? I happen to know you are hard to discompose."

But this was not his burden to bear. "He threatened to hurt someone I love if I . . . well . . . I shall have to marry, and you will have to find another lady to torment."

"Now that would be a shame." It felt like he was teasing, but his lips did not even twitch.

We rode in silence for a minute or two before Mr. Paling spoke again. "Have I ever told you about my father?"

"No." He had never spoken of anything of substance; his entire dialogue consisted of innuendo and bluster. But he was not flirting now. He looked as tired as he had on the balcony of the Paling ball. Broken. Real.

"It's not exactly a secret . . ." He sighed and ran his fingers through his already unruly locks. "When I was a lad of fourteen, I was sweet on one of our maids. She shared your temperament, actually, as fiery as she was beautiful. But she was not safe in our home." He had a far-off look that gazed past his horses' ears, Rotten Row, and all of Hyde Park. "After she was found to be with child, she was dismissed to make her own way in the world."

I waited for him to continue, wondering why he would share something like that with me.

He ran his hand over his hair once more. "At forty-six, my father bedded her, a girl less than half his age who should have been under his protection. But as if that weren't bad enough, her sister was also found to be with child, sired by my father, just two years later." His jaw clenched, and he ground his teeth for a moment. "No women were safe in my home. I watched him break my mother's heart and insult our good name with no recourse." The muscles in his jaw twitched, but he said no more.

"Why are you telling me this?" I asked, my voice hardly more than a whisper.

He studied my face.

I had to look away under such scrutiny.

He shrugged. "I don't know. You remind me of her."

I didn't have a response for that.

"She was so fiery, so spirited. But not anymore. I see her in Lowdham sometimes, around the village or at church. Her eyes are dead. Listless." He turned his gaze to me, his expression kind. "It's how you looked when you said you must marry."

I shivered. Marrying Will would be a death of sorts, but it would still be preferable to the certainty of hell that living with Mr. Smith would bring.

He shook away his far-off look, memories of another woman and another time. "Now that I have told you a little about my own shameful father, would you care to share whatever burden has you looking so gloomy today? Perhaps I can help."

"I am honored, but I cannot speak openly . . . It would not be considered seemly." My tongue grew thick even mentioning such things.

He did not press me but considered his words for a long moment. "Have you ever been to the races?"

"Of course not."

"With any other lady, I would not have bothered to ask, but with you . . ." He chuckled. "Anyway, I love going to the races. And it's not about placing a decent wager, although that is nice too. There are some horses that are born racers. They are spirited and feisty and will not allow themselves to be beat. They are not always the most impressive-looking horses. Not the biggest or the fastest, even. But they have that indomitable spirit. That is how you pick a racehorse, Miss Fletcher." He turned and considered me for a moment, making me want to squirm under his scrutiny. "And you are the most spirited filly I have ever seen. When you have fire in your eyes, I think there might not be anything so beautiful in the world." He grinned. "It's why I tease you so mercilessly. I love stoking your flames, so to speak."

He sobered again, a pained look crossing his face. "I'd hate to stand by while the flame turns to ashes." He shook his head and whispered in a haunted voice. "Not again." He cleared his throat and shook his head. "So, tell me please, why are you forced to marry?"

I had not intended to tell him anything, but I answered that question and the next. Soon enough, he knew everything. He listened, nodding thoughtfully here and there, never once blaming or judging me. The look of genuine concern on his face touched me deeply.

"Do you have a plan?" was the last question he asked.

"Yes, like I told you. I plan to marry Mr. Skinner so he will not bring a brother such as that into Rushden."

He scowled. "I meant a plan where you are not submitting yourself to a life of torture, married to the town vicar."

I wrinkled my nose. "Mr. Skinner is a good man."

Mr. Paling scoffed. "You are forgetting that I have met him. He's an arrogant bore and apparently a simpleton as well if he believes Mr. Smith over you."

I wished I could contradict his assessment. "You must admit that marrying Will is the lesser of the evils."

"Barely," he muttered. I swatted him on his arm, but he continued. "I am sure I can come up with a better solution for you. I just need more time. Meet me here again tomorrow?"

"That is not actually a good idea, Mr. My-no-plan-is-better-than-yours." He smirked at my sauciness. "I doubt my reputation can endure the pleasure of your company much longer. As it is, it might already be irreparably tarnished."

"Balderdash and poppycock. Being seen with me should add to your consequence."

I scoffed. "Not after that waltz we shared. Or have you not heard the rumors?"

He raised an eyebrow. "What rumors?"

"That I am your latest trollop."

"What?" he yelled, flicking the reins over-enthusiastically. The horses jolted, though he soothed them quickly. "I would never." He shook his head. "Flirtations are one thing, but I don't take mistresses and certainly not with a barely-out-of-the-schoolroom miss such as yourself." He ran his hand through his hair again, giving his Brutus coiffure an even more disheveled look than usual.

I crossed my arms in front of my chest. "Too immature even to be a mistress," I muttered, somehow offended that I wasn't his type, though I didn't want to be *that* type to anyone.

"That's not what I meant. I have never had—nor do I ever intend to have—a mistress."

A deep sigh wracked me. At least not every man was as despicable as Mr. Smith.

"I simply meant that I make it a rule to only flirt with women who are above reproach. Dash it all, but I've flirted with half the patronesses of Almack's, and no one has ever dared to insinuate such a thing. Trollop," he harrumphed, then pointed a finger at me accusatorially, as if his flirtations were my fault. "If your reputation weren't so fragile, no one would have dared circulate such a rumor."

I shrugged helplessly. If I could effortlessly add consequence to my name, I would have done so already. "Shy of marriage, there is nothing I can do to improve my fragile reputation. Now, if you would kindly return me to my sister—"

"Wait, that's it!" he interrupted. "You are brilliant."

Umm. I don't think anyone had ever said that to me before. "I am?"

He nodded. "Agree to marry me so I can bolster your reputation."

"What?" I stared at him, stunned, then closed my gaping jaw.

He waved a lackadaisical hand as if marriage were as easy as ordering a hackney. "It will be a temporary understanding, of course, just to give us the time we need to figure a way out of this tangle you and Mr. Smith are in. Under the guise of courtship, we can converse without casting aspersion on your character. Then, after we find a way to protect you and your friends from Mr. Smith's debauchery, you can cry off."

I shook my head. "That is the most harebrained plan I have ever heard."

"No, it's perfect. Mr. Smith will not try to harm you while you are under my protection. And we can figure out how to defame Smith while preventing you from a life of drudgery with the vicar. Then, you break it off with me, and you will be the talk of the Town. Your success in the Season will be guaranteed, and I can finally do something other than sit around and helplessly watch a man like that abuse woman after woman. Again." He switched the reins from hand to hand and drummed his foot upon the floor, obviously excited about the idea.

But I wasn't nearly so sure. "I'm already the talk of the Town, thanks to your attention, and I don't think it's doing my reputation any favors."

He glared at me. "I know. That's why I am offering you my name, so you can be gossiped about as my intended rather than my *trollop*." He squeezed that last word through clenched teeth. "Everyone of the *ton* knows I have no intentions to marry, so they will be intrigued to discover the woman who finally managed to ensnare me." He laughed. "The joke will be on them!"

But I knew that if I subjected myself to this arrangement, the joke would be on me. I was already too invested . . . too attracted . . . A false engagement would tear my heart to pieces, I was sure. "I think my reputation would be safer in the vicar's hands, but thank you kindly for your offer."

He scowled, then chuckled. "I finally bring myself to offer for someone, and I'm rejected!"

I shrugged mercilessly. If it were a real offer, of course, that would be one thing. But this was something else entirely; I felt no compunction to soften my rejection.

But he didn't let up. "Your reputation won't matter one jot if you marry the vicar. Trust me. It's better to have an infamous reputation than none at all. And just think: you will have invitations to Almack's and all the best connections. When you cry off, you will have your pick of suitors."

Perhaps. But was that what I really wanted? If Mr. Paling really took me under his wing, I would have the chance to move in a completely different circle, one that even my mother was not capable of penetrating. And I wouldn't even have to marry Will.

I could certainly see the benefits, but what would Mr. Paling gain from this? Alarm spiked through me as I considered what ulterior motives he might have. "Why would you do this? No man should offer up his name so flippantly."

The muscle of his jaw twitched as he clenched and unclenched his teeth. "I hate my father . . . what he did to those girls . . . what he did to my mother . . . He uses his wealth and position to take advantage of those he should protect . . . and I am helpless to stop him. And I swore, with heaven as my witness, that if I was ever in a position to prevent such abuse in the future, I would not stand idly by. I would use my wealth and position to protect rather than exploit."

He sat still and stoic as a statue. Honesty emanated from his oath, such that I could not doubt his sincerity. This was his true self. Not a flirt. Not a dandy. No. He was a knight errant, out to protect the honor of those weaker than he.

And I was his damsel in distress. I wasn't certain I liked that, though. "But when I cry off, it will tarnish your character. You would sustain that aspersion for a woman you hardly know?"

Though sincerity traced his words, I watched his face for any signs of hesitancy. He gave none but laughed throatily, his eyes sparkling like stars. "Yes, my pristine character must not be sullied by the prospect of a union with a respectable lady. Trust me, I shall be fine." He extended his hand to me. "Partners?"

My hand trembled as I placed it in his, but I shook it firmly, relieved to find someone I could confide in, someone who believed me and would throw his weight into the effort of foiling Mr. Smith's devious plans. I was unable to keep the grin off my face. "You have yourself a deal."

He pulled my hand in closer, whispering, "Do not forget to cry off, my love, or I shall do so, and then you *will* be ruined. I've no desire to be hood-winked into marriage."

I gulped at the truth in his warning. "May it be a short and ineffectual engagement." And may my heart emerge unscathed.

"It's a deal."

Our business concluded, he returned me to my sister. I had been with him too long already. "Do you want to tell her the happy news, or should I?" he whispered.

The blood drained from my face at his words. He seemed to understand my predicament, for he addressed Lizzie without preamble. "I have proposed to Miss Fletcher, and she has accepted." He smiled winningly, the words not at all bothering him.

My sister's eyes shifted from me to him and back again, unable to believe the pronouncement, but Mrs. Bell more than made up for her silence with her incessant congratulations.

Lizzie recovered enough to say, "Anne is not of age, and I am not authorized to approve the connection. You shall have to apply to her father if, indeed, you seek a union."

Mrs. Bell protested. "Of course he seeks a union. Can't you see how much in love he is? He is always stealing glances when she is looking the other way. And I have it on good authority from Mrs. Merryweather that his eyes were never anywhere else but on her the whole of last night's ball. He only danced two dances, both with her, while glaring at every other man that had the mis—"

"That is proof enough. Thank you for coming to my rescue." Mr. Paling raced to cut her off, his voice pitched slightly higher than normal.

But Mrs. Bell continued, unperturbed. "But there can be no reason to blush now that the betrothal has been announced."

A beautiful crimson mottled his cheeks. "Ah, yes, there can be no reason to blush now, can there, if I should whisper sweet nothings into her ear." He bent over me, whispering, "I shall count the favors you owe me by the number of embarrassments I am called upon to endure due to this arrangement. This makes number one."

"It is not my fault you danced with me alone or apparently ogled me whenever my mind was elsewhere. Zero."

He scowled but whispered back, "It's not my fault you are so bewitching or that your sister's friend cannot hold her tongue. One."

My heart leapt at his compliment so begrudgingly bestowed.

He spoke to Lizzie. "I shall write to your Father tonight, but I intend to announce the engagement right away. I plan to drive Anne around in my curricle tomorrow and should like the liberty of doing so without setting tongues wagging."

"Could you not wait for a response from my father?"

Why was Lizzie being so difficult? He was trying to help me, not compromise me. "No," he sighed over-dramatically. "I am afraid I have waited all my life to find a woman like Anne, and I do not wish to wait another day."

Would that my heart could keep beating and my lungs would continue to fill. Even though my brain knew that he was acting a part, my heart did not understand the difference.

CHAPTER SEVENTEEN
Favors

It felt like an age since I had gotten a full night's sleep, thanks to my reccurring nightmares. But tonight was different. Tonight, I lay in bed with a thousand what-ifs parading through my mind. Mr. Paling provided the only what-if that did not end in misery. I would have to put my trust in him.

I growled in frustration and threw off my sheets. I hated depending on other people—especially men. Father had abandoned me to Mother's clutches. Will hadn't believed me. And Mr. Smith! Well, he was the entire problem, wasn't he? I was pinning all my hopes on an immature dandy as incapable of sincerity as I was at holding my tongue.

Heaven help us both.

I stormed out of bed and re-lit the candle. I needed to write to Father and warn him of my engagement. I didn't think Mr. Paling actually meant to write to him but was sure Lizzie would. I decided on the briefest of notes:

Father,
Mr. Paling asked for my hand. I told him I would accept his proposal, as long as he meets your approval. I shall leave it to you to discuss the particulars.
Anne

I wanted to write to Charlotte and Angel to warn them of Mr. Smith's actions but could not commit such words to paper; that admission would ruin my reputation if the wrong hands got hold of it. If I had known Mr. Skinner would be merging their families, I would have told Angel in person of Mr. Smith's attempt to have his way with me. But it was too late for that now.

Now, I had to depend on Mr. Paling.

❧❧❧❧

When he came to call the next day, Mr. Paling was dressed in a modest crimson waistcoat with a simply tied cravat. I had never seen him look more handsome. I drank in the warm scent of his orange-blossom cologne, which wafted over me as he handed me into the curricle. As soon as he set the bays to walking, I asked, "Have you come up with a plan?"

"Right to business, eh? Sure you don't want to engage in a little bit of flirtation first?" He waggled his brows at me, but I swatted him away.

"I don't suppose you could find a cause to duel him, one that is not based on defending my honor, that is."

"Oh, you would like that, wouldn't you? He could kill me, he would be forced into exile, and you would be free from the both of us. No, my darling, I would rather be shackled to your shapely ankles than ten feet under or exiled into a country at war." He sat so close I could feel heat pouring off him, unfazed by the chilly November air.

"Don't call me *darling*," I commanded in a tone that reminded me of my governess.

"But, love, my mother has spies all over Town, and if we should drop the charade for an instant, believe me, she will notice." As if to punctuate his remark, he nodded to a passerby who turned and whispered into the ear of her companion.

Perhaps he was distracted by the beautiful woman, for he hit a particularly large divot in the road, and the carriage lurched. Instinctively, I grabbed his leg to steady myself, inadvertently squeezing the knot of muscles in his thigh. Releasing his leg immediately did not lessen my discomfort. I avoided looking at him, afraid to gauge his reaction or allow him to spy the blush on my cheeks.

"Where are you taking me?" I asked, realizing we were not headed to Hyde Park.

"Well after that display, I believe I shall take you on the road with the most potholes."

I should have some quip ready to punish him for the remark, but his proximity sapped both the scathe and the wit from my words.

He stared at me with a mocking little smile on his face, obviously glad at my discomfiture.

"You ought to keep your eyes on the road," I said.

He casually draped his arm on the seat behind me while his eyes roved over my figure. "But I would much rather look at you." At that moment, though, he found another pothole. He removed his arm from behind me and took the reins in both hands. Under his breath, he muttered, "I ought to keep my eyes on the road." His jaw clenched, and a flush crept up his neck.

"Do you bite back your words when you work your jaw like that?"

"No." The muscles of his jaw continued to twitch. Long after I had given up on procuring an answer, he added in a quiet voice, "I bite back emotions."

"You want to hide your emotions too? Lizzie taught me how to do that, by the way."

"No, my love," he said. My heart quickened at the sobriquet, regardless of his insincerity. "We are not at all alike in that regard. You seek to avoid *displaying* emotions. I seek to avoid *feeling* emotions."

"How unromantic of you."

"You would have me weep at the death of a swan and compose sonnets to lament its passing?" His dimples carved gullies into his cheeks.

"No. But I would have you feel grief at the death of a loved one and feel joy at all the beauties of the earth."

He waved me off. "I have had grief enough in my twenty-five years, and as to all the beauties of the earth . . ." He turned his appreciative gaze to my eyes and then my lips. "I believe myself capable of enjoying them all without the interference of emotions that I might find irksome."

"Hedonist."

He shrugged unapologetically.

I cleared my throat. "Well, now that you have satisfied your flirtatious quota, let's talk of more serious matters. The sooner we puzzle out how to deal with Mr. Smith, the sooner you can return to your carefree existence of enjoying every beauty but caring for none."

His lower lip protruded into a frown as he grew serious. "Right. Firstly, we need to gather more information. What are his habits? Does he gamble? Where does his money come from and where does it go? Has he sired any children? Does he use extortion?"

I coughed, lacking the composure to speak openly of such things.

"I do not mean to offend your sensibilities," he apologized, "but we really ought to discover the size of this threat first. I have already asked my man of business and my valet to search around for all the gossip they can get about the Smiths. And then I can speak to his solicitor and man of business if need be. That should give us something more to go off of." He took my gloved hand in his. "And then we will make a plan."

"Thank you, Mr. Paling." I wanted to say more, but the words would not come while he held my hand in his. I felt safe. Protected. Loved?

"You probably ought to call me Thomas. Would you prefer if I call you Anne, or have you another moniker you prefer?" He looked into my eyes. "Though I could think of a few other titles for the only woman to have ever wheedled a marriage proposal out of me."

I threw his hand away. "I did no such thing. This was your mad idea."

He laughed. "But among your sisters, do you go by Anne, Nan, or Nancy? Or have I missed the mark entirely?"

He had. But he would never hear about how John had once called me Andrew and the name had stuck. "Anne suits me fine."

He instantly contradicted me. "No. I think Anne is too common a name for you, my love. You are really more a Diana or a Helen."

I scoffed.

"What, you don't think your face could launch a thousand ships?"

I rolled my eyes at his flattery. "If I could pick one woman in history to emulate, Helen of Troy would be far, far down on the list. I would rather not start a war that led to the deaths of thousands."

"No? Well, it's good to know you have a decent understanding of Greek mythology at any rate. But you cannot bemoan starting a war, for that is what we have begun. But step one, heart of my heart: espionage."

Heart of his heart? Oh, but I wished my heart could keep up with his shifting levels of caprice. "What do you need from me? What can I do?" I did not want to become a helpless maid in this war.

His grin spread from ear to ear, his dimples gathering in deep creases as he responded. "For starters, you can charm my family." He pulled the lines, and I realized we had come upon Barkley Square, in front of the Paling townhouse. "They are dying to meet you."

I was aghast. "Why on earth would you bring me here? I'm not dressed appropriately for a visit."

He smirked, surveying my attire. "If you looked any more suitable, they would probably procure a special license and have us wedded within the week, and then we would both be doomed."

I crossed my arms in front of me. "I have no desire to meet any more of your relations. We had ample time to discuss our plans, and you can now return me home."

He rubbed his neck, the expression looking sheepish. "Consider it that favor you owe me?"

When he looked at me with that boyish grin, my lips could not form the word *no*. "Fine," I said peevishly. "You abominable man."

Mr. Paling—no, Thomas—helped me alight from the curricle and adjusted my shawl around my shoulders. Standing behind me, he leaned forward, whispering into my ear, "I really am quite abominable." Though his words chilled me, in the next moment, his lips brushed my neck, and I was all at once on fire, from ice to fire with only his lips as kindling.

I whipped around, ready to lash at him for stealing a kiss, but his look stilled me. His mask of insincerity was gone, and his eyes were like deep pools, filled with some sort of pain and regret. Loss, maybe. I knew, looking into those eyes, that he had not meant to brush his lips against my neck. This was his other self, the one that neither flirted nor simpered, but carried unimaginable depths. I had no way to navigate the murky intensity of his eyes, no guide marks or signposts. There was darkness there and trouble, and I wondered what he could have done to think of himself as truly abominable.

I reached out tentatively, placing a hand on his cheek. "You may be abominable, but you are no villain. Thank you for helping me."

His brows rose, questioning how I could judge such a thing. But I knew. I knew in that unknowable place in my soul, where things feel right, that he was a good person. And so I patted him on the cheek and pulled on his arm, placing mine in his so that I could meet whomever it was he cared to introduce me to.

He shook his head, as if chasing off the cobwebs that had gathered in his mind, and escorted me up the steps and through the front door. I had been too distracted during the ball to get a good look at the surroundings, but I could see now that the Paling townhouse left nothing to be desired; it was as grand as it was tastefully decorated. From the butler to the flower arrangements, the home exuded both taste and propriety.

Thomas led me up the stairs to a large withdrawing room, which, I could tell at a glance, was packed full of people. I stalled him before we could cross the threshold, whispering, "Why does your mother claim such a hoard of visitors?"

His whispered response brushed heat down my neck. "Once they heard of my engagement, my whole family came to meet you."

I gasped. "I thought you wanted me to meet *someone*, not *everyone*."

"It's the way my family does things."

People started to notice us standing on the threshold. My palms began to sweat thinking of having to lie to an entire throng of people. "But what shall we say once we call off the charade? Have you no concern for your family's feelings if not for mine?"

He grinned so wickedly, so mischievously, that I felt all my previous misadventures must have only relegated me to a lower level of sainthood compared to him. He leaned forward until our noses almost touched, whispering, "Not in the slightest, my little angel," and sealed that indecorous admission with a kiss on my lips that could be no mistake.

I pulled away from him and looked to the guests, noting with shame how many had stood witness to my first kiss. Unadulterated anger surged in. He would receive no more compassion from me.

I slapped him soundly across the cheek.

The echo reverberated through the room, and I watched what felt like a multitude of heads swivel at the sound, accompanied by gasps. I fled back down the stairs with the flabbergasted visage of Mr. Paling filling my mind.

CHAPTER EIGHTEEN
Insult

"ANNE, WAIT," MR. PALING CALLED. He rushed down the stairs after me, but I refused to comply. He caught up to me before the butler could offer my coat and hat. "Come," he said, placing a hand on my arm.

I shrugged him off. "Don't touch me. I am not going back there."

"And?" he asked, a hand on his hip. "You are going to run home unaccompanied? I think not."

I had not actually considered where I would go, but I did not want to be with him. "I wish I had a horse," I mumbled. I always felt better after a bruising ride.

"You could ride one of my bays, but you're hardly dressed for such." He scratched his chin. "Not that that ever bothered you before."

I glared at him.

"And while I personally would love to see you ride down the crowded London streets astride my bay without a habit—or a saddle, come to think of it—I would advise against it. Especially since I entered this agreement with the sole purpose of protecting your reputation."

Confound it, but he was infuriating. "Are you incapable of taking anything seriously? This is not a game to me, Mr. Paling, not while the reputation and safety of myself and those I love is on the line."

He sobered. "Of course. Forgive me for trying to diffuse my embarrassment with humor. A nasty habit of mine. But I assure you I am capable of serious thought, on occasion." He held out his arm. "Come, I know a place where you can chastise me without all of my family catching wind of what is at stake for you."

I reluctantly accepted his escort. He led me out a back door and down a few steps to a secluded little garden, both desolate and ugly now that the first frost had fallen. "You should not have kissed me in front of your family," I said. Or at all.

"You should not have slapped me in front of my family."

I crossed my arms in front of me. "Why not? They stood witness to my first kiss. Why not witness my temper as well?"

He moaned loudly. "You mean to tell me that was your first one?"

"Of course it was."

He rubbed his hand behind his neck, responding meekly, "I'm sorry."

I scoffed.

"Truly. It's surprisingly easy to forget how inexperienced you are, Anne. You do not blush, dissemble, or reprove when being flattered."

I glared at him.

"Like that, for instance. You carry yourself as a woman rather than a girl, and as a strong, powerful woman at that."

"And that gives you the right to kiss me?"

He chuckled and took a step toward me. "A woman who knows her own mind and will not fail to humble those above her station when they are being unreasonable. You are a force to be reckoned with and . . ." He paused. "I mean no offense when I say I forgot that you were, in that regard, wholly inexperienced. I thought a kiss would be appropriate given both our engagement and the fact that my family would never believe me capable of restraint when faced with beauty such as yours."

I huffed. "And yet somehow you have managed to refrain these past weeks. Your fortitude must be extraordinary."

Though my voice had dripped with irony, his soft response held no trace of it when he answered. "You have no idea." He gazed at my mouth, stepping closer to me.

My heart rate soared. "I am a debutante, not a fool."

My warning stilled his approach. He turned away from me and sat on a cold-looking stone bench next to a bare-limbed plane tree. "I'm the fool," he said.

"And abominable."

He smiled ruefully. "Yes. Of course, I warned you how abominable I am, but you did not believe me."

I huffed. "I thought you were talking of past indiscretions, not future ones."

He chuckled. "Those too." He was looking away from me when he asked, "What would you like to do now?"

"Well, I begin to grow cold. I would like you to take me home."

He approached me, smirking. "Finally Hestia, the goddess of fire, begins to cool." Though his great coat had already been delivered to the butler, he took off his tailcoat and draped it about my shoulders.

I did not hesitate to slip my arms in its sleeves, reveling in its heat and the feeling of being dwarfed. My traitorous eyes could not help but notice how broad his shoulders looked when only covered by shirtsleeves while my double-crossing nose inhaled the citrusy scent of his cologne. But I did not want to find such pleasure in this man's company, nor in his coat.

He continued. "I meant, would you like to continue to pretend that we have an understanding?"

I snorted at the irony of that term. "I do not think I will ever understand you."

He smiled, and my heart rate sped. "Nor I you. But if you should like to call off, this obvious quarrel would be an appropriate time." He returned to the bench, his back to me.

If we called off now, he would not be able to help me. I would have to throw myself at Will and plead for him to marry me instead. But we had at least a few weeks before Mr. Skinner would marry. Perhaps I could continue this torturous farce with Thomas and only throw myself at Will if our plans failed. I sighed. "Would you hate me forever if I did not yet call it off?"

He turned abruptly to study me, but his voice and visage belied nothing. "I could never hate you, Anne."

"Hah." I looked back to the house. "I bet your family does. I wonder what they must think of me."

He shrugged. "They know a lover's spat when they see one." He stood and began walking toward me.

"A lover's spat indeed. Rubbish. They cannot all be such fools."

His honest grin resurfaced. "But if you took the time to know them, my siren, you would know they are. They are expecting us to quarrel and for me to be able to placate you with a kiss." He shook his head as he huffed.

"It was your kiss that got us in this mess in the first place."

He stood an arm's length away, took my hand in his, and looked into my eyes. His dark eyes looked placid. Peaceful. "You deserve better, Anne. I will help you with Mr. Smith, but you need to promise that you will fly far away from me and my painfully foolish family."

His thumb ran slow circles over mine, and though, to him, it was a harmless gesture that indicated he was simply in thought, the sensation sent tingles up my arm.

He shook his head. "You are such a passionate creature. Your first kiss should have been ardent." He looked away, "And not by a man who is using you as a ruse to placate his family's intense pestering that he settle down."

Was that why he had introduced me?

"By a man who sees your strength and not just your beauty, who adores your futile attempts to rein in your passions."

I stepped toward him, my heart pounding. No one had ever adored me for my passion before. It was my failing, not my virtue.

I stepped closer. He still avoided looking at me, though he surely knew that I was now standing inches away from him. I placed my gloved hand on his cold cheek and forced his head to turn to me. I thought, perhaps, he would look at me with the same passion I felt, with that same unmistakable urge to kiss him soundly for accepting and loving who I am rather than trying to mold me and break me into who he needed me to be.

But as I looked into his eyes, they did not mirror my passion. They were full of tears, waiting to burst forth but kept ever so carefully in check. The look was utterly heartrending.

I drew him into me, sliding my arms underneath his and tucking my head into his chest. At first, he responded only with stillness. But I continued to squeeze myself into him. Even if he did not need the comfort, I did, for the look he gave me broke my heart.

Slowly, he returned the embrace.

"It's all right to cry," I whispered. "I won't tell anyone."

He chuckled and rested his cheek on the top of my head. "I am not going to cry, but thank you." We stood there for what felt like an eternity before he pulled away from me.

I wanted to ask him what he was thinking of when he offered that haunted look, but I didn't dare. "Thomas Paling, you are going to be all right. Do you hear me?"

His smirk returned, displaying his delectable dimples. "Yes, Mother."

I did not rise to the bait but nodded my head once in a stern fashion, then shrugged out of his tailcoat and helped him into it, shivering at the intimacy and laughing at myself for my foolishness.

"What?" he asked.

"Nothing," I responded quietly.

"Please, Anne. I like knowing the thoughts that humor you. And I could use a little bit of humor right now."

It was my turn to shrug and tug at my glove self-consciously. "I was thinking of the irony that I could embrace an eligible bachelor without so much as a blush, but helping that same gentleman into his coat felt—." Intimate. But I couldn't actually voice the word. I cleared my throat. "Unnerving. Be glad I am not your valet."

He smirked at me. "I would rather have you—"

"I would burn your waistcoats," I said before he could finish.

He smiled. Not a wolfish grin. Not a lopsided smirk. But an even smile, showing straight teeth and two equally creased dimples. If the smile had not stilled my breath, the words would have. "You are devastatingly adorable."

But there was no passion in his eyes. It was the way a man might love a puppy. And so I forced myself to breathe deeply as he said, "But I have ruined your coiffure." He reached forward and touched the back of my neck, lacing his fingers through the hair which had escaped its bonds. "It's so soft."

"Yes," was my only response. He might be able to pet me with all the disinterestedness of stroking a cat, but every fiber of my being was set on fire at his careless caress.

I stepped away from him and crossed to sit on the stone bench that was as cold as his heart. I stripped my gloves and set them to the side. He crossed to where I was, though still standing, and picked up the white gloves, presumably so that they would not get dirty.

I felt through my hair, which I had pinned loosely this morning, thinking I should keep my bonnet on the whole time. The coiffure was never meant to be seen. I sighed, then went on a search-and-rescue mission for the errant pins.

Thomas stepped closer so I could start depositing pins in his outstretched hand. I worked quickly, scouring my scalp for the prodigals and shaking my hair out of its twists. Finding the last pin, I put it in my mouth, separating it with my teeth.

"Your hair isn't naturally curly, is it?" he asked.

I was trying to ignore his presence at the moment, so I responded curtly, mumbling around the hairpin in my mouth. "No, it is very straight." I grabbed the whole of my hair with both hands and began twisting it into a simple chignon.

"Wait," he said urgently. Had someone spied us here alone? I looked over my shoulder anxiously, afraid of who might be approaching. I saw no one, so I began to rise and tilt my head to look at him when his mouth crashed down upon mine.

The hairpin that had been in my mouth fell to the ground as every passion in my being rose up with that kiss. His hands found my loose hair, and he ran his fingers through it, moaning softly against my mouth. The sound was more than enough to unhinge me, to set me aflame down to my toes, and I drew myself deeper into him, standing fully so I could press myself into the embrace. I couldn't possibly be close enough to him. The feeling was insatiable.

I had no idea what I was doing or how kisses were meant to be. But his hands dropped from my hair to just below my waist, to the front of my hips, and he began pushing me away.

No. Why was he pushing me away now? I wouldn't have it. I needed to be closer to him, so I grabbed his hands and guided them around the back of me, drawing him into me as I advanced slowly toward him.

"Stop," he said, his voice a husky whisper.

I stilled my mouth and backed away enough to look into his eyes. They reflected the gray clouds enveloping us.

"I can't—Anne. I can't—"

He didn't want me. He didn't need me like I needed him. I was only an amusement to him. A distraction from the pains and sorrows of his life. And it was going to break my heart, for as much as I had tried to bridle it, I knew I had lost my heart to him already.

Everyone, myself included, had warned me against Mr. Paling, but my heart had not listened. I was every bit as foolish and naive as my sister had always thought me.

CHAPTER NINETEEN
Prometheus

I DETERMINED TO TELL LIZZIE about the false engagement and the threat of Mr. Smith. If anyone could help steer me through these unnavigable waters safely, it would be her. And any plans she made would surely be better executed than Mr. Paling's harebrained schemes.

But as Lizzie and I sat silently trimming bonnets and awaiting visitors, my mouth grew dry and refused to release the words.

"Stop bouncing your knee," she said in the same detached voice Mother usually employed.

I ground my teeth, but the annoyance loosened my tongue. "You know Mr. Smith?"

"The devilishly handsome gentleman you walked with at Hyde Park the other day?"

My stomach sank as I thought of his broad shoulders that he had used to pin me to the door. "Yes, the devil himself. He . . ." I hated being forced to relive this moment. "You know how Father invited him to hunt after he bought that colt?"

Lizzie nodded vaguely.

"Well, while he was staying with us, he found me alone in the corridor one evening and tried to steal a kiss." This telling felt easier than the last had, even though my throat still tried to prevent the words from escaping. I cleared my throat and opened my mouth to try again, but Lizzie interrupted me.

"Anne, I do not care to hear about all your amorous conquests. In fact, I don't understand why any man of consequence and intelligence could saddle himself with a ridiculous girl, incapable of a modicum of propriety, who is always getting herself into trouble. And how you have secured two proposals in the same number of weeks may continue to puzzle me till my dying day."

I blinked at her words, as if I could bat them away with my lashes. I had been wrong to try to confide in Lizzie. I thought I was coming to understand her—and like her as well—but perhaps we were not quite ready for that. Or maybe this was her jealous nature lashing out yet again.

I tried to gain control over the feelings of betrayal and anger I felt by saying silently, *You are obtuse. I am so much better than you.* But it was her voice that sounded in my head, reinforcing her own superiority.

Though the saying did not work with my sister this time, it proved effective against Thomas when he called. With every one of his dimpled smiles, I forced myself to repeat the mantra. His smiles soon changed to pouts, and I remembered how soft and urgent his lips had been. But I pushed the thought aside and repeated the maxim until he took his leave.

My sister considered me. "Perhaps Mr. Paling will be a good match for you after all. I have never seen you act so proper before."

In my head, I applied the saying to Lizzie before I could respond with a simple nod to her backhanded compliment.

The following day, Thomas spared me the necessity of another such visit by sending a missive and flowers instead.

Anne,

Firstly, I'm sorry. I wanted to say that yesterday but didn't dare—not with your sister watching with all the sympathy of a gargoyle atop Notre Dame. I am sorry for violating your trust like I did. It was folly. Sheer folly. I promise to behave myself in the future.

Secondly, speaking with you yesterday was utterly heart rending. As a friend, I long to repay you with some advice: Do not change who you are because of me. You are a rushing waterfall so loud it deafens all else. Your beauty is in your raw power. Stop trying to tame yourself into a tinkling fountain. Fountains are beautiful, but to see you stoop so low—there is no beauty in that. Please do not retreat into a shell of etiquette and propriety and become a boring husk of the woman you once were. You absolutely take my breath away with your passion. Don't school it.

Thirdly, I need to speak with you about the results of my espionage. I had intended to call upon you today but was afraid your sister would not allow the chance for private conversation. To that end, I have decided to take my sister Mary into my confidence. She has proven trustworthy in times past, and I know she shall keep all your secrets as readily as my own. I shall call on you tomorrow, and with Mary as chaperone, we shall all three go on a walk and discuss our options. I can ensure your safety.

Thomas

Safety my foot. Spending time with him was as safe as playing with lions. He would rend my heart asunder again and again if I let him.

The image of my favorite stuffed rabbit, which I had adored into oblivion, came to mind. It would lose its tail, the beans spilling out while I shrieked and cried. Nurse would fix it, and I would love it again until I loved it with too much vigor and a seam would rip.

I was Prometheus but with my heart, rather than my liver, eaten out daily.

I fortified my heart as well as I could, pouring layers of protection over it. I didn't care how flattering his words were. Telling me to never change and to not stamp out the passion in my eyes was the most foolish advice I had ever received. It would be like telling me to walk into battle naked. I would not allow myself to interact with Thomas without a shield of superiority and a sword of hatred, with maybe a buckler of disgust thrown on as well. I would remind myself that for all his chivalry and pretty words, I was only an amusement to him.

On Monday, Thomas brought Mary with him, as promised. Though Mr. Paling featured brown hair and dark, inscrutable eyes, Mary's golden hair fell in perfect ringlets down her back with cornflower-blue eyes peering at me from under her bonnet.

"Shall we?" he asked, extending a hand to me. "I thought we might walk to the miliners."

I accepted one arm while he gave his sister the other. "How has your spy network fared?" I began without preamble. The sooner we stopped Mr. Smith, the sooner I could escape my Promethean chains.

"A pint of ale was all it took to set tongues wagging. Several servants under Smith's employ have been dismissed once they were found to be with child."

I put a hand to my stomach, but it did not settle my unease. "And Mr. Smith is the father?" I asked.

He nodded. "He did not pay for their silence so they had no compunction about identifying Smith once they were sent to the streets."

"That's tragic."

Mary sniffled.

"Yes." Thomas handed his sister a handkerchief. "A tragedy which occurs all too often, I'm afraid."

"Is there anything we can do . . ." I chewed on the inside of my cheeks. "Can we defame him or bring some sort of action against him?"

Mary spoke for the first time. "A solicitor could press a suit to demand that Mr. Smith pay for his children's upkeep, but the chances of finding one who is willing to prosecute are slim to none."

I was surprised by her authoritative tone; I had hastily relegated her as nothing more than a shy violet. Perhaps I should reconsider.

Mary spoke again, and I was annoyed that I couldn't see her, with Thomas betwixt us. "Unless you happen to know a solicitor personally, a family friend or distant relative?"

"Can't say that I do." Under my breath, I muttered, "Should have formed an attachment to a solicitor."

Thomas smirked. "Don't let me stop you."

I huffed. "Did your spy network find anything else?"

He shook his head. "There were no other hints of anything . . . nefarious. Well, nothing illegal at any rate."

"So there is nothing we can do." The sky darkened, and I wondered if it was my own dejection or if the clouds, which had begun to gather, had finally overtaken the sun.

Mary spoke again. "Unfortunately, a man of means may do whatever he likes without incurring Society's wrath, let alone drawing the law upon him."

"But I . . . I can't just sit around and do nothing while he threatens such—"

"Yes, of course." She graciously stopped my line of thinking. "I didn't mean we should do nothing. I simply said that a man of *means* remains above the law. We must take away his means. Ruin him financially."

I liked the sound of that. "How? Gambling?"

Thomas cleared his throat. "Maybe. But there are no rumors of him visiting gaming hells."

"The races?" I asked. I was fairly certain he intended to race the thoroughbred he had bought from Father.

Thomas shook his head. "Wrong time of the year for horses. And from what I have been able to gather so far, Mr. Smith is a bit of a miser, hardly ever laying a hefty wager, even when he does bet."

When he was a houseguest, we had sat down for an occasional rubber of whist, but even then, he never played for more than pennies. "Too bad he doesn't take to the tables. You could just rob him blind and send him packing."

Mary's laughter sounded oddly like her brother's. "You have obviously never sat down with Thomas for a game of cards. Mr. Smith is not the one who would leave the table impoverished." Somehow that surprised me. Thomas was a man of the Town, well versed in the arts of city life and surely capable of holding his own at the card table. I glanced at Thomas, who was looking peevishly at his sister, but he did not offer up a defense. He must be truly horrid at cards. Odd that, since he read people so well.

Our conversation stalled as we approached the milliner's. Thomas promised to buy Mary whatever she wished, then forced me to try on hat after bonnet, flirting with me all the while. "The wide brim of this hat complements the fullness of your mouth." Or, "No, this bonnet positively hides the fire in your eyes. We would not want to fool anyone into believing you demure."

I suffered his attention with all the patience I could muster. Finally, he settled on a bonnet that he deemed capable of adding to—rather than detracting from—my beauty, and we were able to leave the store.

As we resumed our walk, I linked arms with Mary so Thomas would not obstruct our conversation with his broad shoulders. "So how do we sink a non-gambler's fortunes?" I asked.

"We're not sure yet," Mary responded. "We still need more information. Thomas will have to talk to Mr. Smith's solicitor and his man of business to see what details he can glean."

Thomas walked next to me on the left. "They won't talk to me about another man's confidential business."

Mary didn't offer him a glance. "You are resourceful. Think of something."

He rubbed his chin. "I could pretend to want to do business with Mr. Smith." He scowled. "But I'm not certain his . . . line of business . . ." He cleared his throat. "Is conducive to business contractions."

My stomach squirmed as if I had eaten live worms.

Mary waved a hand nonchalantly. "Yes, fine, Thomas. Do that. Now, Anne, you need to discover what our timeline is."

"Pardon?"

"When's the wedding?"

I cleared my throat. "Well . . . he proposed at your coming out ball, so, if he marries by banns, we have at least three weeks."

"He won't marry by banns," Thomas interjected. "Not when it is only ten shillings for a common license."

Mary nodded. "It did not appear in the *Gazette*, so it may be that they do not plan on marrying immediately." She scrunched her nose in thought. "But even if we have months, it will take quite a bit of time to turn a man's investments sour."

I hadn't thought of that yet. "How long do you think?"

She shrugged and looked at Thomas. "Not my area of expertise."

Thomas grimaced. "It really depends. Fortunes can sink as quickly as a marooned ship in some investments and bleed out slowly in others. But months would be better than weeks, at any rate."

"If we can't ruin Mr. Smith's finances before the wedding, then stopping the union entirely would be the next best thing," I said. "I don't want Angel to have to live with that man as her brother-in-law." I shuddered.

Mary put a hand to her chest as if my statement wounded her. "That would protect your friend, certainly. But if Mr. Smith is abusing girls, he should be stopped, whether or not he marries into your circle of influence," Mary said, a certain amount of vehemence in her voice.

I hurried to reassure her. "Yes, of course. I only mean to mitigate damage in the meanwhile."

A crease formed in between Mr. Paling's brows. "So here is the plan: I shall attempt to speak with Mr. Smith's solicitor and his man of business. Anne, you must write to Miss Skinner and needle any information you can, but most importantly, discover when they intend to marry. And . . ." He looked at me, then shook his head.

"And?" I prompted.

"And I think I shall call on Mr. Skinner myself. You know, gather information about the wedding and a few incriminating stories about you as well."

"You shall do no such thing." There was so much history between Will and me, both beautiful and grisly, that my cheeks flamed at the thought of the stories Will might choose to share.

Thomas leaned in and spoke softly. "That's quite a blush for a woman who had never been kissed until only recently. Why can I not make you blush like that?"

"Why bother blushing when everything you say is a lie?" I whispered.

"I don't lie," he said belligerently.

Mary raised her eyebrows at our whispered conversation but did not interject.

"Oh? Then what do you choose to call your flagrant flattery? You certainly don't mean those things in earnest."

He pursed his lips in thought. My comments turned his mood from sanguine to taciturn, but I willed myself to have no compassion.

"Don't call on Will," I hissed.

"Fine," he snapped back. "I'll not call on *Mr. Skinner*."

The clouds, which had slowly shrouded the sun, lowered, threatening rain, and the three of us quickened our pace.

Mary muttered, "I wish I had brought an umbrella rather than this useless parasol."

Thunder struck in the distance, and the wind picked up, licking my skirts and attempting to steal my bonnet. With one hand lifting my hem and the other atop my head, we sprinted to my sister's townhouse as thick drops began to fall. We ran inside, surprised at how wet we became in such little time. Thomas ordered that his carriage be brought around.

"Did you come in the curricle?" I asked.

"Yes, of course."

"Not a practical equipage for the rain," I said.

"Since when has Thomas ever been accused of being practical?" Mary responded.

Thomas caught my eye before we both doubled over laughing.

"What?" Mary asked, looking between Thomas and me. "What have I said?"

Thomas placated her concerns. "You said nothing wrong, Mary. No one in their right mind would ever accuse me of such a thing." But the wink he gave me was equal parts mirth and affection.

I couldn't ignore the heat I felt, huddled in that cold corridor, soaked to my core. "Here, take an umbrella." I handed one to him, surprised at the lightning that arched between our hands as he grabbed it.

From the look we shared, I had to believe that he had felt it too.

But then he was off.

I shivered in the cold, wondering if I would feel this way every time he left me.

CHAPTER TWENTY
Miss Loveland

I DREAMT I ATTENDED A ball in a gorgeous cream gown with a silver lace overlay. As I spun around, the threads sparkled in the candlelight like a crystal chandelier.

Will claimed my hand, and I apologized profusely for everything I had ever said to him. He forgave me, and we returned to our friendly banter. I wanted nothing more.

Then Mr. Smith came and asked for the next dance. I spun away from him, but the silver overlay of my dress became a spider's web that held me fast. What I had thought were rosettes were nothing more than the carcasses of insects who had already been consumed. I wrestled out of the web, leaving me in nothing more than a torn shift.

I looked around for help, but the room was empty; we waltzed alone. Holding both my hands in his, he spun me out so that I faced the same direction as he. Then he pulled me into him. His arms, still entangled with mine, held me fast, molding me to him. As we swayed together to the eerily lilting music, he whispered in my ear, "I love the ones who fight."

I felt sick. Deeply ill. But instincts crept in, and I stomped hard on his toes. When his arms instinctively loosened, I turned around, kneeing him hard. He groaned in pain, but when I looked at him, it was Thomas I had hurt, Thomas who slowly slid to the ground. I wanted to reach for him, to tell him I had never meant to hurt him, that I loved him. But I was awake before I could.

My hair was limp with sweat, my breathing shallow. I remembered the way Mr. Smith trapped me, claiming he liked a struggle. The more I strained, the more pleasure I brought him.

My body shivered, and I began trembling. I sat up, pulling my knees under my chin, rocking back and forth. After such nightmares, sleep usually eluded me for the rest of the evening. But I had to return to that dreamscape; I needed to see if Thomas was still lying where I had left him. I imagined how I would bend over him, apologizing profusely. I would try to help him up but would trip on the hem of my dress, falling over both of us. Then, crumpled on the floor next to him, he would pull me into his arms, and I would finally feel safe.

When the dreamscape returned, however, Thomas was nowhere to be found. Instead, I was surrounded by the Palings, all of whom looked at me accusatorially. Mrs. Slater displayed enough disdain to make me feel like a rodent. But when I looked at Mary's impossibly blue eyes filled with tears, I knew I had done something reprehensible. I had broken Thomas's heart, and I hadn't even known it had been mine to break.

I lay in my bed and watched the rain drizzle down the window panes in synchronicity with my tears.

Someday, I would have pleasant dreams again.

Atkins brought in the mail, but there were no letters from home. Instead, invitations piled in; I was more sought after as Mr. Paling's fiancée than I ever was as a debutante.

I knew I should accept all the invitations, using this opportunity to further my acquaintance and gain entrance into a realm of Society that had always been closed to me, but I couldn't muster the courage. I would be expected to attend with Thomas, who would eat away at my heart all the while. I already died a little every time he flashed his debonair smile or called me his darling.

Once this arrangement was over, I hoped to salvage enough of my heart to sustain life. I tossed all the invitations onto the bedside table and snuggled under the comforter, seeking the warmth that eluded me.

"Come, miss, or you'll be late for breakfast," Atkins said.

I sighed but dragged myself to my feet.

"The rain will let up eventually. It always does."

It had rained steadily since yesterday's walk, but I didn't bother telling her that the rain was the least of my worries as she dressed me and plaited my hair.

The day continued, every bit as drab and dreary as the morning had, until Thomas was announced. He would surely bring some warmth and cheer into this dreadful day. But when he entered the parlor, I hardly recognized him. His bearing was different. His lackadaisical air had all but vanished. He seemed as cold as the rain which beat upon the windowpanes.

He handed me a letter, saying aloud, "My sister asked me to send you this invitation."

I took the letter graciously and then sat next to him.

"Read it," he whispered.

My sister narrowed her eyes at the way he bent toward me, obviously assuming he said something impertinent, but I ignored her and opened the missive.

I need you to call on someone. I'll explain in the curricle.
For now, please tell your sister that I shall escort you to my mother's house for tea. And bring a calling card.

Espionage? Excitement thrummed through my veins. I gave Lizzie a bright smile. "Thomas has come to fetch me for tea with his mother." I turned to Thomas, "Let me just fetch my coat."

Lizzie sighed. "If you have to take Anne out in this weather, do make sure she stays dry."

Thomas nodded seriously. "Of course."

Lizzie narrowed her eyes again and somehow filled the look with such censure and suspicion, I wondered if she thought we were trying to run to Gretna Green.

I knew Lizzie didn't quite approve of Thomas. Lands! *I* didn't quite approve of Thomas, but I knew he would never do anything so nefarious. "I'll be back before you know it, Lizzie," though the statement worried me some. I didn't even know where we were going.

I grabbed a calling card, put it in my reticule, and put on my pelisse; we were out the door in a trice. Thomas held an umbrella over my head with all the propriety of a butler as he escorted me to his curricle, the top up to protect us from the storm.

"Where are we going?" I asked excitedly, but before he could answer, I added, "And are you sure we should go out in this weather?"

"Around you, I am not sure about anything." I had expected a smile, a wink, some indication of his teasing remarks, but his face belied not a hint of humor. "But as we are already out in the rain, I suggest we go through with it. Who knows when the weather may let up? Plus, Miss Loveland is more likely to be found at home on a day such as this." He urged his bays forward.

"Miss Loveland? Will's cousin?"

"If by that, you mean Mr. Skinner's cousin, then yes," he said, a tinge of annoyance piercing his tone.

"And she is back from Rushden?" Angel had described Miss Loveland's visit in her last letter.

He shrugged. "I was not aware that she had been in Rushden at all."

"Yes, after she completed her stay at Hinwick, she visited the Skinners for a week, so she should have the latest *on dit* about Will's wedding."

Thomas shook his head and offered an enigmatic smile. "Your mission is much more than gossip."

Ooh. "Do go on." Finally, I was given something more to do than sit at home and write letters to which no one responded. Was Angel mad at me? Or had Will forbidden her from writing?

"Mr. Loveland is a solicitor."

I waited for more, but we turned a corner and a cold wind whipped me in the face, dousing me with rain. Thomas grabbed a woolen blanket out of a box at his feet and handed it to me. I draped it about me to shield me from the moisture.

"Come away from the side. You will stay drier in the middle."

I was leery to be so close to him though; I remained where I was.

"Obstinate girl," he muttered. He reached over, wrapped an arm around my waist, and dragged me into his side.

It was decidedly warmer next to him.

"You have nothing but a thin pelisse to protect you from the elements. Not even a muff. I'm trying to prevent you from catching cold, not violate you."

He distanced himself to the edge of the seat, as far from me as possible, where the hood did little good protecting him. The rain poured off the bill of his hat onto one of his many capes.

"But you will be soaked," I protested.

He shrugged. "No worse than the drivers who handle this day in and day out. I am dressed for it. You are not."

I chewed my lip, sorry for all the trouble I was causing him. Almost as sorry as I was for the distance between us, even if that distance was exactly what I had wanted. I shivered, missing his heat, but returned to the topic at hand. "So Mr. Loveland is a solicitor?"

He nodded.

"And? I can't fathom what you want me to accomplish by speaking with his daughter."

"I expected a little more ingenuity from an ingenue," he said drily.

I knew he was teasing me, but his remarks hit a little too close to home. I didn't want to be so helpless.

"We need to find a sympathetic solicitor, and who better than Mr. Skinner's cousin?"

"Their familial connection is not so near as all that." I tried to remember Mrs. Skinner's introduction at the Hinwick ball, but I had been too busy trying to tune out her shrill tone to bother paying attention. "I think they are second or third cousins. They didn't even know they were related until three weeks ago."

Thomas deflated, his shoulders slumping. "We need to try something, since my visit to Smith's solicitor went so poorly." He grimaced.

"What happened?"

Thomas wiped away a drop of rain that had dodged his hat to land on his cheek. "He began friendly enough at first when he thought I might become a future client. But he clamped up completely when I mentioned that I was seeking to draft a marriage settlement like Mr. Smith's. Practically threatened to turn me out. If I tried to snoop about Mr. Loveland's office, looking for information on Mr. Smith, Mr. Loveland would likely toss me out in the same fashion. But if *you* call on Miss Loveland, you can convince her of Mr. Smith's knavery. She won't want to connect her family with his."

"Maybe. Since Miss Loveland spent a week with the Skinners, perhaps she has grown to care for them enough to help our cause, even if she is not a close relation." I considered what I might say to convince a person whom I had only met once—and briefly at that—to trust me. *If* she even acknowledged our tenuous acquaintance. "Wait. Weren't you a guest at Hinwick the same time as she was? I'm sure she would accept your call more readily than she would mine."

He gave a deep growl that rumbled around his ribcage and somehow set my heart running its paces. "There's a reason you found me hiding in the stables, remember?"

I laughed at that sunny memory. "But now that you are an engaged man, you can have nothing to fear from her."

"Hardly," he muttered.

"No stable around so you have to hide behind a lady's skirts?"

He smirked but did not comment. As surly as he was today, I decided not to tease him further.

From that point on, we traveled in silence through the mostly deserted streets until he pulled in front of a drab-looking row. "This is your stop. The one on the end."

I hurried down when he let me out. "I am sorry you are soaked."

If he made a response, I did not catch it.

Standing in front of Miss Loveland's door, I began to feel apprehensive. I was not in the practice of calling on ladies whom I did not know intimately, but I steeled my nerves and knocked soundly. The butler took my card and asked me to wait inside. I threw a glance over my shoulder at Mr. Paling, who huddled on the bench, rubbing his hands together for warmth. The poor man.

Miss Loveland received me more warmly than I had expected. "Why, Miss Fletcher, what a pleasant surprise! I am so glad to see you again, though Angel and Will both talked of you so frequently, it's almost as if you were always present."

Her warm regard made me both grateful and wary. "Thank you?" I said, though I hadn't meant for it to be a question.

She laughed lightly and led me to a small side room where a fire warmed the grate. "Would you like some tea? I believe my mother is visiting with some guests in the sitting room, but I might be able to obtain a cup if you would like."

"No, I left my driver shivering in the cold and will not be able to stay long." I didn't mention who my driver was; Thomas would appreciate the anonymity. "How long have you been in Town?"

"Since Monday, though you will be pleased to note that I arrived without incident, not like the mail-coach robbery you and the colonel endured."

I groaned inwardly. Angel must have shared every detail of my letters with her. "I'm glad you made it safely. But tell me of all the news from Rushden. I haven't heard from Angel since the engagement."

Miss Loveland clapped her hands excitedly. "Oh, congratulations! I just knew you and Will would work things out."

I blinked at her several times. Had she really not heard anything? "No. Mr. Skinner has become engaged to a Miss Smith."

"Miss Smith!" she spluttered. "But that can't be right."

No it wasn't. And it was my fault for pushing the two of them together.

She stared at me for several moments, her face pale and drawn, before she began to snigger. She repressed the sound into a titter, but it erupted into a full-blown laughing fit. "I'm sorry, Miss Fletcher," she said once she composed herself. "I really did try—you see, I promised that I wouldn't say anything." She giggled once more. "Mr. Skinner can't actually be engaged to Miss Smith."

I shrugged. "It took me a while to get used to the idea too."

She gave a sly smile. "That's because it doesn't make any sense. He doesn't know her. He doesn't love her. The only reason he came to London was for you."

Ha! "That's what I had thought, too, but—"

"Of course you did. Anyone with eyes could see it—he moped for a week straight." She shook her head. "But after that letter that you sent Angel? The one where you described not only Mr. Paling's escort home after the mail coach incident, but also his flowers, two visits, and sitting with you at the opera? Will was beside himself with jealousy."

Oh no. "I didn't mean to . . . I never would have tried to hurt him."

She shrugged. "But you did hurt him. And he hoped that if you felt jealous, you would stop hurting him and start loving him back. That's the only reason he proposed to Miss Smith."

"But . . . she accepted. So even if that was his original intention, they are well and truly engaged now."

"Are they, though?" she asked mysteriously.

Her odd tone made me question myself. "Yes?"

"No. I was there when Angel opened his letter. They only entered into a false engagement. Miss Smith promised to cry off as soon as their plan started to work."

No. That was ludicrous. Surely Thomas and I were the only ones foolish enough to subject themselves to such torture. But then I remembered the way Miss Smith had whispered something in his ear right before Will proposed. Had she really promised to cry off, just like I had?

I tapped my hand on my knee, replaying my conversation with Will in Hyde Park. He had certainly wanted—expected even—me to come crawling back to him, hadn't he? I could still remember his look of shocked devastation when I told him I wished I had never met him. "Are you certain beyond any reasonable doubt that Mr. Skinner does not intend to actually marry Miss Smith?"

She smoothed out some imaginary crease in her skirt. "Well now, I have not heard from Angel since I returned to Town, but I suppose it's possible that they may have developed a true attachment in the interim." She paused and wrung her hands. "But you would be better off speaking with Mr. Skinner about that than with me. I'm sure he will tell you everything once you admit your regret at having refused him."

"But . . ." I spluttered. "I have entered into a hasty engagement myself." Though it, too, was a sham, she need not know that. "And I . . ." So many thoughts coursed through my head, I could not iterate any one of them. My very world was spinning. "I have to go."

She laughed merrily, clasping her hands in front of her heart. "Yes, go swiftly. How romantic to be so crossed in love."

Romantic my foot. Aggravating. Abysmal. Tragic.

If Will had connived his engagement, I would wring his cassocked neck.

CHAPTER TWENTY-ONE
Lies

I DENIED MISS LOVELAND'S BUTLER the chance to offer me an umbrella in my haste to meet up with Mr. Paling.

Thomas hopped down to hand me up. Once huddled together out of the rain, he asked, "What is wrong? What did she say to upset you?"

"Miss Loveland thinks it is a false engagement."

He shrugged. "I am sure we could not fool everyone, but what does that matter?"

I laughed. "No, not ours. *Theirs.* Mr. Skinner and Miss Smith. Miss Loveland told me they became engaged so I would feel jealous and be brought to heel."

"As if you were a dog." He chuckled. "I would like to see someone try to bring you to heel." I fed him a look, and he cleared his throat. "If that is the case, he doesn't know you well after all."

"No," I responded in more sober tones. "I suppose he doesn't."

"Shall I drive you home?" he asked.

"Yes, please. I need to send him a letter. I know it is a lot to ask, especially as you have done so much for me already, but would you be willing to act as courier? I would rather my sister's staff remain unaware that I am sending a letter to a gentleman to whom I am not engaged."

"My curricle is at your service, madam." He offered a mock bow and then spurred on his bays.

"Thank you." I was not sure why his behavior to me was so distant today, but it was a nice change. Without his constant innuendos and waggling eyebrows, my heart and anger had been kept equally in check.

When we arrived at my sister's townhouse, he asked, "Did you want me to wait, or will you need some time to compose the letter?"

I bit my lip, thinking. When I looked at him to answer, he was looking at my lips, and I couldn't help but wonder if he wanted to kiss me as much as I wanted to kiss him. The humid air grew thicker, and I noticed how closely we had huddled together to avoid the rain. I looked into his eyes and thought I could see desire in them as he looked into mine, but he did not close the gap between us.

He cleared his throat. "Miss Fletcher, I am happy to wait for you as long as you need, but you cannot begin writing the letter until you go inside."

I giggled, embarrassed that I had been caught remembering his kiss where he obviously had not been so affected. "I would hate to leave you in the rain again. And I might need some help with the letter. Would you mind too much if you came inside? You could at least warm yourself by the fire while I write."

He bowed a little too grandly, and the rain poured off the brim of his hat. "Your wish is my command." He handed me the umbrella. "Would you be so kind as to fetch a stable hand to serve as postillion while we are inside?"

I nodded, opened the umbrella, and dashed inside the door. Simmons immediately helped me shrug out of my pelisse, and I made my demands known: a postillion, a writing table, and a fire in the parlor.

He bowed. "Seeing as your sister is visiting Mrs. Bell, would you like me to summon Atkins?"

Goodness, no. Her chaperonage would be almost as bad as Lizzie's. "No, thank you. I don't think Mr. Paling's visit will be of a long duration."

He narrowed his eyes slightly but bowed. "Very good."

I entered the parlor and stood next to the fire, fanning my splotchy dress so that it might dry faster. When Mr. Paling entered, he stood next to me and leaned upon the mantle.

I removed myself, sitting in one of the wingback chairs that flanked the fireplace, and tried to dry my stockings as indiscriminately as possible. But Mr. Paling did not avail himself of the opportunity to ogle my outstretched legs; he stared into the fire.

"You seem a bit out of sorts today," I said. "Is there anything amiss?"

When he turned to look at me, his eyes wore a haunted quality. He rubbed a hand over the back of his head. "Anne, I . . ."

"Your waistcoat!" I interrupted, noticing the bland fabric he'd kept hidden behind his three-cape coat. "It's gray. The mind reels."

He offered a flourishing bow. "Is it more or less practical than the one I wore at Hinwick?"

I laughed. "More, to be sure."

"Do you like it?" he asked sincerely.

I surveyed him critically, standing and walking a half-circle around him while tapping my chin. I liked everything I saw, but could never tell him that. "I am honestly not sure. It's so different from your . . ." I stopped observing his physique—ahem—waistcoat long enough to look up at his face. "Your eyes. They are gray."

"Yes," he said simply.

I couldn't help but stare into them. The outside ring was a dark charcoal, but the inner eye was more the color of storm clouds when the sun breaks through. Breathtaking. "Have they always been gray?" I asked, then flustered, realizing the ridiculousness of the question. "What I mean is, I could never quite decipher their color before. Perhaps I was only seeing the reflection off your waistcoat." The expression in his eyes had been just as unreadable before, and yet, as I looked into his eyes, I thought I could see a bit of eagerness about them. Was I able to read Mr. Paling? My mind boggled at the thought.

He cleared his throat, reminding me that I had been staring into his eyes for far too long.

"I do like the gray." I coughed. "Of your waistcoat, that is." I went back to the chair and sat, pointedly ignoring his gaze.

I expected him to insinuate something completely too familiar, but he said amicably, "I wanted to tell you about why I brought you to meet all my family."

"And about why you are so surly today."

"I'm not surly," he snapped. "I'm just trying not to flirt with you because, apparently, you think everything I say is a lie." He scowled.

"Well, if I knew there was nothing other than grump behind that veneer of flirtation, I wouldn't have mentioned it."

He ran a hand through his wet hair, curlier today thanks to the humidity. "You drive me crazy, you know that don't you?"

I couldn't tell if he was teasing or serious. "You should have tea with my mother. I'm sure she could commiserate."

He tilted his head back and took a deep breath in, then blew it out with cheeks as puffy as an acorn-hoarding chipmunk's.

The butler entered with a writing table, setting the ink, quill, and sand upon it. "There is paper in the drawer, miss. Will you be needing anything else?"

"No."

He bowed himself out.

I returned my attention to Thomas, who gazed moodily into the fire. "You said you wanted to talk about why you brought me to meet your family?" I prompted, hoping to return to a conversation where he didn't look like he wanted to throttle me. "I thought it was to stop your family's pestering that you settle down."

He offered a sad, broken smile. "There is more to it than that. Ever since I learned about my father's indiscretions, I promised my mother that I would never fall in love or marry. She has tried to change my convictions ever since. After meeting you at the ball, she was so hopeful, so excited, so . . . I thought if I introduced you as my fiancée and then you cried off . . . she would grant me a reprieve from her incessant attacks."

I stared at him for a long while as he gazed into the fire. "Why would you choose to never love?"

His look was unfocused, far-off. "My father adored my mother, you know. Yes, they married for connections and dowry and family duty and all that, but he was a devoted husband. He loved her. But while she was in the family way again and again . . . she became less capable of loving him. She was the one who suggested a mistress." He paused again before taking a different tack. "Here's the thing: God is love, right?"

I nodded tentatively, unsure where this new thought would lead.

"Love is from God, but I don't think He gave us lust," he said. "I think that is the devil's counterfeit. He uses it to corrode our hearts, like maggots, festering and laying waste. My father began having mistresses, but that unleashed an unquenchable desire that snuffed the love out of his heart. Out of Mother's heart. Now he is a wretched maggot of a man, but he did not used to be this way." He paused for a long time, waves of sorrow and anger rolling off him.

I wanted to reach out, to comfort him somehow, but didn't dare.

"I determined I would never walk the path of my father. I would never be so foolish as to allow myself to love or marry."

I scoffed, then covered my mouth at the sound. "I'm sorry, but I must have misheard you. You believe that God gives you a gift—love—and the devil curses that gift—lust. So you shun God's gift of love and embrace lust?"

He scowled at me. "No, Anne. I shun both gifts. I want nothing to do with lust."

"Then why are you such an outrageous flirt? And why did you kiss me?"

He rubbed his hand over his eyes. "I shouldn't have kissed you. I'm sorry." He stared into the fire and whispered, in a voice that would haunt my dreams, "But I am even more sorry for what I felt."

Had he felt his heart hammering in his chest like mine did in this fragile moment? I didn't dare ask. I took a few deep, troubled breaths. "I still don't understand. You have acted remarkably heroic with me in trying to thwart Mr. Smith." I paused. How could I say this without offending him? "And I thank you for it. Thank you for listening to me and being a gentleman. But your reputation toward the fairer sex in general hardly marks you as a man determined not to love or lust or whatever it is you avoid."

His face clouded over, and I thought he might rage at me, but in the end, he rubbed his hand behind his neck again. "My father was a gentleman in the public eye but a monster in his own home. I am trying, Miss Fletcher, to be anything other than him."

"So you prefer to be a monster to the public eye and a gentleman in private."

He shrugged. "If you say so."

I mulled the problem over in my head for a moment. "What if God gives you both gifts? And the lust can only corrupt if it is not equally tempered by love? What if, by denying yourself both gifts, you deny being human? You deny the power of creation? You deny Adam and Eve and the power of God Himself?"

He plopped down on the sofa, leaning his head back and stretching his Hessians out in front of him. "I don't know. I just don't trust love."

Neither did I.

He wasn't intending to eat my heart out daily. He was just broken. And I couldn't fix him. Instead, I sat in front of the writing table and pulled out the paper. I inspected the quill, then dipped it into the ink.

Will,
I need to talk to you. Please call on me as soon as possible.

I could think of nothing else to say, so I read the line aloud and asked for Thomas's advice.

He barked a laugh. "You sound like my mother ordering me about. Would he actually come if you wrote him a missive like that?"

I tilted my head as I thought. "Maybe? If he had been desperate enough to enter a false engagement just to make me jealous." But I remembered the cruel words I had delivered at Hyde Park. "No. The last time we spoke, I told him I had no interest in ever seeing him again. He would throw a note like this in the fire."

Mr. Paling began to pace about the room. "You need to apologize first and then flirt with him."

I grimaced and started again.

William,

I am so sorry. I only said those terrible things to you because I was so jealous. Please, see me as soon as possible. It breaks my heart that I hurt you.

I crumpled the paper and tossed it toward the fireplace. "Apologizing for things I do not feel remotely sorry for is fairly excruciating. I swear, if this was all a game to him, I shall have him strung and quartered."

Mr. Paling stopped his pacing long enough to offer a sardonic look. "Tell him just that, and I'm sure you'll have him back at your side in no time at all."

I was too frustrated to even smile at his quip. "Just tell me what to write."

He smirked. "A love letter to show him you are interested. Use that to lure him to visit you, and then you can discover whether or not his engagement is false."

"A . . . love letter? But I couldn't possibly."

He smiled enigmatically. "Somehow, I doubt that."

"It would be so wrong of me."

He pursed his lips and tilted his head. "If he truly pretended the engagement to make you jealous, then he deserves the deception."

"And if he has actually fallen for Miss Smith?"

"Then your letter will not change anything, and we continue to find ways to disinherit Mr. Smith."

"I don't like it," I said.

He folded his arms across his chest. "Neither do I. But do you have a better idea? Our entire engagement was based off the need to keep Mr. Smith away from you and yours. If Mr. Skinner and Miss Smith have no agreement, then our work is already done. I can continue trying to stop his debauchery on my own without this"—he motioned to me and him—"blasted engagement in the way."

He was right. We could break off our engagement now, and I could spend my time in London with people who were not destined to break my heart over and over again.

I straightened my shoulders and picked up my pen. A love letter. That should not be too hard.

Will,

Please forgive me for the things I said to you in Hyde Park. I was jealous and acted like a fool. I still think of you daily and would love if you would please come visit me at your earliest convenience.

I read the lines to Thomas.

"I still think of you daily?" He chuckled. "It sounds more like an obituary than a love letter."

He was right. I stared at the page, willing words to come, but they would not. I looked up when I felt Thomas's eyes upon me; he did not look away. They were soft, and he opened his mouth as if to speak. I held my breath. Hoping. Wanting. Waiting. But he closed his mouth without a word and returned his gaze to the crackling fire.

Removing a new sheet of paper, I began again without an addressee. The words flowed easily once I pictured a pair of dimpled cheeks and soft, gray eyes.

You must know I love you. I have always loved you. When you are not around, I long for you. I long to understand the depths I read in your unfathomable eyes. I long to know the cause of your smile and of your capricious moods. I long to understand every facet of your soul, and I feel privileged to know the parts of you that you have willingly shared with me. I cannot bear the thought of marrying another when you are the one I was meant to be with. I am sorry I did not know my own mind when you asked me to marry you. I was a fool. I still am. But I am a fool for you. I understand if you will not have me. But I want you to know that I am yours. I am yours forever, whether you will have me or not. And I am sorry for all the hurt I have given you. Please call on me tomorrow to let me know whether or not my hope is in vain before it is too late.

Anne

It sounded believable enough as I re-read it, even though Will's eyes had never been unfathomable to me.

I walked to Thomas and handed him the letter. "Let me know if you think it will do."

He began reading aloud. "You must know I love you."

Though he was only reading my own words back to me, my heart skipped several beats. This had been one of my worst ideas yet. My heart would never recover if I let him read those words aloud. I snatched the letter from his hand. "Here. Allow me. You must know I . . . Oh this is ridiculous. Just read the letter silently, please."

His lips twitched, and his dimples creased as he tried to repress his smile, but he said nothing as he took the letter from my hand and perused it.

I had to remind myself to breathe. Did he suspect this letter was written to him? His face betrayed nothing.

After an age, Thomas looked up, his eyes searching mine. What did he see there? Were my eyes as mercurial as his? "Do you really mean this?"

The rushing of my heart filled my ears. "Every word." Every word except the one I omitted on the top of the page, indicating the recipient. "Will it do?" I whispered anxiously.

His gaze pierced mine before he cleared his throat to respond. "I suppose that depends on what you wish to accomplish. If you want him to fall even more desperately in love with you than he already is, then, yes, it will more than suffice."

"But the problem is, I don't think he loves me at all," I whispered, then walked away.

CHAPTER TWENTY-TWO
Mr. Loveland

IT WAS ONLY MID-MORNING WHEN Simmons announced a caller. I rose to greet Will, anxious to see what he had to say to my letter, but it was not he. "Miss Loveland!" I exclaimed. "Now it is my turn to be pleasantly surprised."

She grimaced. "I hope you shall still think as much after you read the contents of this letter."

She handed it to me, and I recognized the script long before I saw the seal or signature. It was from Angel. I scanned it hastily.

Angel had not only described the falling-out between Will and me, but also his determination to marry Miss Smith in earnest. And as if that weren't bad enough, she then described how excited she was to have a gentleman who looked like he waltzed off a fashion plate for a brother-in-law!

This was bad. This was very bad. I moaned and sagged into my chair.

Angel *knew* Mr. Smith had tried to kiss me and offered me a carte blanche. Of course, I had not told her of his assault—who could possibly list such in a letter that would incriminate me as much as him?—but still, she should be more wary. How the blazes had Mr. Smith managed to win her over so easily?

"Are you all right?" Miss Loveland said timidly. "I'm sorry to have been so wrong . . . and for giving you false hope."

I noticed that she had remained standing and waved her into one of my sister's uncomfortable chairs. "I am not at all saddened by the fact that Mr. Skinner is marrying another. The problem lies with Mr. Smith."

She looked at me querulously, her brows creasing together.

"Are you at all acquainted with the Smiths?" I asked.

She shook her head.

"That is probably for the best." I sighed. If Mr. Smith knew her, he would somehow be able to warp her mind as well. "He is a scoundrel who . . . uh . . .

runs a disreputable business, securing mistresses for the well-to-do. And he has been threatening Angel and me."

Her heart-shaped face grew pale.

"But the man is more cunning than a fox. The falling-out that Mr. Skinner and I had? It was over Mr. Smith. I tried to convince Will that he was not to be trusted, but apparently, Will thinks I am the untrustworthy one."

Miss Loveland bit her lip, obviously not sure whom to believe. "Do you have any evidence?"

I nodded. "Yes, though my fiancé does not think it is enough for a solicitor to want to prosecute."

She perked up. "My father is a solicitor, though . . ." She looked at Angel's letter which I still held. I handed it back to her. "I am not sure my father would want to press a suit against his cousin's family."

"I sincerely doubt that if your father knew all the things about Mr. Smith that I have learned, he would want Mr. Smith in the family."

She stood and held her hand out to me. "Let's visit my father and find out, shall we?"

"At his place of business?"

"Of course. Where else would we find him at this time of day?"

I didn't really know. I had never visited a gentleman before, in his place of business or otherwise. Mother would have had an apoplexy. The thought buoyed me; I jumped to my feet and threaded my arm through hers. "Well, then? What are we waiting for?"

When we reached her carriage, the footman helped us in.

"To Father's office."

He did not so much as blink at the request. I almost giggled. Was she really able to go wherever she pleased without censure? And without chaperonage? "Where is your maid?"

She shrugged. "Probably at home, mending my stockings or some such. Why?"

My mind boggled. "You are allowed to go about town without a female companion?"

She laughed. "I am the daughter of a solicitor, not a duke. The *haut ton* may look down their noses at me for my middle-class habits, but I don't care so much, as long as I can come and go as I please."

Here was someone of my own ilk. "I would love to be given the same latitude."

She shrugged. "It's a trade-off. But now, tell me truly. You really don't mind that Will is marrying Miss Smith?"

I nodded.

"Have you no feelings for Will whatsoever?"

"Oh no." I chuckled. "I have many feelings for Will, though right now, few of them are flattering, and certainly none are romantic. He's like a brother."

She pursed her lips. "I think that aptly describes my position toward men in general. It's why I am so happy for others who find themselves in love. I just can't seem to find that for me."

I hadn't either, until I'd met Thomas.

Before long, we were on a street which I had never seen before, somewhere outside of Mayfair. While certainly not in an unsavory part of town, I felt particularly out of place near all the brownstone businesses. Several men walked about, and a few lounged outside their shops, talking with customers, though Miss Loveland and I were the only ladies about.

No one paid us any heed, until Miss Loveland bought a meat pasty from a vendor.

"'Allo me love. Buyin' a treat for ye old man?"

Miss Loveland nodded. "Hello Benwick. Nice that the rain has cleared."

"Right loverly day." He handed her the pasty, which he had wrapped in several papers. "Be careful it don't drip none on ye linen."

She gave a cheery farewell then escorted me past a few doors to her father's place of business, walking through the shiny black door without knocking. "Come on," she said to me as I dawdled. "There is nothing to be afraid of."

Of course. I wasn't afraid, was I? Just a tad nervous.

Mr. Loveland was sitting at a desk, scribbling, but set aside the parchment when he saw his daughter. "What brings you here, love? Not that I'm not right happy at seeing you."

"Thought you might be hungry." She handed him the pasty. "And Miss Fletcher has some business she wants to discuss with you." She turned to me. "I'll wait in the carriage." And then she left me there, like a bumbling muttonhead.

Mr. Loveland, a shortish man with a rounding belly, seemed happy enough to see me, and even more happy to see the pasty. He unwrapped it and began eating. After a moment, he eyed me. "Come, child. Sit." He motioned me to a chair with his free hand. "What can I do for you?"

I folded my hands in front of me, considering the question. The thing was, I knew little about law proceedings. "I don't really know where to start. I suppose I should say that I have a dear friend whose brother is about to marry poorly."

He sighed. "People do the funniest things for love. Take it from me: there's no fixing it."

"Yes, but the bride's brother is a reprehensible man who has already taken advantage of several ladies and has threatened to do the same to my friend."

He scowled and put the pasty back down on the paper, licking his lips. "Well, that is another matter entirely. Does the groom know?"

I both nodded and shrugged. "He has been informed, but he does not believe me."

"And the evidence?"

"The testimony of several servants who have been turned out of his household once they were . . . found with child." I tried to swallow, but my throat had become too dry.

He ran his fingers over his scant hair, then steepled them in front of him. "I suppose, if I am able to corroborate this story with your witnesses, I could at least write a letter to your friend's brother. People have a funny way of listening to a solicitor's testimony." He winked at me.

"And of disregarding women's testimonies."

He nodded solemnly. "Aye. That too. Now, what's the name of this bloke and the names and addresses of the witnesses?" He picked up a quill and dipped it in the ink.

"Um, well . . . this probably won't be very helpful, since his name is Mr. Smith and I am not quite sure of his first name. Or address."

Mr. Loveland looked unimpressed.

"And my fiancé, Mr. Paling, is the one who spoke with the victims."

"Mr. Paling? The dandy whose every waistcoat is even more outlandish than the last?"

I grimaced. "The very same."

He chuckled. "I didn't guess that man would tie the knot any time soon." He put the quill back down and resumed eating. "Send him in here and I'll talk with him."

It was a clear dismissal. "I shall have him call on you at your earliest convenience."

"Fine, fine," he said.

And though everything had gone better than I could have hoped, I still hadn't mentioned that all this was for Mr. Loveland's cousin. "I'm sorry I don't know Mr. Smith's first name, but Miss Smith is marrying Mr. William Skinner."

He spluttered, little bits of meat spraying out of his mouth. "That's my cousin."

I nodded.

He put his pasty back down, licked his fingers, then began rifling through documents piled on his desk. "Well, now. Well, well," he said as he found one. "Isn't that interesting?" He trailed off as he looked at the document.

"Yes?"

"The other day, Mr. Skinner came to see me about drafting a wedding settlement to a Miss Smith. But rather than sitting with her father and their solicitor as we should have, he brought me a document which Mr. Smith's solicitor had already drafted. He just wanted me to sign it." He tapped the document, obviously thinking about something. "Though everything was in order, it felt a little off."

"How so?"

He shrugged. "Other than not meeting with Mr. Smith or his solicitor? Miss Smith was only given five hundred pounds—a mere pittance—and hardly worth the fee to create a settlement."

"How much does that normally cost?"

"One hundred pounds."

A hundred pounds? For that little document that Mr. Loveland was holding in between his greasy fingers? That seemed an exorbitant sum to me.

He ran his hand through his hair again. "Mr. Skinner assured me he was still eager to wed, even if she was practically penniless, but why would someone with so little to her name need a marriage settlement?"

He looked at me pointedly, but I merely stared back. "I have no idea. You are the solicitor. You tell me."

He chuckled. "They wouldn't. Marriage settlements are solely for the purpose of providing for the bride, else everything they have goes to the groom. Sometimes, yes, the groom himself makes provisions for the bride, but that is rare." He read over the document again then looked at me suddenly. "And why would an orphan with no money to her name have two named trustees?" He pointed to a blot which, from my vantage point, I had no hope of deciphering. "Mr. Cornish is listed here as a trustee."

He shook his head and then wrote down something on a sheet of paper. "Have that fiancé of yours visit me. In the meanwhile, I suggest you find out who this Mr. Cornish is. He may be able to help you even more than I can."

Interesting. I nodded gratefully and took the slip of paper. All it had was Mr. Cornish's address. I dipped a deep curtsy. "Thank you for your help."

He waved me off and returned to his pasty.

CHAPTER TWENTY-THREE
Jealousy

"ANNE, WHY ARE YOU WEARING that hideous dress?" Of course those were the first words my sister had for me as she came in from her errands and primly settled next to the fire.

"I like its cheer." It was the clear blue of a summer sky, and it matched my mood. With a solicitor on my side, things were looking more hopeful.

Surprisingly, she accepted this response without censure. "Is your fiancé coming over today?"

"He promised to call closer to dinner."

"Oh," she said, sitting up straighter. "Shall we set a plate for him? I didn't order anything special."

"No, that won't be necessary."

She cocked her head to the side. "Why haven't you invited him for dinner yet?"

I tried not to fiddle while she observed me. "He is busy, I'm sure."

She gave me an arched look. "Too busy to dine with his fiancée? That does not bode well. Once James and I were engaged, he cancelled everything else to spend time with me."

I looked into the fire. Nothing about our strange relationship boded well, least of all his harebrained idea to have me write a love letter to Will, especially since his false engagement had already turned into a real one. The idea of him reading my letter now was mortifying.

"Find out what day he is available, and we shall have him to dinner. We will not allow him to refuse."

I nodded but stared into the fire.

She cleared her throat. "I want to check on Maria. She has had pains lately and fears she may be nearing her confinement sooner than she had anticipated.

If your beau comes by before I do, send a servant over to fetch me so I can act as chaperone."

Once she was gone, I tried to return to my book, but worries assailed me. I removed myself to the library and sat to pen another letter, the letter I probably should have sent to Will in the first place.

Dear Will,

I have always admired you.

However, I have hardly slept a wink since that day in Hyde Park where Mr. Smith detailed his plans for ravishing your sister. You cannot possibly marry Miss Smith and bring that monster into your family. You simply cannot. I have been desperate since he threatened her, dreaming nightmare after nightmare.

Yesterday, Miss Loveland told me your engagement is nothing more than a ploy for me to grow jealous and fight to have you back. But may I offer a bit of advice? Please assume a woman is capable of knowing her own mind. If she refuses you, it is not considered polite to threaten her with a monster intent on ravishing her and her best friend. She will not take kindly to the manipulation. She may even, in a state of desperation, pen a love letter intended for another and address it to you. I am sorry for the deception, but I do not love you. I simply said that to keep Angel safe.

Before I could finish, the butler announced Mr. Paling. I hastily spread sand over the words, hoping to obscure their contents. "I had not expected you yet."

"Yes, I came a bit early." He stopped in his tracks to look at me.

I glanced down to ensure that my fichu covered me properly and that I had no ink on my person.

"Why, Anne, you look ravishing in blue."

I winced at his term, which only reminded me of Mr. Smith's threats.

"Does this mean you are ready to thwart fashion's tyranny and embrace color once again?" he asked.

"Perhaps it does."

"Welcome to the club." He offered me a ridiculously courtly bow, flourishing his burnt-orange waistcoat. "I came earlier than expected to announce that my services as courier have yet to be fulfilled, though not for want of trying." He extracted a letter, which he had tucked into his waistcoat, and handed it to me. It was still warm and smelled of orange blossoms.

Relief flooded me as I peeked at the humiliating words I had written. "Thank you. I never should have penned this in the first place, especially as I now have it on good authority that Will has every intention of marrying Miss

Smith." I crossed past Mr. Paling to throw the letter in the fire, but he caught my wrist.

"No, Anne. Don't burn it." His look bored into me.

I had removed my gloves to write and couldn't help but feel a sense of shock as his cold leather touched my sensitive inner wrist. "Whyever not? It was cruel of me to pen such a thing. I'm glad you were unable to deliver it."

With his other hand, he reached over and plucked the letter from me, secreting it back inside his coat somewhere. "Because it would be a shame to destroy such poetry."

"Mr. Paling." I reached for the letter, but my hand hovered an inch away from his buttons. I could hardly pat down his pockets and remove the letter myself. "You must destroy that letter."

He grabbed my hand. "Careful, love," he whispered. "I am quite ticklish."

He stared into my eyes, but I turned away, crossing my arms over my chest. "Promise me you will not deliver that letter."

"You have my word as a gentleman."

I released a breath I had not realized I had been holding and crossed back to the table, picked up the quill, rinsed it, and patted it dry.

Thomas returned to the discussion at hand. "As to Mr. Skinner, his lodgings were empty, and the landlady said she had no intention of his coming back."

I shrugged. "Will is a vicar. He probably wanted to be back in Rushden for services."

Thomas pouted, his lower lip protruding dangerously far, positively begging to be kissed. "Why is it that you use Mr. Skinner's given name but not mine? I am, after all, your fiancé."

I chose not to respond, not wanting him to understand why I needed as much distance between the two of us as possible. "You never asked me how I knew *Mr. Skinner's* engagement was now in earnest."

He raised his brows, waiting patiently for the tale.

I told him everything and gave him the paper with Mr. Cornish's address.

"Brighton, huh? What do you think the chances are that this Mr. Cornish actually came to London to sign the settlement?"

I shrugged. "You think his signature was forged?"

"It could be."

I grabbed a fresh piece of paper and laid it before me on the writing table. "We must write him at once. What is the address?"

But Thomas did not answer and instead walked toward me predatorily. My heart thudded painfully at the heat in his eyes. I thought—hoped—he would stride forward, grab me by my shoulders, and kiss me soundly, but he stopped on the other side of the writing table. Maintaining his steady gaze, he asked, "Do you plan to pen another love letter? Perhaps you could declare your ardent love for this presumably rich Mr. Cornish like you did to Mr. Skinner." He slowly retrieved the letter I had penned from his coat pocket. "Or perhaps this letter would suffice. I noticed you did not address it to anyone in particular. You could just write 'Mr. Cornish' on top."

I made to snatch the letter, but Thomas caught my wrist with his other hand and held me there. His eyes blazed into mine, and his low, throaty words sent shivers down my spine. "Careful, darling. Words like these might turn a man jealous. And jealousy can do strange things to even the most resolute of men." He maintained my gaze but ever so slowly returned the letter to his pocket.

When he released my hand, my lungs remembered how to breathe.

Then Thomas picked up the second letter I had written Will. The letter that admitted I had penned the original missive with another in mind. My throat constricted, and I spat out a choked cough.

He tilted the paper so the sand fell onto the table in a neat line, tapped the missive sharply, then blew on it before handing it to me. "Your second love letter to Will is dry."

So he had at least read the name atop. "It is not a love letter. It is the scathing rebuke I should have sent him yesterday." I folded it before he could spy the incriminating words I had written upon it, then busied myself with returning the sand to the pot. "No more lies."

He removed his glove, then tilted my chin up, forcing my gaze to his. "No more lies," he promised. He took my bare hand in his and raised it to his lips.

It was not heart-crushing madness that crashed upon me like it had in his mother's dead garden, but something else entirely that passed between us. With that kiss, he seemed to display respect, honor, and even, just maybe, the tiniest bit of love.

He looked down at the folded letter. "You won't let me read this one?"

I scoffed. "I wouldn't want you to grow jealous, now, would I? I hear it does strange things to a man."

He laughed, and the spell was broken. "No need to write Mr. Cornish. I fancy a trip to Brighton myself." He gave me a curious look that I would never be able to interpret. "Have you heard from your father?"

I shook my head. "No. Am I supposed to?"

He looked affronted, but I could not tell if it was real or pretended. "He hasn't agreed to our engagement yet."

I guffawed. "You actually wrote him?"

He stood straighter and whisked away an invisible piece of fluff on his sleeve. "Of course. It wouldn't be a proper engagement otherwise."

I snorted. "So the more people we fool, the more proper it becomes?"

"Precisely." He nodded.

"That's rich. In any case, I doubt my father will reply. Any response will come through my mother." I stood and crossed the room, needing to put more distance between myself and Prometheus. If only he weren't so handsome. Or charming. Or so devilishly . . . "Is there anything else of a sensitive nature you would like to discuss?" I asked. "Lizzie made me promise I would send for her when you arrive. She's just visiting with Mrs. Bell."

Thomas grinned mischievously. "You weren't expecting me for a little while yet. Surely there is some other way that a courting couple might while away an hour whilst unchaperoned."

"Right then." I left the room in order to find the butler and have Lizzie sent for.

Thomas's laughter followed me. But, thankfully, he did not.

CHAPTER TWENTY-FOUR
Objections

THOMAS LEFT THE NEXT DAY, promising to track down Mr. Cornish and come back as soon as he could. And though Mary Paling called on Monday, she had no news of her brother. We simply had to wait.

I hated waiting.

On Tuesday, Miss Loveland called, and while I thought her a refreshingly delightful friend, she likewise had no news.

On Wednesday morning, however, Lizzie had a letter from home. She looked up from her letter when I entered for breakfast. "Father will not approve of the marriage until he meets Mr. Paling in person."

I sat on the edge of my seat and plucked off my gloves, wringing them in my hands, anxious to hear more. "Does Father mean to come to London?" He hated the sooty, sulphury city.

"No, Mr. Paling will have to travel to Rushden in order to meet him."

That would never happen.

"But Papa is well," Lizzie continued, "and the windows have all been replaced. Mama and Charlotte plan to arrive on Friday."

No! I had hoped to release Thomas from the engagement before Mother came to Town. After learning of his property and influence, she wouldn't allow me to cry off. Then Thomas would have to break the engagement, my reputation would be shattered, and Mother would lock me in my room for the remainder of my days.

Lizzie kept reading the letter. "They would come sooner, but your vicar is getting married tomorrow and Mother feels it her duty to attend."

I stared at her, my mind reeling. "Will marries *tomorrow*?"

She scanned the parchment again. "According to Mama, yes."

"But it is so soon." I needed more time. "The wedding never even showed up in the *Gazette*," I argued weakly. There was no need for such haste.

Lizzie ignored me, trying to decipher Mama's cramped script.

I stood. "Excuse me, but I'm not feeling quite the thing." I fled to my room, not caring for once about the strange look my sister sent my way.

I called Atkins to me and began penning a hasty letter.

Mr. Paling,

I have learned that Mr. Skinner marries tomorrow. I cannot let this happen. Thank you for your help thus far, but there is no more time to plot and scheme. I need to go back to Rushden. I will do whatever it takes.

Anne

Atkins entered. "Did you need me, miss?"

"Yes. Pack both our bags. We are traveling to Rushden by mail coach. Right now."

"But . . ." Her eyes grew large as saucers, then darted from this thing to that, taking in the enormity of the task.

"If I ask you to leave everything except one change of clothing, can you be ready in the next fifteen minutes?"

She closed her jaw and dropped a curtsy. "Yes, miss. Let's go home."

Home.

I was going back.

I didn't cry as Atkins and I pulled away from the Ascough townhouse, from the place where I assaulted Thomas with my satchel after he made some innuendo. I didn't cry on the mail coach as I squeezed between Atkins and an older man who leered at me with an unmistakable gleam in his eye. I didn't cry when we changed horses at the same inn where I flattened the colonel's cravat. I didn't cry as we passed Hinwick House and I remembered how ridiculous Thomas had looked riding sidesaddle. I didn't cry at the look of disapproval Mother gave me when she learned that I incurred such a cost to travel just to attend the vicar's wedding. I didn't cry when I was told that my bedchamber was being aired and I would have to sleep in the west wing. I didn't even cry when I realized the room which had been prepared for me was the very same room Mr. Smith had dragged me into.

But after Atkins left me, I turned the key and sank against the door—the same door that Smith had pinned me to. That same door that featured in nearly every one of my nightmares. I sank to the floor in front of that door and sobbed.

I sobbed for the past, for the coincidence of having met Smith alone in the corridor that evening. I cried for the fear inside me, that he would do that—or worse—to people I loved. I cried for the love I left behind. I cried that I had ever loved at all.

I hadn't thought I could sleep on the hard oak floor, while the draft reached its cruel tentacles into my soul, chilling my bones, but that is just what I did. I dreamt of being trapped in a room no bigger than a closet, with Smith pressed against me, pinning me to the door.

"Anne, stop fighting it," he whispered against my lips.

I knew, somehow, that if I gave him what he wanted, he would take me out of that space I was trapped in. And I kissed him.

I awoke with a start and shivered, not for the cold, but for the fact that I had kissed him this time. I had kissed him. And I had enjoyed it.

I crawled to the bed and wriggled into the covers. There. In the same bed that Smith had once slept in. I curled into a ball and pulled the covers over my head, cocooning myself in the acrid smell of gunpowder that still hung about the sheets. The pillow, which I used to muffle my sobs, smelled of a lightly scented pomade.

I shivered and wept but did not sleep. Once the sky began to lighten, I arose. I knew it was time to act; I had to talk to Will.

I didn't bother to dress but buttoned my pelisse over my chemise and shuffled into my shoes. Though I was sure my hair must look a mess—what with waking in a cold sweat after tossing and turning—I didn't risk lighting a candle to survey my unruly state; I combed through my hair with my fingers and re-plaited it in the dark. I did not need a candle to guide my steps as I sneaked through the east door.

Though the morning was still an inky blue, with clouds obscuring the moon and starlight, I picked my way down the well-worn path, lifting my hem so it would not catch on the underbrush. A barn owl hooted its morning prayers, but the only other sound was my ragged breath that billowed in front of me in thick plumes.

I reached High Street, as silent as it was dark. I walked to the rectory, but there were no lights peeking through the windows. I crept through the hedge to the window that I knew belonged to Will's bedroom and knocked lightly upon it. Though to me, the sound broke the night's stillness as if it had been thunder, he did not come. I knocked again to no avail.

I sat in the hedges, contemplating my fate. I needed to find Will before the wedding. I pressed my face upon the cold glass. By the light of a few orange coals that still sat in the grate, I looked to the four-poster mahogany bed that I feared I might one day have to share with the vicar, though marrying Will was my last resort for protecting Angel and Charlotte.

But the curtains on the bed were open, and Will did not lie upon it. The covers were still drawn up; it looked as though he had not slept at all.

I rushed down the steep cobblestones to Will's second home, St. Mary's. He had to be there. But the church was as dark as a tomb. Where was he?

I remembered how much time he spent in the little schoolroom above the church where he taught a few boys in the village how to read. He used it as an office now and again. I circled north, where the faintest hint of a fire or candle shone in the schoolroom above the north porch. The old wooden steps creaked as I ascended them and knocked softly.

After only a few moments' pause, Will opened the door. His mouth dropped open, and he stood frozen upon the threshold, the bitter wind licking up the loose folds of his shirtsleeves and exposing more of his chest and throat than I ever wished to see.

I shivered. "May I come in?"

He startled and reached out to touch me, surprise filling his gaze when he made contact.

"Honestly, Will, it is beyond cold. May I come in?"

He stepped aside and allowed me to enter. I crossed the room and rubbed my hands in front of the remnants of the fire still living in the grate.

"I had honestly thought you were a ghost coming to haunt me on the morning of my wedding," he said as he came next to me and threw some kindling into the fire.

Perhaps I was. "Miss Loveland informed me that your wedding was nothing more than a ruse. What happened?"

He blushed to the tips of his ears, then bent down to place some small logs on the fire. The blaze ate the dry wood, licking it with its flames. "I fell in love." He combed his hair with a hand. "Julia is wonderful. Mother adores her. I know she will make a respectable clergyman's wife."

"What about me?" I said weakly.

He frowned. "And you would not."

I huffed. He had come to the right conclusion at the wrong time. "But you said you loved me."

He rubbed the back of his neck. "I think I had grown so accustomed to defending your atrocious behavior to my mother that I never stopped to really see you. I loved the dream of you, maybe, but that's all it ever was."

I let out a silent puff of air. He finally saw me clearly? His timing was impeccable. "Are you really marrying this morning?"

He nodded. "A few more hours, I think." He licked his lips then turned from me to look into the fire.

I struggled with what I could say to him. I had already told him of Mr. Smith's actions, and he hadn't believed me. What good would telling him again do? "I wish I could take it all back—all those words I said to you."

He turned to look at me, thousands of emotions swirling across his face.

"I wish I had never left Rushden." Mother had been right. I had never found anything better in London than what I had here. Yes, I had found love. But an unreciprocated love was exactly what Will and I had shared for years. My heart broke, knowing what Will had felt all that time.

His eyebrows twitched, and his lips curved into that familiar lopsided smile. "It's a little late in the game for wishful thinking, Anne."

"Is it?"

He gave a nervous chuckle.

I took a step toward him. As he did not step away, I advanced again until we shared the same breath. "I'd like to object to the wedding," I whispered.

"Anne, don't do this." But he did not step away.

I smiled, a little wistful, a little sad. "As vicar of this parish, I would like you to hear my objections."

He looked at me, full of terror.

Poor Will. But I continued, for the sake of his sister and mine. "The groom is not allowed to marry because he has already been promised to me. He told me that if I returned from London with my hand and heart unscathed, he would marry me. And here I am."

"But I heard it from Mr. Paling himself." His voice squeaked. "You are engaged and I have moved on."

I carefully considered my words. I did not want to lie to him. Again. "My engagement was a ruse. Just like yours."

"A ruse for what?"

I turned from him and looked toward the fire, forming the most truthful words I could summon that would serve my purpose. "A ruse to stop you." The fire sizzled and cracked.

"Stop me from what? And don't tell me that you were jealous, because I won't believe that."

"From bringing Mr. Smith into your family. He is a degenerate, profligate scoundrel of the worst kind."

"I know."

Wait. What?

Our discussion was stalled by a knock upon the door.

Will looked around like a startled bird.

"Perhaps we could ignore it?" I whispered, afraid of being caught alone with the vicar.

But the visitor knocked again, even louder.

"Is there another way out?" I looked about the small schoolroom. There were no cupboards, pantries, or hidey-holes visible. Just a few tables and stools.

"No," he whispered, beckoning me to a wingback chair by the fire. "If you have even an ounce of wisdom, you will keep yourself hidden."

I did not need the warning. I sat, pulling my feet up so that, angled as it was toward the fire, it completely hid my form.

Another knock. "Mr. Skinner, I know you are in there," a muffled voice called.

The door opened. "Can I help you?"

"Yes. I'm looking for Miss Fletcher. You wouldn't happen to know where she is?" the familiar voice asked. A chill ran down my spine that had nothing to do with the open door and the cold air it permitted into the small room.

Mother.

CHAPTER TWENTY-FIVE
Epiphany

"I thought Miss Fletcher was in London?" Will said.

"She arrived in Rushden late last night, but her bedchambers were found empty this morning."

"I will help you find her. Let me get my hat and coat." The sound of shuffling indicated he did just that.

"That won't be necessary." I heard Mother step into the room. The door closed. The floorboards creaked as she approached my hiding spot. When she began pacing the room, I thought I might escape her scrutiny, but then a claw wrapped itself onto the arm of the chair. I shrunk from it, like a snail's eye does when touched, but the movement was futile. She loomed over me.

"Well, hello, daughter. How strange to find you closeted with the vicar hours before his wedding." Her eyes took in the sight of me. With my knees tucked under my chin, my pelisse fell down on either side; it was easy for her to see that I wore nothing but a shift. She clucked her tongue and shook her head. "I knew you would try something like this. I should have locked you in your room."

I wanted to speak, but words would not form. I jumped to my feet and over to Will for support, but his face shone a ghastly white; he looked ready to faint. "Miss Fletcher just came to congratulate me."

"In her negligee?" Mother asked.

Will winced.

"Of course not. We are both engaged to other people," I said.

"And yet, here you are." She gestured to the two of us.

She made an irrefutable point.

Mother paced back and forth with her hands laced behind her back. "What a bumble-broth we are in now. Somehow, I doubt the rector would be pleased to hear that the vicar planned a final assignation on the morn before his wedding."

Will flinched.

"There was no assignation, Mother," I said through gritted teeth. "You can't malign his character based on my actions—"

Mother slashed a hand through the air as she cut me off. "Mr. Skinner, I am sorry to inflict my daughter upon you, and on the morn of your wedding no less, but as a man of reason, you must see the prudence of such a course."

Will's shoulders sagged, and he looked to the floor, but he nodded his agreement.

"I'm sorry, Will," I whispered. "Truly."

He did not look up from his feet.

Mother took a deep breath and stood straighter, brushing her hands together. "Well now, let's get you home, Anne, before all of Rushden sees you in this state. The vicar's decision to marry you over Miss Smith will already tempt scandal." Mother walked toward the door.

Before following in her wake, I placed my hand on Will's cheek and lifted his eyes to meet mine. "It will be all right, Will. I promise to be a good wife to you." I expected him to put on a brave face, perhaps even give me a tilted smile at the ludicrous prospect that I could be a good wife to anyone, but there was no twinkle of humor in his eyes. His listless gaze was fixed to something beyond me. In his variegated brown eyes that so often pulsed and breathed with life, I saw only death.

And it was my fault. I was preventing him from marrying the woman he loved. My own reckless nature had ended up dooming us both to a marriage as loveless as my mother's. She had been right to try to tame that recklessness out of me. But now it was too late.

Something broke within me. "No."

Mother and Will both snapped their eyes to mine.

"Not like this. I will not make Mr. Skinner suffer the consequences of my mistakes." Again.

"But you have no choice," Mother said plainly. "You will do what I say."

"I always have, haven't I?" I advanced toward her. "All my life, I only wanted to please you, to make you proud of me, sure that someday, I would be able to earn your love. But I was never good enough."

She rubbed her temples. "Dealing with you always gives me a headache."

I ignored her dismissive comment. "Even when I announced my engagement to a man of the first water, you never wrote to tell me how proud you were. You didn't even congratulate me when I came home. No warm embrace or approval. Just disdain."

She crossed her arms in front of her. "What is there to approve of? If you had an engagement worth anything, you wouldn't be having this dalliance with Mr. Skinner."

"A dalliance? Mother!"

She continued as if I had never spoken. "Lizzie warned me what kind of man Mr. Paling is. A man like that may offer an arrangement of sorts but not marriage. Mark my words, Anne, he means to break off the engagement and pick you up as a mistress once your reputation is in shatters. Marrying the vicar is the best you could possibly do for yourself."

I stared at her, stunned. She could think what she wanted of Mr. Paling. She didn't know him. But me? Her daughter? "How could you think so poorly of me?" I whispered.

Her dull eyes surveyed me for a moment before she swept her arm, indicating the room. "Because you do things like this, Anne, and then I am forced to tidy up after you."

I staggered back a step. "Mothers should tidy up after their children. Am I not your daughter?"

She gave a mirthless laugh. "Oh, yes. You are very much my daughter. As obstinate and foolhardy as I was at your age. But I learned my place, and it's time you learned yours. You cannot command love or respect until you change your impertinent ways. School your emotions."

Her words brought to mind the letter Thomas had written me. What had he said? I had read those words over and over and could almost imagine the way they would sound in his voice. *Do not change who you are . . . You absolutely take my breath away with your passion. Don't school it.*

"No." As soon as I said the word, a weight fell off my shoulders, and a warmth swept through me that left me feeling light and buoyant. "I am not going to change who I am to please you."

She lifted her hand to slap me across the face, the same as she had countless times before for my "willfulness," but this time, I caught her arm by the wrist, then tossed it away.

"No," I said again, straightening to my full height, and only then did I realize that I towered over my mother by a full head. "You can choose to love me and respect me or you can continue to despise me. But I will not cow to you any longer."

As I uttered the words, a sense of rightness enveloped me. A sense of peace . . . and power. My own worth was no longer tangled up in her opinion. My heart, long hobbled with feelings of doubt and inadequacies, expanded enough to break its fetters. I wanted to cry or laugh or sing. But I wouldn't give Mother the satisfaction.

Mother scrunched her face into a sneer and pointed at me. "If you think I will let you drag our family name through the mud—"

But I did not back down. "You have no power over me anymore." I took a long, deep breath, then laughed hysterically at how easy breathing had become.

"Stop that hideous noise. You will be thrown into an asylum if you laugh so maniacally." Mother backed away from me as if I were feral.

I laughed the harder. I felt . . . happy. I had found happiness. And it wasn't in London. It wasn't even in Thomas's arms. It was here. In me. I was happy. And I was free.

But Mother shook her head and narrowed her eyes. "If you don't marry the vicar, you will become a pariah."

"I would rather be a happy pariah than stuck in a loveless marriage, enslaved to propriety's necessities, just as you are."

She scoffed. "You only say that because you have never seen the inside of a workhouse."

"Are you threatening to cast me off, Mother?"

She shrugged, unmoved. "I might if you don't marry Mr. Skinner."

"But you are the only one to have witnessed me in this compromising state. You could save everyone a great deal of pain by pretending you had not."

"And be saddled with your willfulness, your wonton behavior the rest of my life? You think that nothing you do has consequences. But you cannot waltz into a man's presence in nothing but your negligee and assume that your assignations will go unnoticed."

I pulled my coat closer around me. "There was no assignation, and Mr. Skinner truly loves Miss Smith, something that you cannot possibly understand."

Mother scoffed. "And you do?"

Oh, I knew what it was to love. And I knew heartbreak. I would not wish that pain on Will any longer. "I refuse to allow you to manipulate me anymore, Mother. Mr. Skinner and I both deserve better than this." I grasped her about her shoulders, spun her around, and shoved her away from me. "Feel free to inform whomever you like that your daughter is a worthless light skirt and lock me in the room for the rest of my days, but I will not have you ruining Will's chances at happiness. Now, if you'll excuse me, I have a wedding to save."

With one hand, I pushed her out the door while the other hand slammed it in her face. I threw my back against the door, lest she decide to not go quietly. By the way my heart hammered in my ears and my entire body felt alive, I doubted she could force entry with a battering ram.

"That was magnificent," Will said in a reverent voice.

I huffed. "I'm afraid it was rather foolish. I have no idea what repercussions await me, so let's make this quick. I am sorry to hear you are in love with Miss Smith because her brother is a monster. You cannot bring the influence of such a man into your home."

"I know, Anne. I know everything." He scowled and clenched his fists, that vein pulsing across his forehead like it did whenever he was angry. "I'm sorry I did not believe you before, but I do now. And I promise I will protect you, Angel, and everyone else from his debauchery."

The weight of trying to shield Angel and Charlotte all by myself lifted off my shoulders. "How?"

He gave a tilted smile. "I can't explain right now, but you'll know soon enough." He winked at me. "So . . . do you release me from our understanding?"

I laughed. "Of course I do."

"Good. I should very much like to get married now." He blushed. "To someone else. Not you."

I rolled my eyes. "I know, Will. Sorry for almost forcing you to marry me."

His face scrunched up as if he'd eaten a lemon, but he nodded in acceptance. "Like I almost did to you."

I smiled. "Yes, well . . . thank you for *not* doing that and for giving me the chance to go to London, out from under my mother's—" I gasped. "Mother. I'd better make sure she hasn't readied the horses to abduct us both and carry us off to Gretna Green."

Will grimaced. "She would do it too."

"Oh, I know she would. Enjoy marrying the love of your life. I may have to physically restrain Mother from coming to object, in which case, I'll miss the wedding." I swung the door and called over my shoulder, "But know that I wish you well!"

If he made a response, I didn't hear it before the door closed.

The sun peeked up between the houses on High Street as I rushed home. I slipped through the side door and up to the guest chamber, calling for Atkins; she could discover Mother's whereabouts and plans faster than anyone. I threw on my spare dress while I waited.

Atkins knocked, then entered, silently helping me tie the ribbon behind my back. "You should not have snuck out, miss. Your mother is in a rare mood."

"I'm afraid you're right, Atkins. I need you to discover . . ." As I turned to face her, I recognized all too well the bright outline of a handprint across her face. Atkins had taken the punishment I had refused. "Oh no! I'm so sorry."

She said nothing, just bobbed her head.

"Did she dismiss you?"

Atkins shook her head but did not raise her gaze to mine.

"I'm sure Mother was just so furious—" I was about to excuse her behavior as I had at least a million times before, but I caught myself. "Mother just wanted to punish someone—anyone under her power—now that I stood up to her."

Atkins beamed beatifically. "Did you, now?"

I nodded, and before I knew it, Atkins had wrapped her arms around me. "I am so proud of you."

I had never heard those words applied to me before. Finally, someone was proud of me. I hugged her back, enjoying the sensation of being held. Of being loved.

She pulled away and held me at arm's length. "You've turned into a beautiful young lady, Miss Fletcher. In spite of your mother."

"Perhaps." I spoke quickly. "But the fact remains that I have angered her terribly, and I'm afraid that not only you but also Mr. Skinner and Miss Smith shall suffer for it. Tell me what her plans are."

Atkins stared at me blankly.

"She wants to force Mr. Skinner to break off the engagement and marry me instead," I explained.

Atkins gasped but did not ask for more details. She was smart enough to put two and two together.

"But I can't let her," I said. "Please, find out what her intentions are."

Atkins bobbed a curtsy. "Right away, miss."

After my maid ran off, Charlotte barreled into the room, enveloping me in a hug. "Anne, when did you arrive? I have missed you terribly."

She smelled of rose water and talc. I had missed that smell. I had missed her. "Late last night. And I never thought I would say this, Charlotte, but it's good to be home."

She hugged me again, then held me at arm's length. "I want to hear all about Mr. Paling." She wagged a finger at me. "And I can't believe you never told me you were engaged. I had to hear it from Mother, of all people."

I sighed. "There was too much to tell. You never could have afforded the postage."

She crossed her arms and tapped her foot impatiently.

"Charlotte, it will make a lovely story, and I promise to tell you all of it soon, but not now."

She pouted but did not press me.

"How have you been, Lottie?"

Charlotte gave me the coy smile that only a seventeen-year-old could command. "I have never been better." She plopped onto the bed and sighed.

Oh? "I would think you never missed me at all."

She pouted. "Of course I missed you. It's just that no one ever paid me any attention while you were around. The last few days have been . . . enlightening."

The last few days? "How long has Mr. Smith been in town?"

She twirled a long, golden lock around her finger and smiled. "Not long enough. He's so handsome."

Handsome. And vile. Remorseless. My breathing grew heavy.

"I think he means to offer for me. He asked me to come to the church early today so he could have a chance to talk to me in private."

Poor, naive Charlotte. "Has he asked Father for permission to court you?"

She frowned. "I don't think so. Mother keeps him at arm's length, though I'm sure I don't know why."

I do. She may be unfeeling, but at least she had heeded my warning about him. "It's because she knows his intentions are less than honorable."

Charlotte sat up straight, her eyes wide. "What do you mean?"

"In London, I learned that Mr. Smith has seduced several women."

"No." Her dainty chin trembled.

"And left them destitute. I'm sorry, Charlotte."

She rubbed her nose, and I reached forward to comfort her. She waved me off. "I didn't have enough time to fall in love with him, you know."

I hugged her anyway. "I am glad you still thought he was a good man. That means he hasn't hurt you."

She pulled away, her luminous eyes wide. "Do you think . . . today . . . he meant to hurt me?"

Indubitably. But I did not want to alarm my sister. "With a man like that, who knows what he may have wanted? Perhaps nothing more than a kiss or two." I shuddered to think of what else he might have planned. I pushed Charlotte away, holding her at arm's length. "Do you still want to see him today? I will go with you if you want to deliver a few choice words."

She laughed. "No, that's more your style than mine. I think I shall let him stand there looking the fool."

I laughed with her. "You have a good head on your shoulders, you know. Even if you try to hide it behind a book."

Atkins entered, a panicked look on her face.

"Charlotte, I need to speak to Atkins for a moment. Do excuse us?"

She offered a carefree shrug and shut the door as she left.

Atkins whispered, "Her maid was as tight-lipped as they come. Wouldn't tell me a blimey thing. But I heard from the butler that your mother left already. She was headed toward the church."

No! Why couldn't she leave well enough alone? She should just lock me away somewhere and be done with it. "Thank you, Atkins." I fished a few coins from my reticule and pressed them into her palm. "It's not much, especially if Mother sacks you, but it's all I have."

She didn't waste a moment in pocketing the change, and I didn't waste one in heading out the door. I had to meet Mother before she had the chance to ruin Will's happiness—and my reputation.

CHAPTER TWENTY-SIX
Fisticuffs

I RACED DOWN THE HILL to the chapel, the rosy dawn testifying that I did not have much time. In another hour, villagers would assemble outside the church so they could wish the vicar well in his nuptials.

But when I turned the corner, High Street was still deserted. I rushed down the cobblestones and up the steps toward the chapel door. A dark figure stepped out of the shadows right in front of me.

Mr. Smith. He had been waiting there for Charlotte.

My stomach lurched.

"Miss Fletcher? I thought you were in London."

I tried to catch my breath after my run, made all the harder by the band of constriction that wormed around my throat when in Mr. Smith's presence. "I was, but I had a wedding to attend and a seduction to stop."

He cocked an eyebrow. "Sounds like a busy day. It's a pleasure to see you again."

I pushed past him and tried the door, but it was bolted shut. I pounded on it, hoping that Will or the curate would stop speaking with my mother and answer my summons swiftly. But then I was situated, once again, between Mr. Smith and a large, impenetrable door. My chest hurt, as if someone had rolled a millstone upon my sternum, and my breathing became even more labored.

"I look forward to seeing you with more frequency now that I have family in Rushden." He leaned in, placing his palms on the door on either side of my head.

"We have been in this position before." Though my voice trembled, I managed to continue. "It did not end well for you last time."

He chuckled but straightened and looked around for passersby. When none were to be seen, he leaned closer.

"My fiancé will not take kindly to you stealing kisses," I said.

He cocked his head to the side, inches from my face. "Yes, I heard Mr. Paling actually came up to scratch. Congratulations. But he is not here now, is he? And since you stole my chance with Charlotte this morning, I have to assume that you sent yourself as tribute."

I tried to knee him as I had once before, but he was wise to me and kept his legs away, allowing his long frame to pen me in. He leaned forward, brushing his lips against mine, when the bolt scraped in the lock, and the door swung in. Mr. Smith and I ended up in a tumble on the floor.

I tried to push him off me, but the man was like a sack of rocks and did not seem inclined to remove himself. I spied Will standing there quite numb to my dilemma. "Will, this cur just pinned me to the church door and kissed me. Get him off me!"

Someone yanked Mr. Smith up with a growl. "You kissed my fiancée?"

Thomas! He had come. When I looked at him, the blood in my veins started doing strange things, tingling my extremities as if I'd replaced my blood with champagne.

I sprang to my feet in time to watch Thomas plant a facer on Mr. Smith. "Stop!" Will cried. "Not in the church." He ran up and pushed Thomas and Mr. Smith away from one another.

Mr. Smith's upper lip curled into a snarl. "This wanton little wench—"

Thomas lunged for him again. "Don't you dare."

Will interceded. "Everyone, calm down. We have a wedding to celebrate. We can clear up this misunderstanding later."

Mr. Smith brushed the dust off his otherwise immaculate ensemble and blotted his bleeding lip with a handkerchief.

"Smith, there are some documents the curate wants us to sign before the ceremony," Will said. "Let's head into the vestry and see to that."

Mr. Smith shot Thomas and me a withering look before following Will to the vestry.

Thomas threw an arm around me, drawing me to him. "Are you all right?"

"Yes." I snuggled into him. "Now that you are here."

"That's good," he murmured. "I heard you had a busy morning."

Mr. Smith had said the same thing. I shivered. "Where did you hear that from?"

Thomas tucked a strand of hair behind my ear, then traced my jaw with his thumb. "You had an assignation first with the vicar and now with Mr. Smith. Busy, busy."

I pushed him away from me. "Don't joke about something like that. It's not funny."

He sobered. "Sorry."

"Wait, how did you know that I met with Will?"

"I met your mother. Charming lady." He grimaced. "Which reminds me, you will want to peek into the vestry. I have a little surprise waiting for you there." We walked down the aisle toward the room, but Thomas tugged on my arm before we reached the doorway. "This is close enough, love," he whispered. He scooted close behind me, resting his head on my shoulder so he could watch too. I wondered if he could feel my heart thudding erratically, but I did not pull away. I had to force myself to focus on what was happening in the vestry.

From my vantage point in the corridor, I saw curate Brownrigg sit at his oaken desk, nodding kindly to someone. He cleared his throat. "Mr. Smith, I presume? Good. I am glad you were able to arrive well ahead of the appointed hour. There have been some developments that need to be discussed."

What was this? I looked to Thomas, who offered a debonair smile.

The curate picked a piece of paper off his desk and handed it to someone. "This claim suggests that you are not Miss Smith's sole guardian. Apparently, a Mr. Cornish shares that responsibility with you?"

"Yes," Mr. Smith said. "But he is in the West Indies and has left my sister's guardianship in my hands."

"Still . . ." Mr. Brownrigg glanced toward an outside door. "You admit that Mr. Cornish shares duties as Miss Smith's guardian?"

"Yes, of course," Mr. Smith said. "Though I hardly see why that matters."

A swarthy man I did not recognize blustered into the room from the outside door. "It matters to me that you tried to swindle my niece out of her inheritance."

"Uncle Cornish!" Smith blanched. "When did you return?"

"Just in time, it would seem." Mr. Cornish did not take a seat but remained by the door, leaning his bulky body against the frame.

Thomas pulled me back into the chapel and gently pressed me against the wall. "Wait here a moment," he whispered before tiptoeing closer to the doorway.

Though my line of vision was completely obstructed, I could still hear Mr. Smith's nervous chuckle. "I was ensuring that my dear sister was able to marry for love. If word of her inheritance had leaked out, she would have been surrounded by fortune hunters who would use her abominably."

Someone grunted. "And so you used her abominably instead? Offered her a mere pittance for a dowry? And what of the money that you have been pilfering from her trust fund? Those were all spent for her benefit too, no doubt."

"Yes," Mr. Smith's voice squeaked. He cleared his throat. "Every farthing. I recorded every expense in the ledger. I can show you easily enough once we return to London."

"Good," Mr. Cornish said. "Now, Mr. Skinner, I have no objections to you marrying my niece, but a new contract must be made up."

There were sounds of shuffling feet and a small scuffle. The next thing I knew, Mr. Smith sprawled across the floor in front of me. Thomas knelt on his back, pulling Mr. Smith's arms behind him.

Mr. Cornish strode through the doorway with the curate and my mother fast on his heels. "Thought he might try to run, the cur," Mr. Cornish muttered.

A man I did not recognize came from the vestry, extracted a pair of handcuffs, and knelt beside Thomas. He locked Mr. Smith's wrists behind his back. "We'll be throwin' you in gaol now that you tried to get a run on us."

"But you can't! I've done nothing wrong!" He struggled against the cuffs. "Get off me, you cretin!"

"Nothing for it," Mr. Cornish said. "We don't want you running overseas with that little nest egg you've spent so long to develop, now do we?"

Smith dropped his head, the accusation sapping his desire to struggle. The same man who had cuffed him hauled him away.

Mr. Cornish grunted and turned to Will. "I'm sorry, son, but your wedding will need to be postponed. I will need a solicitor to write up a proper marriage contract, and with that mongrel as one of her guardians, it may take a while."

Will nodded to Mr. Cornish. "I understand. We shall wait as long as it takes."

Mr. Cornish nodded, then added to Thomas, "We'd better make sure my nephew doesn't weasel his way into the inspector's good graces. Wouldn't do if he gave him the slip before we recover the money he embezzled, now would it?" Mr. Cornish adopted a swagger as he and Thomas strode out the doors of the church.

Will offered a tilted smile. "Told you that you would find out soon enough." Dark shadows rimmed his eyes, and I guessed that I fared no better. I hadn't even taken the time to re-plait my hair.

"But I would have enjoyed knowing about this scheme even sooner."

He shrugged. "Mr. Paling said we had to wait for the Bow Street Runner, who wouldn't arrive until this morning."

There was a story here, surely. Thomas must have been busy if he'd been to Brighton and back in time to arrive in Rushden to stop the wedding. But before I could inquire about it, my mother approached me with a formidable look in her eye. "Just because you've gotten out of this scrape doesn't mean that I've forgotten about this morning," she hissed.

Will stepped in front of me, intending to shield me as he had so many times in the past.

But I whispered to him, "This is my battle. Let me fight it."

He took a moment to consider this before he withdrew, wisely pulling the curate aside as well so Mother and I could engage in a private conversation.

But she did not start with the vehement censure I expected. "I came here with every intention of stopping the wedding, but both Mr. Skinner and that fiancé of yours wouldn't hear of it."

I snorted. Me not marrying Will seemed like the only thing those two could agree on.

She raised an eyebrow but changed the subject. "Mr. Paling seems . . . respectable."

"Yes, he is."

"More respectable than I had previously given him credit for. And . . . well . . ." Mother fiddled with her skirt in an uncharacteristic show of nerves. "I thought Mr. Skinner was the best person to tame your wildness, but Mr. Paling . . ." She looked at me with her head cocked to one side, as if examining a bug she found under a rock. "Mr. Paling actually likes your willfulness. And your impertinence. Or so he says."

I laughed. "Yes. He told me that as well."

She blinked rapidly. "I thought I was helping you." She wiped her hands and took a deep breath, then turned away.

It wasn't quite an apology—more of an olive branch—but it was an improvement over being forced to marry or being imprisoned for the rest of my days. And it was probably the best I would get. But I didn't know how to accept her peace offering. Anything I said might rile her up rather than pacify her. So I remained silent.

After a long moment, she turned to face me again. "You should know that I told Mr. Paling what I saw this morning. And the curate."

I blushed. "I am not sure I shall be able to endure one of Mr. Brownrigg's sermons if he thinks me a temptress."

"You are not worried about what Mr. Paling thinks?"

I shrugged. "Not really." He knew exactly what I was about. "He trusts me."

The doors opened, and Mrs. Skinner, Angel, and Miss Smith walked in. I ran to Angel and threw my arms about her. "I missed you. How come you never wrote?"

"Anne, I can't believe you came!" She hugged me back. "Mother wouldn't let me write."

Figured. The woman had long despised me.

"Will told me you would not be able to make it back for the wedding."

I grinned at her exuberance. "I almost didn't."

"Well, isn't that lovely," Mrs. Skinner said, though she paid me little attention while her eyes scanned the church and she wandered to Mother.

I leaned forward and whispered into Angel's ear, "Mr. Smith hasn't bothered you, has he?"

She wrinkled her nose. "He leered at me a few times, but that is all."

I pressed her hand. "Good. I know neither of us would want him as a brother-in-law."

Mrs. Skinner's shrill voice filled the church. "What do you mean, they shall not marry today?"

Will tried to placate his mother. "They discovered a problem with the marriage settlement, and the wedding will have to be postponed."

"What problems? Why am I always the last to know everything!" As the local gossipmonger, Mrs. Skinner grudged having to depend on others for the *on dit*.

Will handled her with a miraculous amount of patience. "In this instance, my bride is the last to know anything," he pulled her to his side protectively, "and as the problems impact her most particularly, she deserves to hear everything first."

Mrs. Skinner huffed. But everyone looked to Miss Smith, who looked as white as her dress. "What do you mean?" she asked Will in her soft voice. "What's wrong with the contract?"

My heart broke a little, knowing the terrible news she was about to receive.

But Will knew exactly how to handle her. He took her hand in his, and said, "Julia, dear, you will never believe who has come to the wedding. Uncle Cornish!"

She gasped. "Really? I haven't seen him since I was a child." She looked around. "But where is he?"

"Ah . . ." Will cleared his throat. "He will be back momentarily. Did you know that he shares guardianship over you?"

"No. I mean, I think I heard something about that once but . . ." She shrugged.

"Yes, well, he is one of your guardians, but he allowed your brother to take care of your guardianship since he was in the West Indies. Mr. Cornish informed me that your mother was quite an heiress."

Her dark brows drew together. "She was?"

Will nodded. "And she left it all to you."

Miss Smith's eyes looked like they might bulge out of her head. "My brother told me it was his mother who had the money."

Will shook his head and opened his mouth to speak, but it was Mrs. Skinner's voice which pierced the reverence of the church. "Sakes alive! An heiress?" And then she fainted.

Will bent over, fanning her with his hands, while Angel, aware of her mother's nerves, rummaged through her reticule until she found the smelling salts. She waved the pungent concoction under her mother's nose until she came to.

Mrs. Skinner immediately began speaking, as if she had never fainted at all, her discordant voice bouncing off the arched ceiling. "Oh, my son, my sweet baby boy." She reached up and pinched Will's cheek. "You have made a wonderful match to an heiress! I always imagined you fancied that lusty Fletcher girl, but you bypassed her lures and went straight for the golden goose."

Quick as a Newmarket horse, Angel returned the salts under her mother's nose, causing her to cough and cease her embarrassing prattle.

Angel looked to both me and Miss Smith, apologizing profusely. "Forgive my mother. She must have hit her head. She does not seem to know what she is saying."

But I laughed. "She knows exactly what she's about, and I couldn't agree with her more." I turned to Miss Smith. "Congratulations to both of you."

Miss Smith still looked a bit too white. "I'm still not quite sure I understand."

After helping his mother to stand, Will led Miss Smith to one of the wooden pews and insisted that she sit. "You are an heiress, my love. Now, the bad news, of course, is that your brother knew very well what he was doing when he signed that wedding contract, delineating nothing more than five hundred pounds for your dowry. If we go through with the wedding right now, the inheritance wouldn't go to you. We need to have another contract signed . . . if you will still have me, of course."

Miss Smith's face turned red. "Of course I will. You are the best thing that has ever happened to me."

Mrs. Skinner started clapping.

Will glared at his mother until she stopped. "Better than learning you are an heiress?"

She nodded vigorously. And then he kissed her soundly.

Angel and Charlotte both sighed. "It's almost as wonderful as watching a wedding," Charlotte said over-dramatically.

But I wondered where Thomas had run off to and when he would return.

Mrs. Skinner stood and clapped her hands sharply. "Though we are unable to celebrate the marriage today, the wedding breakfast will not keep. I propose we walk to the vicarage and break our fasts together, in celebration of Miss Smith and Mr. Skinner's *upcoming* nuptials."

"Capital," Will said, and he and his betrothed led the procession. "I didn't sleep a wink last night and I'm famished."

But I held back. There was someone I needed to see. Angel tugged on my arm, but I shook my head. "I would rather not subject myself to any more of your mother's gloating about how Will finally escaped my evil clutches." I laughed like a villain to seal my point.

"But we still need to hear all about your fiancé," Charlotte said.

Angel pointed an accusatory finger at me. "And I know you haven't told me the half of it."

"I think I shall wait around to redirect the other well-wishers. Why, I haven't even seen Father or John yet, and they'll both be cross if they miss breakfast."

"True," Charlotte said.

But Angel waved away my argument. "Someone else can do that. I'm sure the curate wouldn't mind."

I massaged my temple. "I've a bit of a headache and would rather not countenance our mothers at the moment. But once everyone is gone, I shall tell you both about my misadventures in London."

Angel threaded Charlotte's arm through hers. "Come on, Charlotte. It would seem that Anne has made up her mind, and once she's done that, there is no deterring her." She tossed a look over her shoulder. "Not even Bath buns."

She knew me so well. But though it felt like an age since I'd eaten, I had other, more pressing matters to deal with.

I waited in the church for over an hour, redirecting well-wishers to the vicarage. But Thomas never came.

CHAPTER TWENTY-SEVEN
The Death of Me

As soon as I returned home, I flung myself on the bed. I could swear the pillow still smelled of Mr. Smith's pomade. I wiped my mouth with the back of my hand but couldn't remove the memory of his taste.

He was locked away—for now at least. I should feel a sense of relief, but instead, I cried. Because Thomas had come. But he hadn't come for me.

When I saw him in the church, I had allowed myself to hope. After all, he had traveled all the way to Rushden. He had saved the day, as any knight errant should, but rescuing a damsel in distress and loving her were two different things. And he had no notion of marrying or ever falling in love. I could not change that. I could not change him. He had fulfilled his part of the bargain, and now I had to fulfill mine. I had to cry off. He had thwarted Mr. Smith, but I had lost Thomas.

I thought I would rejoice at the end of this Promethean charade, but perhaps joy would come in time. Now was a time to mourn.

I pulled the covers over my head and allowed myself to sob. I cried for all the people whom Mr. Smith had hurt. I cried for Thomas—that his father's indiscretions had taught him to distrust and even fear love and marriage. That he was as broken as my heart.

Sobbing like a child, I lulled myself into a blessedly dreamless sleep.

I was startled to hear a knock on my door. "Miss? Are you in there?"

Atkins. I decided to ignore her.

She stormed in and pulled the covers off me. "There is someone here to see you."

I yawned, sleep fogging my thoughts. "I've not had a good night's sleep for a month at least." I yawned again and snuggled back into the pillows. "And I do not care to see anyone right now."

She planted her hands on her hips. "I would lay ten to one you will care to see this particular someone." She grabbed my hand and pulled me up. "But you will have to hurry. Weatherford is intent on turning him away."

Him? As I hurried into the hall, a familiar laugh echoed toward me. My heart opened at the sound of his voice. "Miss Fletcher has developed the nasty habit of denying me entry even though I know she is at home."

"That can hardly recommend you now, can it?" the butler said. "You would be best advised to leave your card."

From the top of the stairs, I could see Thomas patting his pockets but coming up empty.

"Why, Mr. Paling!" I rushed down the stairs to greet him. "How is it that you, a man of the Town, could be found without your calling card? Unspeakable." When I reached the door, I could see his eyes dancing with humor, the corners of his lips curling upward barely enough to dimple his apple cheeks.

"I was in a bit of a hurry to get to Rushden before the wedding."

My heart pounded recklessly, in direct contrast to his tone of nonchalance. I adopted the same demeanor, casually looking him up and down. "I suppose we can overlook the breach in etiquette just this once. Please, do come in."

Weatherford frowned but allowed him to enter. We claimed the parlor and sat next to each other on the sofa, maintaining proper distance. "When did you and Mr. Cornish arrive? Was it last night or early this morning?"

He laughed. "You will steal the telling of a great story if you start that way."

"Sorry." I folded my hands primly on my knees. "Go ahead and spin your yarn."

"No," he said petulantly, pouting his lower lip. "Now you have ruined it."

"Please?" I begged.

He sighed dramatically. "If I must." He cleared his throat before launching into the tale with gusto. "I visited Mr. Cornish's estate in Brighton, but his steward said that Mr. Cornish was in the West Indies. I asked him if he knew anything about Miss Smith, but the man was as tight-lipped as the Smith solicitor—that man was complicit in Mr. Smith's plans to filch money from his sister's trust fund, by the way."

"Mr. Smith's solicitor?"

Thomas nodded.

"Ah. So that explains how Mr. Smith convinced him to write such an unfavorable settlement for Miss Smith."

Thomas stretched his legs out in front of him. "Yes. And also why he was so wary of me when I claimed to have visited him on Mr. Smith's recommendation. He had been aiding Mr. Smith in pilfering Miss Smith's money from the time her mother died some twelve years ago. Anyhow, just as I was about ready to give up on learning anything in Brighton, Mr. Cornish blusters in with his sea legs still on him, freshly returned from the West Indies."

I clapped my hands appreciatively. "And he was more open than his steward?"

He nodded. "When I told him of his niece's five-hundred-pound dowry, he was livid." Thomas smiled and leaned back. "You should have seen him, Anne. I've never witnessed a human turn so purple in the face. Almost apoplectic."

"I'm glad he wasn't. Then we would still be in the dark."

He nodded. "Too true. But Mr. Cornish is made of sterner stuff. Even though he had just arrived from a long voyage, he had no compunction about traveling with me to London to talk to his nephew."

"But Mr. Smith wasn't home."

Thomas glared at me. "Are you telling this story or am I?"

I folded my hands apologetically. "Sorry. Do go on."

He raised his eyebrows, daring me to interrupt him again. I didn't.

Finally, he continued. "But, as you so astutely surmised in your interruption, Mr. Smith wasn't home. Apparently, he had already left for Rushden. So Mr. Cornish decided to do some digging. I took him to visit Mr. Loveland, and together, they gained access to the ledgers that detailed the moneys withdrawn from Miss Smith's trust."

My eyes narrowed. "You were back in London, and you didn't even send a note?"

Thomas held his hands in front of him defensively. "I was very busy determining that Mr. Smith's abuses of his sister's accounts were criminal."

I brightened. "Criminal? As in, Mr. Smith will spend time behind bars?"

He nodded seriously. "I believe so. Mr. Loveland said he would remain in prison until he repaid every farthing to his sister." He chuckled. "It will take him a while. He withdrew five thousand pounds for Miss Smith's coming-out alone."

I gasped at the mind-boggling sum Miss Smith had never benefited from. "So, let's see. Where was I?"

"You had just determined that Mr. Smith's embezzlement was criminal. What day was this?"

He scrunched his forehead. "Tuesday. And we didn't find out about the wedding plans until yesterday. It seems that Mr. Smith was a bit paranoid that someone like us would try to prevent the wedding from happening, which is why their wedding was so secretive and rushed."

Ah. That made sense. "I wasn't aware of the date either until Mother's letter. I never would have imagined he would marry so quickly. Why, they have only been engaged a fortnight."

He looked deeply into my eyes, whispering, "So have we. Longest two weeks of my life." He winked.

I nudged his knee. "Mine too," I teased so that he would not know I was in earnest. "So then you arrived last night?"

He nodded. "But first, Mr. Cornish and I stopped at Bow Street and made a plan with Inspector Blakely. He said he had some business to take care of and wouldn't arrive until late last night. He told Mr. Cornish and me not to approach Mr. Smith until he was at the wedding; he was afraid he would try to run."

"Which he did."

Thomas nodded. "That he did."

"But you told Will about your plan. Did he believe you right away?" Anger boiled up inside me when I thought of how much strife could have been avoided if Will would have just listened to me in the first place.

"It's hard not to believe a person when they bring irrefutable evidence and the law with them."

Fair point. I sighed. Now that the threat of Mr. Smith and the urgency to stop him had been lifted, I felt exhausted, as if all the sleepless nights finally caught up with me.

"Are you alright?" Thomas asked.

I nodded. "Thanks to you." I gave a tired smile. "My knight errant arrived in the nick of time."

His brow furrowed. "Not in time to save you from that cockroach. Did he really kiss you, right on the threshold of the church?"

A bitter tang filled my mouth, and I wanted to spit. "Yes."

"What a cad." He cracked his knuckles and flexed his hands. "A pity you did not have a satchel full of apples on hand."

I laughed at the memory. "Yes, but hauling him off like that was an even better idea. How can I ever repay you?"

"I can think of a few ways." He leaned closer, biting his lip while gazing at my mouth, but I looked away and cleared my throat.

"You saved Miss Smith, you know. If she had wed without a marriage contract . . ."

"I think it would be more aptly put to say that *we* saved Miss Smith. Together."

I scoffed. "I tried to marry the vicar. *You* saved Miss Smith."

"About that . . ." He leaned forward, placed his elbows on his knees, and steepled his fingers. "I would rather my fiancée not throw herself at a man while she wears nothing but her negligee."

My cheeks heated. "I was wearing a coat."

He raised his eyebrows at me. "You do not try to refute the fact that you visited a man without a chaperone, in your negligee, in the middle of the night?"

I hung my head. "I thought it would fix everything—well, no. Not everything. Mr. Smith would still be at large—but he wouldn't be able to prey on me and mine any longer."

Thomas sat up and draped his arm across the back of the sofa. "You little pea-goose. I told you at the onset that was a terrible plan."

"It was a fine plan. And maybe I shall marry the vicar after all," I teased. "As an heiress, I'm sure Miss Smith could do better for herself than marry a country vicar."

He offered a gentle smile. "How is it that you could marry the vicar while you are still engaged to me? There are countries in the world that allow that sort of thing, but England is not among them."

"Now that you have rendered Mr. Smith incapacitated, our understanding is also at an end." I stuck out my hand, expecting him to shake it as he had when we entered our agreement, but he gently raised my gloved hand to his lips instead, tilting my hand so that he kissed the inside of my wrist. I pulled my hand away, lest he continue; the fire that coursed through my veins pained me sufficiently.

"So does this mean that . . . wait. I have it here somewhere." He ruffled through his pockets and extracted my letter. His eyes scanned the first few lines before he cleared his throat. "You are still deciphering the meaning of Mr. Skinner's unfathomable eyes? You still yearn for him when he is not around?"

I scoffed. "You know, Thomas, I really tried to love Mr. Skinner, but I could not do it, no matter how long I begged my heart to obey."

He laughed heartily. "Now that we are no longer engaged, you call me Thomas, and he becomes Mr. Skinner?"

I shrugged.

"I think you have that backwards." He wagged a finger at me. "And you told me you had meant every word of this letter." He carefully folded it and secured it away once more.

I looked into his stormy eyes and said softly, "I did not lie."

"Anne," he said sternly, "either you loved him, *you have always loved him*"—he pitched those words in a mockery of femininity—"or else you could not love him, even though you wanted to. Which is it?"

He had been breaking my heart for so long, perhaps simply telling him the truth would be the best way to end my suffering. Mother would not allow me to return to London anyway, and I would probably never set eyes on Mr. Paling again. "I meant every word. But I have never loved Will, I have never found his gray eyes unfathomable, and I never put *his* name atop that paper."

Thomas sucked in his breath, then grasped my hand in his, looking earnestly into my eyes. His penetrating gaze seemed to scour my soul, weighing every interaction we had ever shared.

It was too much for me. Tears pricked my eyes, and I turned away from him, humiliated. I was certain he would laugh at me for having fallen so desperately in love, when this whole arrangement had been no more than a guise for his noble quest.

"Do I dare believe?" he whispered. "Do you truly love *me*?"

I could not look at him, but neither could I stop the words from falling off of my lips. "You must know I love you. I have always loved you." Curse my tongue for always being so straightforward.

But he recited the words as smoothly as if he still had the love letter in front of him. "When you are not around, I long for you. I long to know the cause of your smile and of your capricious moods." He gently cupped my cheek and turned my head so that he could look into my eyes.

My heart pounded so painfully against my ribcage, I thought it might burst. "Are you quoting my own letter at me? That is not very original."

He laughed and caressed my cheek with his thumb. "I couldn't help it. You seared those words into my heart, Anne. I had refused to love, but the words in this letter have haunted me both day and night. I have not been able to sleep for thinking you may have written them for another when it is *you* whom I love. You that I cannot bear to think of in another man's arms. You may have penned them, but they are my words now."

I gasped. Did he really, could he honestly return my regard? I didn't dare believe in his sincerity. Thomas was nine parts flirtation after all; maybe he was just borrowing my words so he could use them to woo his next victim.

He dropped his hand from my cheek and pressed his hands into my own once more. "I cannot bear the thought of you marrying Mr. Skinner when you are the one I was meant to be with. I am sorry I did not know my own mind when I asked you to marry me. I was a fool. I still am. But I am a fool for you,

Anne. I understand if you will not have me. But I want you to know that I am yours. I am yours forever, whether you will have me or not. Please marry me, Anne."

I blinked at him several times, hardly able to believe his words. *My* words. Of course I had given him my heart long ago, that was not the question. The real matter was whether or not I could forgive him for all the pain he caused me, and trust that he would not break my heart again. But if I didn't respond, my heart might burst entirely.

"Please, Anne. I love you. Marry me?"

My tongue answered before receiving permission from my brain. "I thought you would never ask." I laughed. "Again. I thought you would never ask me again."

"Is that a yes?" He reached out and wiped a tear that had escaped its confines and coursed down my cheek.

"Yes."

Unlike his last kiss, where he had unexpectedly crushed his mouth to mine, Thomas first removed his gloves and brought his hand to my jaw, then paused. "May I kiss you?"

"Not if I kiss you first." I leaned into him, closing the distance. His lips were soft and warm, not nearly as urgent as last time, but sweet and supple. When I needed to breathe, I rested my forehead atop his. I could feel his lips spread into a smile, and finally, blessedly, I kissed each of his smiling dimples.

His mind must have been racing just as quickly as mine, for he asked, "What do you think about having a short engagement?"

I nodded over-eagerly. "We've been engaged two excruciatingly long weeks already."

"Amen to that."

I pulled away from him. "It was hard on you too?"

He huffed. "You have no idea."

But I rather thought I did. At least that feeling had been mutual.

He took off my gloves and trailed his own gloveless fingers lightly up mine, sending tingles all the way up my arms and down to my toes. "You tried to love Mr. Skinner. And I tried so hard not to love you when you inserted yourself into my life at the Hinwick Ball. But you made it so blasted hard for me."

He placed my gloveless hand atop his so that our palms were together, "I was disarmed at first by your bravery," he tipped his pinkie finger down, curling it around mine, "your willingness to flout convention, your wit, and your sense of humor." With each attribute, he curled another one of his fingers over my own. "In those stables, I was taken with your boundless energy," there went my thumb, and he took my other hand in his, "your grace, and your transcendent beauty." The caress he gave my pinkie and ring finger made it hard to pay attention to the attributes he was listing. "I had built up so many defenses, and you blew them down as if they were but feathers."

He drew the back of my remaining three fingers across his lips, kissing them ever so lightly. "I had hardly any defenses left when you plowed down Colonel Thoroton, but there you surprised me with your strength, your fire, and your unwillingness to back down." I yearned for him to stop so I could kiss him. "You captured my heart before you had even reached London, and I found myself constantly thinking of you, wanting to know what you were doing, what you were thinking. Wondering if the things you said and did would ever stop surprising me—"

I cut off his words with a kiss, this one not as tender as the last. He pulled away to say, "Like that, for example. Who could've known you would have—"

I grabbed him by the cravat to pull him in for another kiss but ended up choking him instead. He gasped, then broke into a coughing fit.

Oh, bonnets! I ran to the sideboard to retrieve some claret. After his coughing subsided, he wheezed, "Or like that. I knew you would be the death of me, Miss Fletcher, but I hadn't expected strangulation." His silver eyes twinkled all the more for the tears coughing had brought them.

I handed him the beverage. "I cannot promise that I will not be the death of you, Thomas Paling, but I can say that loving you has been the greatest torture of my life."

He raised the glass of claret. "I could drink to that."

CHAPTER TWENTY-EIGHT
Freedom

MOTHER CLEARED HER THROAT AS she and Father entered the parlor. "Mr. Paling, I am glad you have come to see my daughter, but kindly refrain from visiting her unchaperoned."

"Yes, ma'am." He stood, then tossed back the claret and handed me the glass so he could shake Father's hand. "Mr. Fletcher, I am so glad to finally meet you."

Father grunted and sat on a chair across from Thomas.

"Take a seat, please," Mother said.

I walked to the sideboard to replace the glass, unsure whether her invitation extended to me as well. Thomas's pleading look decided for me, and I returned to my original seat, leaving a respectable distance between Thomas and me.

"I would very much like to marry your daughter."

Father said nothing.

"I am glad to hear it, Mr. Paling." Mother smiled warmly, though I didn't know if she was happy for me or gleeful that I would no longer be her charge.

I looked to Father to say something, but he took out a large knife and began paring his nails. I couldn't be sure if the move was intended to intimidate Thomas or just give Father something to do.

I cleared my throat. "I'm glad you recovered from the explosion, Father. I imagine staying indoors all that time must have been quite the trial."

Father grunted again but made no inquiries as to how I had spent my time in London. Which made sense, really, since he probably didn't care.

"Mr. Fletcher?" Thomas prompted. "Have you any objections to my marrying your daughter?"

Father looked at Thomas for the first time. "Where did you say you are from?"

"Lowdham, sir, in Nottinghamshire."

"Nottinghamshire, eh? How fares the hunt up there?"

I suppressed a groan. Father would bring up hunting now? As if that were any indication of a man's merit.

Thomas's brows creased into a question for a second, but he replied placidly, "I ride to hounds every year."

Father grunted. "Yes, those vermin are everywhere. But what of whoopers like this one?" He indicated a large stuffed bird on the wall. "Shot that one on my own property. Do you have game like that up north?"

"I don't think I have seen that particular specimen before, no."

"Well then. There you go."

Thomas's lips twitched in tandem with his jaw. He looked at me to glean some meaning from Father's cryptic words.

Keep going, I mouthed to Thomas. Father could speak about hunting for hours if given a chance.

"Does that mean you will consent to my marrying your daughter?"

Father continued perusing his nails. "Yes, of course. I have no use for daughters anyhow."

The muscle in Thomas's jaw twitched, but he nodded and stood. "Fortunately for both of us, then, I do have a use for your daughter." He extended his hand to me, and I stood and took it. "Right now, for example, I have an engagement present I would like to show her. If you will please excuse us?"

Mother and Father stood and bowed, and Thomas pulled me down the hall toward the entry.

"What sort of present can you have for me?" I said. "If it is Mr. Smith tied up in chains, that might be a fraction morose for an engagement gift."

His lips twitched upwards. "No, dearest. That was the gift to end our false engagement. We need something else to celebrate the real one." Thomas stood behind me while I put on my gloves. "Close your eyes now. No peeking."

I dutifully closed my eyes and allowed him to gently pull me toward the door. "Don't run me into the doorframe."

He chuckled. "Now, Anne, I know how hard this is for you, but you will have to trust me." The great oaken door creaked open, and he helped me down the front steps. Only after I heard the pea gravel crunch underneath my boots did he instruct me to open my eyes.

The most beautiful black stallion stood before me with my saddle upon his back. "For me, Thomas?" No one had ever given me a gift of this magnitude before; I wasn't quite certain how to respond.

"No, he's mine."

My heart deflated. I knew it was too good to be true. But, with my saddle on the stallion's back, it was obvious that Thomas intended to allow me to ride him. I cheered at the thought.

But then Thomas approached the horse and grabbed onto the pommel, as if to hoist himself up. "I purchased him so I could master the art of riding sidesaddle," he said over his shoulder, winking at me.

I laughed and pulled him away from the stallion before he could hurt himself. "Don't break your neck until after the wedding, please."

He chuckled. "If you insist. And of course I bought him for you."

"Oh, Thomas." I threw my arms around his neck and kissed him on the cheek before ignoring him so I could inspect the animal. I knew I shouldn't look a gift horse in the mouth, but of course, that was the first thing I did. His pearly white teeth were barely as long as my first knuckle; the horse was the epitome of health. "He's beautiful," I whispered. "He looks just like Phillip."

"That's because he is Phillip."

I snapped my head to Thomas. "You bought him off Mr. Skinner?"

He nodded. "Turns out he didn't really need him. He only bought the stallion to impress a certain horse-loving girl, and his current fiancée doesn't much care for horses."

I snorted.

"Do you want to ride him now?"

I grinned. "Yes, let me just go and change, if you don't mind waiting."

He chortled. "I have waited for you all my life. Somehow, I think I will be able to manage a few minutes more."

My heart melted at the sincerity of his words. I ran to my room and found my riding habit still hanging amongst the things I'd not taken with me to London. I fingered the blue velvet, remembering the dread I had felt at riding unaccompanied with Will so he could propose.

There was a small tear on the fabric from when it had caught on the pommel of my saddle. I laughed, remembering the bumble-broth I had gotten into, and the way Mr. Paling had brought laughter instead of censure. I had needed that. I had needed him. And somehow, he had needed me too.

Atkins helped me dress, and I bounded back down the stairs to the love of my life.

"Would you like a leg up?" Thomas asked politely.

I nodded, and he assisted me before mounting his own bay.

We started them on a gentle walk, Price following behind us discreetly. "Well," I paused, wondering how to ask this. "What do you think of my family?"

He laughed. "It's nice to know I'm not the only one with imperfect parents. But I was thinking of talking to your father about a business venture. We could use Phillip to start raising our own horses if you'd like."

I gasped. "Would you want to? Could I ride all the horses?"

"I think you might have to. I have never broken a horse before."

I couldn't keep the grin off my face. "Horses need a lot of land." I looked at him, but he evaded my gaze. "You wouldn't happen to own a lot of land, now, would you?"

He turned a beatific smile on me. "The one thing we have aplenty in Nottinghamshire is land. But would you want to live in the country?"

I had hoped London would be a place where I could finally feel like I belonged, but the only thing I had really enjoyed about being there had been Thomas. "I prefer the country. Do you think anyone in Lowdham would mind if I rode astride?"

He shrugged. "If they did, would it stop you?"

"Only if you didn't approve. I wouldn't want you to be embarrassed by me."

He grabbed Phillip's reins and stopped both our horses. As he leaned forward, I thought he might try to kiss me, but he propped his forehead against mine. "Nothing you can do will ever embarrass me, Anne. Nothing. You could ride Phillip bareback in the woods wearing only a shift, and still, I would not be embarrassed."

"Is that a promise?" I whispered. "Or a suggestion?"

"Both." He brushed a kiss over my lips before languorously whispering, "I will beat you to the copse of trees."

He took off.

"That's not fair!" I called after him as I fumbled for my reins. But in spite of his head start, Phillip and I beat Thomas handily.

When Thomas reached me, we were both winded. "I'm afraid I will never be able to offer you a fair race. You practically flew over that field."

I nodded. "It feels like flying. Like freedom."

He smiled, his dimples creasing into deep lines, his eyes as shaded as the storm clouds that gathered in the west. "Like loving you."

EPILOGUE

THOMAS CAME INTO THE BREAKFAST room holding two letters. I jumped up to snatch them, but he held them up and away from me. "Ah, ah, ah. Not without proper payment." He tapped his cheek with his free hand, indicating the desire for a kiss.

But I made my own rules, tickling his sides and exposed underarms.

He giggled like a toddler and dropped his hands defensively.

I snatched the letters from him and settled at the breakfast table.

"You play dirty," he said.

"You should know that by now, love. And I know you like it."

He laughed and headed to the sideboard to fill up plates for both of us while I opened Charlotte's letter.

"And how does Lizzie dearest fare? Has she delivered that baby yet?"

I glared at him. "Let me read it first, then I shall tell you."

He set a plate in front of me and turned his attention to his breakfast while I read. "The doctor says she is well, but the baby is taking his time. Most of the letter details the beaus that call on Charlotte."

He smiled. "Of which there are many, I presume. She is going to make quite a splash this Season."

I nodded. "Let's see . . . A Mr. Beuregard has begun calling on her, as well as Mr. Ascough. And she has also received quite a few visits from your friend the colonel."

"Really?" He cocked his head to the side. "I couldn't get him to pay attention to any ladies while I was there, but now that I'm gone, he calls on your sister, of all people. I wonder if they should suit."

I handed the letter to Thomas. "You should read it and see what you think. Charlotte seems oblivious that all these men are coming to call on her and not Lizzie."

He skimmed over it while I turned my attention to my eggs.

"Charlotte is as clueless as you were. How could your mother have raised both of you to be so guileless?"

I snorted. "Guileless? I was absolutely convinced I was hopeless. Do you think I should tell Charlotte that none of those gentlemen called on Lizzie even once in the month I stayed with her?"

He laughed. "Don't. I'm sure nothing could be more attractive than a woman with unassuming airs."

I wrinkled my nose. "Are you sure?"

He stood and nodded to the footman, motioning for him to leave us alone for a moment. Thomas prowled forward, placing his hands on the table on either side of me. "Mrs. Paling," he whispered, "I know for certain. There is nothing more attractive than a woman who, for whatever reason, is wholly unaware of her attractions. I might need to thank your mother for not cosseting and preening you into a pretentious twit."

"Is that so?" I turned to face him, mildly affronted.

He placed a gentle kiss on each of my eyelids and the tip of my nose before settling on my mouth. For the first time, I was grateful to the mother who had taught me how imperfect I was.

I pulled away from him. "And I'm grateful that you determined not to love, else I'm sure you would have married long before I barged into your life."

He laughed. "And what an entrance it was. I was utterly done for from that moment on."

I sighed as I looked into his pale-gray eyes; they held tints of purple, courtesy of today's waistcoat. He leaned forward, but I kept my lips just out of his reach so I could whisper, "And yet, you wouldn't even dance with me."

He kept leaning slowly toward me, until my head was practically against the table. "You are the only woman I will ever dance with ever again." He kissed me soundly, bracing my head with his hand—until the doors reopened. I shoved him away, and we hastily resumed a more decorous position at the table.

Thomas's mother entered, seeming none the wiser. "And how is Thomas's sunshine today?" She came forward and pecked me on the cheek.

"Happier than I have ever been."

"I'm glad to hear it. You've egg in your hair, though, dear." She headed to the sideboard without offering censure.

If blushing down to my toes was possible, I did in that moment, though I couldn't tell for sure due to my stockings and slippers.

Thomas guffawed, then stood and chivalrously picked the traitorous bits of egg out of my hair.

Mrs. Paling returned to the table once she had plated her food. "And remember, if he ever gives you any trouble at all, just send him to my estate. I'll wallop him for you."

I assumed Thomas must have finished grooming me like a monkey when he sat down. "Anne is fully capable of thrashing me without your help, Mother. You should see the punishing left she employs with her satchel."

I tried to ignore both of them by opening and hiding behind Angel's letter. Only once I had read it several times—and the heat from my cheeks abated—did I put the paper down. "The new Mrs. Skinner plans on starting a lace industry."

Thomas stretched back, lacing his arms behind his head. "What does an heiress need with a lace factory?"

I shook my head. "Not a lace factory, a cottage lace-making industry. She tracked down the servants her brother took advantage of and hired a local lace-making widow to teach the girls how to make lace. And she will be starting a school for the children to attend free of charge so the mothers can work while their children are being cared for." I wondered if I could find the illegitimate children of Thomas's father and send them there as well. I'd have to talk to Thomas about it when his mother wasn't around.

"How charitable. She sounds like the ideal wife for a vicar," Mrs. Paling said.

"Better than me, surely." I tapped the letter on the table, reliving my humiliation. "My own charity visit to that same lace-maker did not fare well."

Thomas laughed. "Quite an understatement, love."

I hoped that the subject would drop, but Mrs. Paling was too observant for her own good. She dabbed her mouth with her serviette before speaking. "It would appear you have a rather entertaining story to share, my dear. And I do love to be entertained."

For heaven's sake, the apple hadn't fallen far from that tree. But surely his mother would appreciate this story no more than mine had.

Thomas grinned. "If you don't tell her, I shall." And he would. With embellishments.

I sighed and started my narrative. "The lace-maker Mrs. Skinner is employing, Mrs. Moulton, was recently widowed. When her husband died, I went to visit her."

Mrs. Paling smiled. "Very kind of you, I'm sure."

"I was trying to see the pattern of the lace she was working on, but her tiny cottage was lit with only one rank tallow candle. I held the candle very near the lace as I bent to look at it—and the candle spluttered acrid smoke into my nostrils. I hastily blew on the offending wick, but it did not blow out." I paused dramatically.

"Go on. Don't leave it there," Thomas said.

"The candle, mad at my attempts to snuff it, retaliated by peppering my face with wax. I was so surprised I dropped both the candle and the lace, and the whole spool caught fire."

Mrs. Paling barked out a laugh, then covered her face with her palm.

"Hours of labor. Days. Months of work, maybe. Destroyed in seconds by my beautiful wife," Thomas said.

"I take it you paid the lace-maker for her losses?"

I nodded.

"That was very kind of you, dear, to have purchased all that lace. She surely needed the income. And it prepared you to marry my son."

"In what way?"

Mrs. Paling's pale blue eyes sparkled with the same look of mischief that so often blanketed Thomas's eyes. "Now you know how to burn his hideous waistcoats."

"Mother!" Thomas gasped, straightening his eggplant-colored satin.

I laughed. "I would, but they have too many memories attached to them now."

"Pity," she mumbled.

"Hey!" Thomas protested, pointing his finger alternately between his mother and me. "You two had better not start ganging up on me. Life is hard enough to adjust to as a newlywed. If you keep it up, Mother, we will send you on your way."

"Thomas!" I said. "How could you say such a thing? I would kick you out before I ever did your Mother."

Mrs. Paling pinched my cheek. "That's my girl."

My heart swelled with pride.

"No," Thomas said, putting his arm around me protectively. "She's my girl."

Mrs. Paling tapped her son's knuckles with her spoon, and he withdrew his arm. "She is your wife, you cotton brain, but she is my girl. And I have to thank her for making you happier than you have any right to be, Thomas, especially after the cruelty you put her through. It's a miracle she ever accepted your proposal. And twice, at that."

Thomas pressed a kiss on my cheek. "It is a miracle." He lowered his voice to a whisper. "Do you want to make another miracle? A little girl of our own?"

I pushed him away, heat flaming my cheeks as it never had with his insincere innuendos.

He brushed his fingertips across my cheekbones. "Finally. I made you blush."

FACT OR FICTION

Palings: John Paling (Thomas's father) and Anne Giles are my sixth great-grandparents. John sired two illegitimate children through his servants Anne and her sister Elizabeth; they were both minors, less than half his age. Thomas, Edith, and Mary Paling were just three of John's nine legitimate children. The Palings were likely tenant farmers, similar in social status to the Martins of Austen's *Emma*. In other words, they were not nearly as affluent as I depicted in this book. Unfortunately, this means that Thomas likely never became a dandy with poppy-colored waistcoats.

Fletchers: The Fletcher family owned Rushden Hall from 1755 to 1820. They are described as typical Georgian squires, interested in hunting, shooting, and horse racing. Mr. Fletcher really did stand too close to the fire with his powder horn on and blew out the double windows in that room. Both he and his son, John, walked away from the accident without serious injury. After his father's death, John Fletcher seemed to have gambled away the estate, which was sold to creditors, and he ended up dying in a poor house. Anne, Charlotte, and Lizzie are fictional.

Skinners: William Skinner became the vicar of Rushden in 1807. Little else is known about him.

Thomas Brownrigg: Thomas served as Rushden curate until 1816. He performed the majority of weddings and christenings in Rushden during this time. Little else is known about him.

Widow Moulton: Sarah Moulton was widowed in 1812, leaving her with three boys, ages seven, five, and one. In all likelihood, she probably had a cottage lace-making industry, though there's no record of her lace ever being burnt during a charity visit. She is my fifth great-grandmother.

Orlebars: The Orlebars built Hinwick House in 1710, modeling it after Buckingham House (later Buckingham Palace). The house remained in Orlebar possession until 1995.

Mail-coach robbery: On October 26th, 1812, the mail coach was robbed a few miles outside Rushden.

Colonel Thoroton: Colonel Thoroton of the Coldstream Guards was called home from the war when his father died in 1813. At the age of twenty-four, and already in possession of Flintham Hall, he was one of London's most sought-after bachelors.

All other characters are fictional.

ABOUT THE AUTHOR

AFTER EXHAUSTING HER READING LIST during a banal bout of bed rest, Alene Wecker tackled the tedium by attempting a novel of her own. She fell in love with writing. As a mother, voice teacher, and opera singer, she must have a penchant for fun but poorly-paid professions. She likes to pretend that her experience and master's degree in vocal performance come in handy as she describes debutantes who, like herself, speak several languages and are frequently forced to display their mediocre skills at the pianoforte.

Alene lives in a century-old, Craftsman-style home in Lehi, Utah, with her husband, six children, and a prankster of a ghost whom she has affectionately named Casper.